Leabhair ar iasacht ar feadh 21 lá ón dáta eisiúna.

Fineáil ar leabhair thar ama: 10c ar gach seachtain nó cuid de sheachtain, móide costas an phostas san aisghabhála.

Books are on loan for 21 days from date of issue.

Fines for overdue books: 10c for each week or portion of a week plus cost of postage incurred in recovery.

THE SIXTH SOUL

MARK ROBERTS

CORVUS

First published in hardback, trade paperback and e-book in Great Britain in 2013 by
Corvus, an imprint of Atlantic Books Ltd.

This paperback edition published in 2013 by Corvus, an imprint of Atlantic Books Ltd.

10 9 8 7 6 5 4 3 2 1

A CIP catalogue record for this book is available from the British Library.

Paperback ISBN: 978 0 85789 789 3
E-book ISBN: 978 0 85789 788 6

Printed and bound by CPI Group (UK) Ltd, Croydon, CR0 4YY

Corvus
An imprint of Atlantic Books Ltd
Ormond House
26–27 Boswell Street
London
WC1N 3JZ

www.corvus-books.co.uk

For my wife, Linda

How beautiful you are, my darling!
Oh, how beautiful!
Your eyes are doves.

Song of Songs 1:15

PROLOGUE

In her dream, Julia Caton held her newborn child in her arms and was filled with the deepest love she had ever known. Slowly, the dream dissolved. At half past three in the morning she woke up and carefully positioned herself on the edge of the bed. She folded her hands across her swollen middle and whispered, 'Baby.' She stroked her bump. 'I need the bathroom.'

There was no need to switch on the bathroom light because of the amber glow from next door's brash security light, triggered by a yowling tom-cat.

She thought, *This is a good rehearsal for all that getting up in the night.* A smile spread across her face at the prospect of holding and feeding and loving her baby.

Next door's security light clicked off automatically.

The bathroom was sunk into a darkness all of its own.

The door swung back silently behind her aching spine.

Julia made out the outline of her head in the mirrored cabinet above the bathroom sink. Outside, the tom-cat made a sound like a baby crying and the security light flared into life again. In the mirror, a shadow shifted. Her hands stilled at her side, her eyes two points of light in the glass. And beyond them, another pair of eyes glinted in the mirror.

She felt a sharp pain in the back of her left forearm, something suddenly piercing her skin. She opened her mouth and drew breath.

His hand flew to her face, his fingers digging into the privacy of her mouth, pressing down hard on her tongue and forcing down her lower jaw, stealing the scream from within. A hint of teeth flashed and the whites of his eyes shimmered in the dark surface of the glass.

As she slumped into his arms, a chain of cold thoughts flashed through her mind about the stranger in her bathroom.

She was the fifth pregnant woman he'd attacked. He was going to take her away. And she would never return.

And as the door closed on her senses, a voice whispered into the void. 'I did not come out of darkness. I am darkness itself.'

1

On the way to Brantwood Road, just after he'd burned through the third of four red lights, Detective Chief Inspector David Rosen had been pulled over by a pair of constables in a BMW Traffic Car. With the engine still running, he'd shown his warrant card to them as his window slid down. Their conversation had been to the point.

'Herod, fifth victim, Golden Hour.'

They waved him on.

Minutes later, at the cordoned-off scene of crime, Rosen braked hard. In spite of the need to move fast, he was frozen for a moment by a memory of the funeral he'd attended yesterday. He could still hear the raw grief of Sylvia Green's mother as her daughter's coffin disappeared behind a curtain in the crematorium. It was the fourth funeral he'd been to in as many months. And with each murder, the interval between killings was growing shorter.

Four victims, their faces and names, their lives, all constantly jostled inside his head.

Four dead women, and the killer was as far away as he had been from the first. He tried to breathe slowly to release the solid band of stress around his chest.

'Go!' he said to himself.

He hurried from his car to the back of the white Crime Scene Investigation van, where Detective Sergeant Carol Bellwood was standing, already suited and ready to enter 22 Brantwood Road. He snatched a white protective suit from the metal shelf of the van.

Light beads of rain had settled on Bellwood's black hair, arranged in plaited rows tight against her scalp.

'How long have you been here?' asked Rosen, dressing.

'Three minutes,' replied Bellwood.

Rosen took a mental snapshot of the scene.

It was just past seven o'clock on a dark March morning. Two rows of large 1930s semis faced each other across an affluent suburban road. The pavements on either side were lined with trees, and each house had three metres of garden between the front door and the fence that bordered the pavement.

To the east, the crescent moon over Brantwood Road wasn't the only source of light. Number 22, the house they'd been called to, was floodlit by the NiteOwl searchlight on the roof of the Scientific Support van.

Rosen glanced at the house next door.

'Number 24,' he said. 'It's the only house I can see with the lights out.'

Its windows were black. All the other houses, from the teens through to the thirties, were lit up, the neighbours awake and aware of a rapidly growing police presence.

Rosen, dark-haired, thick-set and middle-aged, was in a hurry to get his latex gloves on, but the more he hurried, the more he failed.

'Here,' said Bellwood, gently. 'Time is of the essence.' She unrolled the bunched tangle on the back of his hand and Rosen felt a tingle of embarrassment at a young woman's touch. 'Curtains are flapping.'

'I hope someone's seen something,' said Rosen. 'Let's find out what the uniforms have come up with.'

Rosen stepped into his overshoes without any of the fuss the gloves had caused him.

Three uniformed officers, a sergeant and two constables, stood at the gate of number 22, guarding the blue and white cordon, grim-faced, silent.

'Chief Inspector Rosen,' said the sergeant.

'Sergeant,' replied Rosen, knowing his face from somewhere but not his name. 'Who was here first?'

'The constables responded,' the sergeant informed him. 'I took over the scene on arrival.'

'Who's in the house?' enquired Rosen.

'Scientific Support.' The sergeant gave his book the merest of glances, checking the names on his running log of those he'd allowed through. 'DC Eleanor Willis and DS Craig Parker.'

'Where's the husband?'

The sergeant nodded towards a nearby police car, its back door wide open, where a big man in neat blue overalls, feet planted on the pavement, head down, vomited into the gutter.

As Rosen watched the husband, he noticed a newly promoted detective constable, Robert Harrison, leaning against the passenger door of an unmarked car, staring in his direction. Caught in the act, Harrison turned his head away.

'What did the husband tell you?' Rosen directed his attention at the constables.

'That he was called out at twelve minutes to three this morning,' the first constable replied.

'Twelve minutes to three? That precise?'

The second constable pointed at a green van parked near by, a skilled tradesman's Merc. 'If you look at the van, sir.'

'I clocked it on the way in,' said Carol Bellwood. 'It says on the side of the van, "Phillip Caton 24/7 Bespoke Plumbing Central Heating Engineer". There's a mobile number and a picture of Neptune wielding his trident and barking the waves down into submission. Mr Confident or what?'

'Or what.' Rosen observed Caton wiping his mouth on his sleeve.

'He gave us a time,' said the first constable. 'And then he fell apart.'

'We had to frogmarch him out of the house before he threw up all over the crime scene.'

'Any sign of a forced entry into the house?'

Their silence was enough. Caton raised his eyes from the puke in the gutter to the gaggle at his gate.

'Robert!' Rosen broke the moment and beckoned him over. Harrison came to the fence.

'David?' said Harrison.

'Carol's going to talk to the husband.' Rosen pointed to Phillip Caton. 'Listen to her questioning him, make notes, no butting in.'

Rosen turned to the sergeant.

'I'm taking over the crime scene now. Thank you for what you've done. Please stay on the door and allow only DS Carol Bellwood here over the threshold until otherwise instructed.'

JUST AS HE stepped into the house, he could hear behind him a man crying out in renewed distress. Rosen was glad it was Carol Bellwood, not he, who had the task of extracting information from Phillip Caton. After so many years as an investigative officer, he could not help but wonder if he was witnessing a man in profound torment, or the performance of a magnificent actor.

2

Scientific Support had worked hard and fast.

From the front door to the stairs, and up each step to the bathroom and bedrooms above, DS Parker and DC Willis had laid down a series of aluminium stepping plates. Rosen picked a path across the makeshift walkway, into the heart of the hall, any evidence left on the carpet being protected by the raised metal plates.

Rosen paused at a picture. On the wall was a framed photograph, a wedding portrait of Phillip and Julia Caton: she veiled and pretty in white, he awkward in top hat and tails. But their smiles were broad that day and the sun had shone on them, just as it had done on him and his wife, Sarah, many years earlier.

Rosen headed up the stairs with a renewed sense of sorrow.

On the landing at the top of the stairs, DC Eleanor Willis, pale and red-haired, used a pair of long-handled tweezers to drop a hypodermic needle into a transparent evidence bag and then peered into it.

'There's blood on the needle,' she said to Rosen as he passed.

'But it won't be his,' he replied.

DS Craig Parker was on his knees, cutting the thick, green carpet with a Stanley knife where it met the skirting board at the bathroom door. The carpet showed a fresh drag mark from the bathroom towards the top of the stairs. Parker pointed this out to Rosen.

'He got her in the bathroom,' he said. 'Dragged her to the stairs.'

'I love the sound,' replied Rosen, 'of a Geordie accent on a cold, gloomy morning.'

'And a very good morning to you, you cheerless Cockney git.' Parker peered at Rosen above his mask and added, 'Are you OK, David?'

Rosen stooped. 'Come here often, Craig?'

By way of answer, Parker smiled sadly. 'We can't find a point of forced entry.'

Craig Parker's face was the human equivalent of a bloodhound's. His weary eyes had seen enough and the bags underneath betrayed a tiredness that was three months short of retirement after thirty years in the Met.

'Eleanor!' Parker got to his feet slowly as his assistant appeared from the bedroom and handed the bagged hypodermic to Rosen.

There was a little fluid left in the chamber. 'Pentothal, no doubt. Herod's anaesthetic of choice. The hypo must've fallen out as he got her out of the house,' said Rosen.

Willis stood opposite Parker. On the count of three they raised the piece of carpet in a single clean lift and carried it into the nearest bedroom, an empty space at the back of the house.

'Anything in the bedrooms?' asked Rosen.

'Nothing so far.' *Nothing* was certain; *so far* was full of hidden promise.

'Craig, how long to go through the whole scene: house, gardens, street outside?'

'Three days.' Parker's voice echoed in the back room.

'If the pattern stays the same,' said Rosen, 'she'll be dead by then. No sign of forced entry, you say?'

'First thing we looked for. Nothing.'

'Next door, number 24?'

'No one lives there,' Willis observed, heading to the bathroom, 'judging by the back garden, the state of the windows and the paintwork outside.'

By contrast, the interior window frames of the bathroom of number 22 were sharp, their brilliant whiteness highlighted as Willis dusted them with dark fingerprint powder.

Rosen looked around at the closed bedroom doors. 'Which one's the baby's room?'

Willis pointed with the bristles of her fingerprint brush.

Being in a nursery made for a baby who would probably never sleep in there, or play, or cry, or breathe between its cloud-daubed walls, filled Rosen with utter sorrow. His failure to do anything so far to stop what was happening was almost unbearable.

Rosen caught the ghostly outline of his reflection in the glass of the window, the boy-like tangle of black curly hair contradicting the jumbled network of wrinkles and shadows on his pale face.

He looked out on the neat suburban road, at the desirable cars and the enviable houses, and focussed on DC Robert Harrison standing behind Carol Bellwood as she tried to talk to Phillip Caton. His gaze wandered.

The trees in the street were tall and broad and narrowly spaced apart. It was a discreet road, a secluded avenue, a nice place to *live*.

Rosen called Craig Parker, who joined him at the bedroom window.

'Can you see across the street through the trees? Can you?' asked Rosen.

'No, I can't see much, David,' replied Parker.

'And that's exactly what he banked on. I'm going into number 24.'

I want to get out of here.

'Why?' asked Parker.

'No forced sign of entry. No pregnant woman in London's going to open her front door in the dead of night, not given the current climate, not given what's happened. I'm going next door. I'm looking for a point of entry.'

'David, man, how could he get into number 22 through number 24—'

Rosen held up a hand. 'I need to check.'

When Rosen reached the street he noticed that, while he'd been inside number 22, Caton had turned a curious shade of yellow, the colour of wax. A terrible idea crossed Rosen's mind. He hoped Caton's anguish would not be compounded by having made an easy mistake as he left the house to go to the job.

On your way out, Rosen wondered, *in the dead of night, did you accidentally leave the front door open?*

3

Each panel in the fence between numbers 22 and 24 Brantwood Road was old but perfectly intact. The decision to widen out the crime scene came from a combination of experience and instinct. Back in '99, Rosen had been at a scene of a crime where there was no evidence of forced entry, but it had become evident that the killer had entered through a vent between adjoining flats.

He looked up at the roof of number 24: a patchwork of slipped and missing slates, making the house and loft space vulnerable to the elements.

He glanced at his watch. Eight o'clock. Time was flying. A whole hour had passed in what felt like a minute.

To the front of the property, a locked garage attached to the side of number 24 blocked his way to the back garden. Taking hold of the top of the fence separating numbers 22 and 24, he steadied his foot on the thick knot of a shrub and hauled himself over. The fence panels creaked under his weight as he jumped down into the garden next door.

He watched his feet. The ground was littered with the faeces of several types of beast. At eye level and within an arm's length, a bird flew out of a bush.

'All right in there, David?' Bellwood's voice came from the garden of number 22.

He called back, 'Yes!' but wasn't sure that this was the truth.

Rosen turned to the sound of Bellwood climbing over the fence. She jumped down gracefully into the garden of number 24.

A bin, long overturned by some fox or other scavenger, lay on its side near the house. The rubbish – food packaging and newspapers showing headlines and sporting triumphs and disasters from eighteen months ago – lay matted on the earth leading to the back door.

Rosen felt his pulse quicken as he got closer to the door. He looked at his watch again: it was a few seconds past eight. He thought of his wife, Sarah, and her appointment with their GP. Time was marching on. He wanted to go with her, he'd promised he would and then this . . . Herod's fifth miserable excursion into other people's lives.

Something lurched inside him. Every nerve was made jagged by what he saw.

The back door of number 24 was slightly open, a glass panel in the door absent from its frame, cleanly removed.

Someone had gone to the trouble of not bashing the door down, not attracting the attention of the neighbours. Rosen eyed the area around the missing panel. It was a cautious job well done.

'Carol?'

'Yes?'

'Can we rule the husband out at the moment?'

'His story held up. I called his client. He was in Knightsbridge, as he said.'

'There's been a break-in. Who's here from the team now?'

'Harrison's on float, DS Gold is with Caton, Corrigan and Feldman are here and knocking on the neighbours' doors. David?'

'Yes?'

'Harrison's a liability.'

'What did he do?'

'Just when you were going into number 22, Caton said, *Do you think Herod's got her?* And Harrison chimes in, *It looks like that, yeah.* Caton went into hysterics. I don't like him, David.'

'I understand.' It explained Caton's sudden sobbing fit. 'Did Caton say anything – anything useful?'

'He kept asking if we knew what Herod was doing with the foetuses.'

'And you told him what?'

'We didn't know for sure. I avoided the forensic psychologist's word *trophy*. Do you buy that rather obvious speculation, David?'

'No,' said Rosen. Unable to offer an alternative theory about the absent babies, he went for something practical. 'Go and call for a second Scientific Support team for number 24.'

Using the tip of the little finger of his left hand, he pushed the door open at its top right-hand corner.

It was an old lady's house.

There was an aura, as if someone had died there long ago, undisturbed by compassion or duty, hidden in the muffled light.

———

IN JUST UNDER twenty minutes, a second Scientific Support team had arrived, pulled in from Shepherd's Bush. Silently and efficiently, they had plated the main passageways from the back door of number 24 to the front door, the stairs and each of the main doorways, upstairs and down.

As the second officer came down the stairs, he said to Rosen, 'There's a cadaver in the bed, main bedroom, front of the house. It's been there some time. We didn't touch it.' The team looked in a hurry to leave. 'We really need to talk with DS Parker next door, sort out a game plan.'

The Scientific Support officers left. Rosen, alone now, felt oppressed. Something of the earth, something foetid, perhaps a fungus, was growing in the fabric of the house, feeding on the wood its spores burrowed into, irrigated by the damp that seemed like an indoor weather system unique to number 24.

Where were her relatives? A five-bedroom semi in Brantwood Road added up to a big inheritance. Where were the claimants to this legacy? Why had no one attempted to even clear the house, let alone sell it?

He imagined his wife Sarah, old and alone, dying, and her death going unnoticed, their home crumbling, broken into by some lunatic, then explored by policemen desperate for clues.

He tried the light switch but the power was dead. As he moved further into the house, it became dimmer still. The red-flocked wallpaper, turning green and brown from the damp, seemed to be dissolving into the deepening shadow.

Persian rugs shifted under Rosen's feet, reminding him of the uneasy sensation of the bogus floors of a fairground funhouse. But he could see no physical sign of an intruder, just an old lady's world frozen in time. Somewhere else, in another room, a well-made mechanical clock still ticked, a heartbeat to the house.

A patch of yellow light appeared on the wall, its source directly behind him. Rosen span round and Carol Bellwood stepped from the shadows.

He was pleased that the newest member of the team was backing him up.

'How's Caton holding up?' asked Rosen.

'Not good, but we're done with him for now.'

As they ascended the stairs, years of stale air formed a backdrop to dust motes that shimmied in the torchlight.

Rosen stopped near the top. Every door upstairs was closed, except one.

He walked towards the open bathroom door.

Weary light filtered into the gloom through the frosted glass.

'David? Are you OK, David?'

He was staring, lost in thought, looking directly up at the ceiling, at the wooden door to the loft space.

'Let's check the bedrooms,' he said.

————

IN THE MAIN bedroom, the top of a human head was visible on the pillow. The quilt on the bed was raised, giving the impression of a relief map, with the outline below that of a human body. Rosen tugged the edge of the quilt but it was stuck to the sheet on the mattress. When he pulled a little harder there was a tearing sound, cloth from cloth, surface from surface. Bellwood entered behind him, her torchlight illuminating what was left of the body.

I'm sorry, thought Rosen. *I'm sorry you've been left here without anyone to mourn you or mark your passing.*

She lay foetal in death, a frail skeleton, knees tucked to elbows, carpals to teeth, her skull nestled on a clump of grey hair.

Rosen lowered the quilt.

Whatever had caused her death, she'd been left to rot into the bedding and dry out. The thought angered and saddened Rosen in equal proportions.

Tweed. There was a half-used bottle of Tweed perfume on the old lady's dressing table and an ivory hairbrush in which a gathering of grey hairs remained for ever trapped in the network of bristles. Her jewellery box was open, neatly arranged, undisturbed. On the dressing table next to it was a gold, heart-shaped locket. It was open. On one side of the heart, a picture of two children, a teenage girl and a small boy; on the other side, a small lock of dark hair.

'Who are you?' Rosen asked the children in the locket.

'And where are you now?' Bellwood stroked the locket with her light.

'What about the other bedrooms?' asked Rosen.

'All empty save the one next to this. Shall we?'

The room next door to the old lady's room was a museum piece. A teenage girl's room, early to mid-1970s, *Jackie* magazine open on the single bed, an early stereo system with an RAK 45 record of Mud's

'Tiger Feet', and posters on the wall of David Bowie as Ziggy Stardust and Paul Gadd as Gary Glitter.

'I wonder?' said Rosen, eyeing a framed photograph of a skinny thirteen-year-old girl. He picked up the frame, speculating as to what had become of her.

'Maybe the old lady was hanging on to a moment in time, the girl grew up and—'

'Maybe.' He looked at the photo – the girl's clothes, her blonde hair in a feather-cut, and figured it was around 1973. 'She was a few years older than I was back in 1973. Not that our paths would have crossed in a million years,' said Rosen, wistfully.

'How come?' asked Bellwood.

'I grew up in Walthamstow. This kind of street, this neighbourhood, was beyond my dreams.'

Rosen was quiet for a long time as he stared at the girl's picture. He sighed; the dusty air was thick with memory of a time before Carol Bellwood was born.

'I had a daughter . . .' Rosen stopped articulating the thought that had escaped unchecked from his mouth and averted his eyes from the bewilderment in Bellwood's face. He turned his mind away from the thought of Hannah, the baby who'd once slept in his arms, and raised his voice a little. 'Come on, let's crack on. I think I've seen a precedent for this.'

Rosen walked back to the bathroom, Bellwood following.

'Back in 1999, in Battersea, a thwarted boyfriend used the flat next door to get to the woman he both loved and hated. It was an ugly murder.'

Rosen looked around the bathroom, pausing on the ceiling for a beat, considering a possibility. He almost smiled as his eyes returned to Bellwood's face.

'Carol, I think I know how Herod got into number 22.'

4

Ten minutes later, back in the bathroom of number 22, Eleanor Willis arranged a set of folding steps beneath the loft door.

'David, if you're right about the loft space,' said Parker, 'you could have enough material up there to tell us what size shoes his granny wears.'

'Am I going to get that lucky?' asked Rosen. 'I haven't had much luck so far.'

As soon as he said it, Rosen thought of Phillip and Julia Caton, and the four other broken couples, and he deeply regretted the note of self-pity.

'However, it depends upon the state of the loft space. It could be almost impossible to retrieve, for instance, a single relevant human hair from all that fibreglass insulation, decaying newspaper, life debris, and whatever crap's been up there since the thirties when these semis were built.'

Wearing latex gloves, Parker mounted the steps to the loft space, lifted the unhinged door and carefully removed it from the hatch, an enigmatic smile forming on his lips.

'What is it, Craig?' asked Rosen.

'He sure had a good view of life in the Caton's bathroom,' said Parker, eyeing the loft door as he lowered it down to Eleanor Willis. As she took it by the edges Rosen resisted the urge to say, 'Be careful.'

'Thumbnail-sized hole in the wood,' said Willis. 'Enough, I guess.'

Willis raised the door carefully in front of her face, closed one eye and peered through it directly at Rosen.

He mounted the steps into the chill air and considered: *a hole in the board covering the loft entrance. Enough to see through? Right into the bathroom. A good view into the most intimate of moments.*

He climbed another step and, raising his head above the loft entrance, shone a beam of torchlight into the darkness. A trivial combination of sensory details were indelibly stamped on his memory: the distant roar of a bus, caught in the acoustics of the loft, and the intense cold trapped in the rafters. Then the rain started.

There was an adjoining wall between numbers 22 and 24, supporting the weight of the roof of both houses. A skin of fresh dust lay across the newly panelled floor of the loft of number 22. In the middle of the shared wall, there was a small hulk of darkness where bricks were missing. He shone a light on the wall and took a close look at the gap. It was large enough for an average-sized man to squeeze through.

Rosen eased his way down the ladder. 'The mortar in the adjoining wall's addled by the look of it, probably due to the state of number 24's roof. It can't have been a big task to get the bricks out. He's tunnelled his way through into here from next door. He broke into number 24, got into the loft and took the bricks out from that side.'

He turned off his torch.

'This is his fifth time round, but it's the first time he's abducted from within the victim's home. Either this isn't Herod's work at all or he's got the dangerous daring urge now. This could be costly to him, very costly. Maybe all of a sudden he believes he can be as reckless in abducting his victims as he is in dropping off around London what's left of them.'

Rosen picked up Willis's sigh behind her protective mask, the subtle tightening of her body language. He noted too that Bellwood had noticed her colleague's reaction to Julia Caton's probable fate.

'Carol,' he explained, 'DC Willis was the first officer to see Herod's handiwork with her own eyes, with no warning, no prior knowledge of what to expect.'

Eleanor Willis propped the loft door against the bath and took a string of pictures of it with her digital camera, then turned to Bellwood.

'I was first to arrive at the scene when Jenny Maguire's body was discovered,' said Willis. 'The surgical removal of the baby was clumsy, the work of one nervous butcher. We found out from the autopsy that he'd used a surgical scalpel, but it looked as if he'd hacked away with a blunt tin opener. His technique improves each time, the line of incision straighter, cleaner.'

The steady rain now fell harder on the shared roof of numbers 22 and 24 Brantwood Road. The noise of the rain clattering on the tiles echoed in the loft space above them.

'David, Carol, come and have a look at this,' Craig Parker called from next door.

Rosen and Bellwood followed the sound of Parker's voice to the door of the smallest of the five bedrooms, used as a boxroom. Parker made a theatrical gesture towards an assortment of junk and said, 'Voilà, man!'

'What am I looking at, Craig?'

Parker pointed directly at a set of aluminium ladders propped against the wall. 'Herod gets down from the loft, then uses Caton's ladders to straighten up the loft entrance, putting the ladders back in place here in the boxroom before he swoops off with the missus.'

'What do you make of it, David?' asked Bellwood.

Rosen glanced at his watch. It was twenty past nine.

'His nerves have settled and he's reached the stage where he's absolutely buzzing from what he's doing. What do you think?' Rosen batted the question back to Bellwood, Parker and Willis.

'If he's changed course midstream,' said Bellwood, 'and he's stopped taking women from public spaces to start making home visits, can you imagine how that's going to play in people's heads when it comes out?'

'How many pregnant women are there in Greater London?' asked Parker.

'Ninety thousand or thereabouts,' replied Willis.

'Ninety thousand women like sitting ducks in their *own homes*.'

Rosen imagined the public terror this new development would cause and hoped, in the face of the evidence, that this was not the work of Herod. But when he considered everything that had happened in the Catons' home and in the house next door, he could not see how it could be otherwise.

'This hasn't been some random choice. This home visit's been a ninety thousand-to-one call. Herod knows this building better than the people who live in it.'

5

Rosen stood outside the kitchen door of 22 Brantwood Road at the side of the house. A trio of newly arrived uniformed officers, dressed in protective suits, approached him.

'Sir, where do you want us to start? Front garden or back?'

'Back garden, number 22. Then, move it over next door. I apologize in advance. It's an absolute mess. But that was the run-up to his point of entry.'

The rain was steady and cold. Alone again, Rosen scrolled to SARAHMOBILE on his phone. It rang.

His wife had recently had sharp abdominal pains, leading her to take time off from her teaching post. She had only ever been off work once before for a protracted period of five months' sickness. Anxiety gnawed at Rosen about what might or might not be causing her such pain. He wished that he believed in God so that he could pray it wasn't anything life threatening. But he didn't believe in God and neither did she.

'Hi, David.'

She sounded bright.

'Have you been in to see the doc?'

'Yes.'

'And?'

'He thinks – he's pretty certain it's a peptic ulcer.'

'Good!'

'Good?' Sarah laughed.

'It's not good in itself . . .'

They had briefly discussed the possibility of cancer on a few occasions and it had played constantly on Rosen's mind ever since.

'Yes, I know what you mean. It could've been a whole lot worse.'

'Where are you?' He changed tack.

'I'm in the car park at work, summoning up the courage to face 10M, today's lesson, "Where is God in the face of evil?" Where is God in the face of 10M?'

In the middle distance, Phillip Caton got into the back of an unmarked police car with DS Gold up front. It would be taking him to Isaac Street Police Station for a more formal interview.

'A peptic ulcer,' said Rosen. 'So what's next?'

'He's referred me to Guy's. I've got to have a barium meal and a scan just to clarify if his diagnosis is correct. Oh, oh God . . .'

'Sarah, what's up?'

Her car door opened and he heard the sudden lurching of his wife being sick on the car park tarmac.

He waited for what felt like a long time.

'I've just been sick,' she confirmed.

'Any blood in it?' he asked.

'No.'

'Good.'

'David, you're starting to annoy me. Intensely.'

'I'm sorry. Maybe you should go home.'

'I might as well be in discomfort but surrounded by people and busy, than sick and at home alone. Besides, I don't think I'll be sick again.'

'When's your appointment?'

'The GP has to contact the hospital, and the hospital send for me when they have a space in clinic. I'll have to go whatever the time.'

The wind shifted direction and a blast of rain hit Rosen directly in the face.

'How's it going there?' she asked.

'Another abduction, another death, no doubt,' answered Rosen.

'Where is God in the face of evil? Answer: there is no God, just a whole lot of evil,' concluded Sarah.

'And you the head of RE in a Catholic school, Mrs Rosen.'

'Don't pipe it too loud, David. Remember, two salaries are better than one. What time will you be home?'

'I'm not sure.'

'Then I guess I'll see you when I see you. Sometime late tonight perhaps?'

'I'll be late, yes, and I'm sorry I couldn't be with you this morning.'

'Don't worry. Others have it worse than us. I love you, mate.'

'I love you, too.'

'Gotta go. Oh, 10M, what a life . . .'

He ended the call, watching the rain. She was bearing pain and discomfort with a spirit that reminded him of one of the many reasons why he loved her from the pit of his being. If it was him with a peptic ulcer, he'd have griped to Olympic standard.

Pocketing his phone, Rosen felt the sudden and subtle weight of a presence behind him.

He turned his head slowly to see DC Robert Harrison walking towards him from the back garden.

'What are you up to?'

Harrison held up the digital camera in his hand.

'Using my initiative, sir. Photographing the back garden in the absence of a direct order and with nothing else to do.'

'How long have you been there?'

'Where?'

'Behind me, Robert, behind me?' *Listening in on my phone conversation.*

'I've just come out of the garden.'

The open gate to the garden swung back against the fence, slamming against the wooden frame and making the wind and rain seem suddenly sharper, even ill tempered.

'OK, Robert. Go next door. You can be in charge of the fingertip search of number 24's back garden.'

Silence.

'Sure.'

Harrison walked away. 'I love you, too,' he muttered.

'What was that?' asked Rosen.

'Just thinking out loud, sir.'

6

Julia Caton was woken by the kicking of her baby inside her womb.

For a few clouded moments, she thought she was dreaming. And in those seconds, as the baby moved, she felt his shifts, rolling and turning, the pressure of his hands and feet pressing the sides of the amniotic sac. It was these gathering sensations that made her realize that, even though she didn't know where she was in that bizarre dream, she and her baby were alive.

Julia opened her eyes to pitch darkness. She ached all the way down her left side, from her shoulder to her ankle. She blinked a few times and strained to see but there was no relief from the dense blackness. She wondered if she'd gone blind.

She was floating on the surface of lukewarm liquid and her baby was moving with the growing impatience of a life waiting to be born. How could her bed be so liquid? *Because it was a dream, that's how, like a dream after too much wine.*

As she grew more wakeful, she became aware, without checking, that she was naked.

She raised a hand close to her face, disturbing the surface of the liquid as she did so, but she couldn't see her fingers even as they brushed the tips of her eyelashes.

The back of her hand came into contact with a smooth surface that felt curved and plastic. The word *lid* slipped into the front of her mind. Lids may lift.

She raised her other hand, palm up, and pushed with both against the cool plastic. The lid didn't budge. Julia knew that they were locked in a container of some kind, floating, floating.

She closed her eyes and took a deep breath to fight down the rising panic, the unwanted gift of delayed shock. She listened to the air rushing into her nostrils, felt her ribcage rising with the intake, and this was all she could hear.

The baby – she had learned it was a boy on the second scan – stilled inside her. It was as if he was obeying some secret command telepathically delivered from mother to son.

'Good boy,' she whispered. 'Don't move.' Her voice was ethereal in the liquid silence. Talking was a mistake. The physical action of speech set off a taste in her mouth and she felt the urge to be sick.

As the sound of her voice sank into the darkness, and smell and taste overtook her senses, memory erupted in nuclear flashes in her mind's eye.

In the bathroom, she had felt a sudden sharpness in her forearm and a hand in her face. The sense that she was dreaming evaporated as the stone-cold wind of reality thrust her into wakefulness.

He didn't come out of darkness, he was darkness itself. The thought assailed her, and the thread of then and now connected.

'Jesus!'

She dipped her fingers into the solution on which she floated and sniffed them.

There was no perceptible scent. Slowly, she opened her lips and allowed her fingers to touch her tongue. Salt. Salt water. They were floating on a solution of salt water, locked in the dark with no sound coming in.

She recalled a name: Alison Todd, the second mother to go missing just over seven months ago, the discovery of her body filling the news headlines on the day Julia had learned that she was pregnant.

Of the four murdered mothers, Alison's case had affected Julia most deeply, the thought of her mutilated body casting a long shadow over their celebratory supper.

Phillip had tried to dismiss Julia's fears, but they had remained all through her pregnancy, sometimes singing loudly, sometimes muttering darkly, but always there.

There were sides to the thing that they were locked inside. Her fears took a collective breath and started screaming inside her head.

'Oh my Jesus!'

Julia could feel the blood draining from her limbs, the lightness in her brain.

A stressed mother stresses an unborn baby!

A received wisdom from the antenatal clinic she'd attended came back to her like a radio signal from deep space, a message from a distant world that she and her baby were now no longer a part of.

A stressed mother . . . stresses . . . an unborn . . . baby.

She couldn't get her breath.

She heard her heart beat against her ribs, picking up pace by the second, and felt it as a pulse behind her eyeballs.

Instinctively, she folded her arms across her middle, covering her baby with the armour of flesh and bone.

Phillip had tried to talk over television news broadcasts that had reported the discovery of Alison Todd's body and the growing details that were released by the media. But Phillip wasn't around all the time, as when he was asleep in the pit of night and she had wandered downstairs and come across the BBC twenty-four-hour news channel.

Footage from the scene of the discovery of a body: blue and white tape cordoning off an area around Lambeth Bridge; the grimness of the reporter's face as she recounted from the place where *a second body, believed to be that of Mrs Todd, was found by a man walking his dog at dawn.*

The police were refusing to reveal whether the mother was dead or alive when the killer performed a forced Caesarean section to remove the baby, along with pieces of the womb. The precise cause of Alison Todd's death was unknown; there had been a media blackout on the detail, to weed out crank confessions.

Rather her than me.

Her own words burned a hole in her memory.

She wept in the darkness, using all the strength in her diaphragm to still the scream, the cry from her heart and her throat. When her baby gave a sudden sharp kick, her willpower collapsed.

The lid was low and her scream bounced back into her face. She drew in another breath and cried out for her mother, plummeting into hysterical tears as the word died on the lid inches from her face.

7

K*now Your Enemy . . . London's Drug Dealers and Addicts.*
The bank of faces on the wall of the open-plan office of
Isaac Street Police Station gazed into the fluorescent silence. In
contrast with the faceless Herod, they looked like a reasonable bunch of
boys and girls. As with budgets, space was tight and the office doubled
up as the incident room for the ongoing murder investigation.

It was nine o'clock at night and DCI David Rosen had been on duty
for just over fifteen hours. Reaching the point of fatigue that should
have sent him home for food and sleep, he remained in the office, held
there by an uneasy instinct. He'd phoned his wife Sarah, apologized
for his absence. It was nothing new to her, and she was up to her eyes
in marking her pupils' exercise books.

Spread across Rosen's desk was a colour map of London, on which
abduction points were marked with red crosses and numbers. The
body drops-offs, the blue crosses, seemed to form no discernible
pattern. Jenny Maguire, victim one, in the lake at St James's Park.
Alison Todd, victim two, under Lambeth Bridge. Jane Wise, victim
three, at the corner of Victoria Street and Vauxhall Bridge Road. Sylvia

Green, victim four, outside the Oval cricket ground. Where would Julia surface? Rosen pored over the map, hoping for inspiration.

He opened Outlook Express. There was one potentially meaningful email, with an attachment, from Carol Bellwood.

> David, I loaded all the significant information from this morning's scene of crime at 22 Brantwood Road and 24 Brantwoood Road into HOLMES. Two hours later and every data permutation possible, I'm sorry to say there have been no matches.
>
> Sorry, Carol
>
> PS check att, with regard to this morning's talk, is this what has happened to the babies?

HOLMES contained all the recorded data for every reported crime, solved and unsolved, in the United Kingdom. If Bellwood, the best HOLMES reader Rosen knew, couldn't squeeze something useful out of the database that cross-matched details from all crime recorded in the UK, then no one could. It was a blow and he swore sourly as he breathed out.

He clicked on the attachment, opened it and muttered, 'Jeez!' at the picture on his screen. It was a stock image of a foetus preserved in a specimen jar, the whiteness of its perfect skin patterned with an elaborate network of veins. The world around him fell away. There was something unbearable about the picture.

He shut the image down. Exhausted and disturbed by what he had seen, he left the office to make coffee in the small, adjoining kitchen.

When he came back to his desk, the red light of the answering machine on his desk blinked continuously. He filled his cheeks with air and blew out.

There was a message. Rosen pressed play. There was a lengthy silence at the beginning of the message and then a voice.

'My name's Brother Aidan Walsh. I'm the abbot of St Mark's, a Dominican community near Faversham in Kent. One of our community, Father Sebastian, thinks he can help you with your current investigation into the abducted women. Perhaps you could ring me.'

Brother Aidan Walsh left a number and the blessings of the Lord Jesus Christ.

Faversham in Kent. Rosen knew the countryside around there well and was intrigued by the message. He dialled the number he'd jotted down on a spiral pad and waited.

The phone rang. He lost count of how many times. They'd probably all be in bed by eight o'clock, rising in the dead of night to pray, no doubt. He decided to give it a few more rings and then he'd hang up. He could try again in the morning.

The phone stopped ringing as the receiver at the other end was lifted. Silence. And then, 'Yes?'

'Is that Brother Aidan?'

'No. I'm afraid he's just gone to evening prayers.'

'I'm Detective Chief Inspector Rosen, London Met. I'm returning Brother Aidan's call. Who am I speaking to, please?'

As the man at the other end replied, the line crackled.

'I'm sorry,' said Rosen. 'It's a poor line, can you speak up?'

'I'm Father Sebastian'

'Brother Aidan mentioned you on the message he left.'

'Could you play the message back for me?'

Rosen ignored the request.

'Technology's a big thing when you live a simple life as we do.'

Rosen looked at the scowling faces of London's drug dealers and addicts, and said, 'Brother Aidan said you could help.'

'Yes, perhaps I can.'

From his desk, Rosen had a view of the closed door of Chief Superintendent Baxter's office; it was a door he disliked, to the room he loathed, of a man he hated.

'Fire away.'

'I think I might have some information for you.'

'Regarding?'

'Could you come to St Mark's?'

'To St Mark's? Brother Aidan mentioned you're near Faversham . . .'

'Do you know the area?' asked the priest.

'Indeed I do,' replied Rosen, scenes from his childhood tumbling in the back of his mind. 'When would you like me to come to see you?'

'Time's not on your side, Detective Rosen.'

'It's normal for people assisting an inquiry to come here to Isaac Street.'

'There's nothing normal about this . . . situation. I gather you need help,' said Father Sebastian. 'Herod accessed the Catons' house through the adjoining property. Didn't he, Mr Rosen?'

In a single movement, Rosen sat up and shifted his weight, hooked by the detail Flint had so casually supplied. It had been withheld from media reports of the fifth abduction. First thing in the morning, Rosen decided, he would be at St Mark's.

'What else do you know, Father Sebastian?'

'A motive, a concrete motive for doing these appalling . . . acts.'

A motive? A concrete motive? He'd have walked naked down Oxford Street for a concrete motive, upside down on his hands if necessary. But there was a glitch with this information and offer of help.

'Father Sebastian, the only person who knows the killer's motive is the killer himself or someone who knows the killer, is a trusted confidant of the killer and . . . and is shielding him.'

'I disagree. We don't live in a vacuum, sealed off from each other, unaware of the wider concerns of the world in which we live and the universe in general.'

'I've got some time tomorrow. Is eight o'clock good for you?' asked Rosen.

'Oh, you know, I'm not so busy.'

'I have to ask you, how do you know what his motivation is?'

'Some years ago, in the mid-nineties I was based at the Vatican. I was the pope's key adviser on all matters relating to the occult.'

So far, three forensic psychologists had independently ruled out the occult motive. Four of them agreed that Herod was the emperor of woman-hatred, with a *Christian* string to his bow.

But the priest on the other end of the phone had an assurance that Rosen found persuasive.

The voice on the phone fell silent. Rosen nursed the silence.

'You'll have to trust me, Detective Rosen. I can help you. You do want me to help you, don't you?'

There was a photograph of Sarah on his desk, smiling in the sunshine. It had been taken the summer after her nervous breakdown and hospitalization. Depression had stopped her eating and drinking, following the winter when their daughter Hannah had died. Two years old, she had been taken from them, without warning, by cot death. Sarah had tried so hard to fight it but depression was the stealthiest demon. He picked up the picture. It was a snapshot of love, of all he held dear, his reason to keep going. It had been a difficult birth and, after two short years, an unbearable loss to both of them.

'Do you know where we are?' asked Father Sebastian.

'I know where you are. I used to pick hops there when I was a kid.'

'For pocket money?'

'No. My mother was on her own with six—' Rosen curbed the sudden and inexplicable compulsion to give personal information to a stranger. 'See you in the morning, then,' he said. 'At eight.'

He went to put down the receiver when he heard Sebastian's voice once again. 'Mr Rosen, just one thing.' An afterthought.

'Father Sebastian?'

'After he's finished with Julia Caton and her baby, I believe he's going to do it one more time. One more mother, one more baby.'

'Are you going to tell me you're psychic?'

The priest laughed. 'Don't be ridiculous. You know as well as I do that the only entity that knows the future with certainty is God.' Father Sebastian hung up.

'I believe in the future,' said Rosen to the drug dealers and addicts of London. 'But I don't believe in God.'

It was time to go home, to catch a few hours' sleep before hitting the road to Faversham. In reaching for his coat, his attention was drawn to Chief Superintendent Baxter's door; sound was condensing behind it, two voices. The door opened.

'Well, thank you for keeping me in the picture.'

Baxter stepped out, clearly surprised by Rosen's presence.

'Working late, David?'

'Fifteen- to sixteen-hour days as per.'

Baxter moved to one side and Detective Constable Robert Harrison emerged from the office. He didn't look at Rosen as he marched, with the overconfidence of the under-intelligent, across the open-plan office, puckering his lips to whistle but failing to form a tune.

'David, I think we need to talk,' said Baxter.

Baxter went back into his office, leaving space for Rosen to follow. He hated Baxter almost as much as he hated the smell of hops.

8

Every so often, a sharp hiss punctured the darkness in which Julia Caton was trapped. It happened when the vice-like tightness in her chest became a fire.

It slowly dawned on her, as she heard the hiss and felt the rush of fresh air into her body, that Herod was throwing her scraps of oxygen, just enough to keep her alive but not enough to allow her to think clearly.

Julia Caton was in a state of self-doubt about what was real and what was not, whether she was awake or whether she was moving through a dream.

All sense of time had disappeared, and she wondered, as she slipped off to sleep, how many days or years she'd been in the dark.

In the silence that swallowed her and the endless darkness before her eyes, Julia was jolted by the sight of a distant star.

It appeared distant at first, though it moved slowly towards her in an elegant curve. If she were asked, as she was sure the starry starry night would, she could no longer tell whether she was awake or asleep, but she had the strangest notion that she was coming slowly to a standing position, moved by some invisible force of nature outside her physical body or mental will.

'We three Kings of Orient are . . . '

The same line over and over, sung by a creature somewhere under the water's edge, near her head. Or was it three creatures? Normally, she was scared of nature; creatures that lived underwater were sometimes good to eat but never while they were still alive, and sometimes creatures under the water thought people were good to eat, but they were too busy singing, just around her hipbones now.

'Field and fountain, moor and mountain . . .'

And then it hit her. The singing was coming from inside her, it was her baby. *Clever boy, must've heard the song at Christmas and remembered the words*. Strange she'd never noticed him singing before.

'Good God!' She couldn't believe her eyes. They were travelling straight towards her, two on sand-coloured camels, the black one on a camel the same colour as the new flooring of her bathroom, which had cost a bloody fortune, and it was a good job Phillip could plumb that suite in; how much his labour would have added to the price Christ alone could tell.

'Julia?' The Chinese king, or were they just Wise Men? The Chinese Wise-King-Man spoke to her in Cantonese, the language of Yum Yums, her favourite takeaway. 'Julia? We have travelled far.'

'I know, I've heard the song.'

His Cantonese she couldn't understand but he was speaking in English and smoking an opium pipe, so it didn't really matter.

The black king, well spoken, the product of an English public school by the sound of it – her child would be privately educated – said, 'We have come from afar to worship the baby.' He had the face and voice of her consultant gynaecologist.

'Have you seen Herod yet?' asked Julia.

'He told us to return, to tell him where you are. How did we come so far?'

'You followed the star, you followed that star above my head.'

'Herod told us where you are, exactly,' the third Wise-King-Man, a man with no face, just a rip for a mouth, told her. He dipped a hand inside a vent in his robe and pulled out a mean-looking snake.

'What kind of snake is this?' she asked, calmly.

'It's a carpet viper,' said Ripped Face.

He set it down on Julia's leg. It slid up the inside of her thigh, up the slope of her belly and up between her breasts.

'Star of wonder, star of light . . .' Baby's voice bubbled, and the snake stopped and remained perfectly still.

'We come bearing gifts,' said the snake, only with Phillip's voice.

'Gold, frankincense and myrrh. Let us see the baby, mother, so that we may tell Herod, to come worship the baby.'

'I don't think so.' Julia felt suddenly nauseous, the snake's eyes pouring an invisible substance that felt like warm sky under the curve of her eyelids. 'Where am I?'

'In a sensory deprivation chamber in the palace of King Herod.'

She reached out to touch the head of the carpet viper and it exploded into a million points of green light.

The kings were fading into the darkness behind the shimmering patterns of light.

'Let us bring Herod so that he too may worship the baby.'

In the tight space, she raised her fists to the lid and hammered, calling at the top of her voice to those cruel and faithless kings who had now faded into the pitch black.

'Come back! Come back for us! Take us with you! Help us, please!'

9

Chief Superintendent Baxter had framed family photographs on his desk: wife with three children, shipshape and anchored around Dad. Rosen arched his neck as he sat across from Baxter and noticed that the pictures had, very gradually, turned over time, so that they were facing more outwards to the room than towards the owner of the desk. There was, Rosen noted, no photographic record of the WPC from Islington whom Baxter had been screwing for over two years.

'Like to talk to me about today?'

Not particularly.

Head back, pencil pointing, body stretched in a straight line. Rosen had, for a long time, tried hard to find something to like in Baxter, but even his shoes demanded disdain.

'Which part of today do you mean?'

'Which part do *you* think?'

'Early morning, Brantwood Road.'

'Correct,' said Baxter.

'Is there a problem?'

'You tell me, David.'

'Apart from the obvious problem of another missing mother and child and a murderer we haven't caught yet . . .'

'There is a *problem*.'

'Go on, Tom.' Rosen smiled briefly, falsely.

Baxter held a hand up, fingers curled into a fist, thumb extended. He looked set to start counting with the assistance of his digits. Problem? Problems.

'One, you went over a fence at a scene of a crime to get into the garden of number 24. Had that area been examined by Scientific Support? Don't answer. It couldn't possibly have been, given the timescale, so, effectively, David, you contaminated a potential mine of information during the golden hour.'

Rosen made a show of digesting Baxter's words.

'I understand your concerns, Tom. However, I was in charge of the scene, I took a calculated risk. That risk led me to the attic, the means of entry and a potential mine of information in the golden hour!'

A tide of red was rising past Baxter's Adam's apple, heading for his face. Rosen perceived that this was clearly meant to be a lecture, not a debate.

'Two, David, and it's a general point that's not gone unnoticed by the team; two, you're losing your focus.'

'Explain, please.'

'Your mind's not on the case.'

'For example?'

'You're a million miles away.' He pointed at his own head and then at Rosen.

'Could you give me an example?'

'Making personal phone calls at the scene of an abduction.'

'Ah, DC Robert Harrison.'

'I have several sources—'

No, you haven't, thought Rosen, *you've got Harrison*.

Baxter smiled and shook his head slowly.

'Look, David, how about you put in a request? Maybe a fresh pair of eyes on the case, maybe if you make room—'

'Tom, please stop right there. It's no secret this investigation has been dogged by sheer bad luck. But if you pull me off the case, you're going to set matters back. Nobody has my overview of events. A fresh pair of eyes will mean going back to square one in managing this investigation.'

'Fine. But I must tell you what's going to happen. I'm going to initiate a peer review of the way you're handling the case. I'm going to bring in Steve Charlton and Tom Ellis from Hammersmith to review the way you've been doing things. It will be a fair and very public exploration of your actions and strategies these past months.' Baxter fell silent, waiting for a reaction that Rosen didn't deliver. 'You can go now.'

Between the desk and the door, Rosen mentally counted off seven senior investigating officers who had suffered directly at Baxter's hands; seven men and women whose achievements had been whitewashed over and whose minor failings had been orchestrated into symphonies of negligence and incompetence. He was good at that sort of thing, Baxter.

Rosen stopped in the doorway, turned.

'Tom. When Parker and Willis have finished their work, let's sit down with two pieces of paper.'

'I'm busy.'

'We'll make a list of all the forensic evidence—'

'Did you hear me?'

'—recovered from the loft space and, on the—'

'Not now!'

'—other piece of paper, we'll make a list of what was recovered from the garden. One list will be long, one will be short.'

Baxter was on his feet, almost dancing.

'I've listened to you, please listen to me,' insisted Rosen.

Rosen held his hand up, fingers curled into a fist, thumb outstretched.

'I checked with the sergeant's log about my time of arrival and double-checked my time leaving the scene with Parker, Willis and my DS. I was – bodily *speaking* – there for two and three-quarter hours. You can speculate until you're blue in the face about my state of mind, but I was at the scene fast and I stayed until I couldn't squeeze another drop from it. Remember the scene-of-crime log audit that your glorious predecessor inflicted on us? When you were a senior investigating officer, you averaged one hour fifty-five in initial arrivals over ten separate murder scenes. By the light of presenteeism, I have the edge on you, Tom. Why not make a pair of comparative graphs and email them to the CC?'

Baxter, the expert statistician who used statistics to bully, embarrass and punish other officers, said, 'You've told me everything I needed to know. Goodbye, David.'

10

When Rosen arrived home, Sarah was in bed. He showered and slid in beside her somewhere between ten and half past. She was in a deep sleep and didn't stir. Within minutes David, too, was fast asleep.

At a quarter to two in the morning, the electrical rhythm in his brain shifted and he began the slow ascent to wakefulness. With his arm beneath the duvet, his hand travelled into the cold space beside him where Sarah should have been, but found only emptiness.

His feet hit the floor.

'Sarah!' he called, as he went out onto the landing. All the bedroom doors were closed. Light filtered from the crack at the bottom of the bathroom door.

'It's not locked,' she said.

Sarah stood at the sink. She smiled at him in spite of the discomfort that creased her face. Her blue eyes were dulled with fatigue, her shoulder-length blonde hair tied back in a ponytail.

'I'm forty-one,' she said, wincing in the mirror. 'But I only look ninety.'

'You look great,' Rosen countered. 'How are you?'

'It's really uncomfortable,' she explained. 'Go back to bed, there's nothing you can do, David. I'll be fine.'

He sat next to her on the edge of the bath.

'When did the GP say your appointment would be?'

'He didn't. As soon as possible was as accurate as he could be.'

'I'll come with you.'

'If you can; but don't worry if events overtake us.'

It was a rerun of the conversation they'd had over her GP appointment.

'What are you going to tell them in school?' asked David.

'I'll reassure them. I'm not going off my rocker again. I'm taking my lithium like a good girl. No need to book in a long-term supply teacher. What's happening with you?'

'Baxter's ordering a peer review—'

'Oh, the slimy little toe-rag. What a waste of time, what a waste of money.'

'It's a humility exercise. For me.'

'Which will conclude that there's nothing more that you could have done to catch this Herod.'

She laid her arm across his back and settled a hand on his shoulder. They looked at each other in the mirror on the wall.

'It's at times like this I wish I was twenty-four and still in the TA.'

He smiled, recalling that when they'd first met, he'd thought she was kidding him when she told him she was in the Territorial Army.

'OK,' he said. 'Why the sudden urge to step back in time?'

'I had access to a gun back then. I'd go and put a bullet in Baxter for you. And on behalf of quite a few other people.'

'The things we forget . . .' He looked at his wife and remembered the young woman who was top of her squadron on the firing range, who couldn't be beaten at darts.

'Are you looking at my wrinkles, David?'

'You're not well; you look uncomfortable, not old.'

'Old as the bloody hills my granny played on as a little girl.'

'But not as old as me. Come back to bed?'

'Just a little longer. I still feel like I might throw up. Any other news?'

'Yeah, I'm revisiting a former childhood haunt in the morning. Kent . . .'

'Kent? Why?'

'Like beggars, desperate coppers can't be choosers.'

'Who are you going to see?'

'A Catholic priest. Father Sebastian. He claims he has a specific insight into the killer's motive.'

'Isn't that what the forensic psychologists get paid for?'

'I guess.'

He felt a deadness creeping into the backs of his thighs, from his hard perch on the edge of the bath.

They were silent for more than a minute.

'I think it's settled down a bit. Let's go back to bed. I'm growing sick of the sight of the toilet. If I feel the need to be sick, I'll run.'

He followed her, turned off the bathroom light, glanced into the darkness and turned the light back on to make the way back easier if it was needed. He drew the quilt over Sarah and tucked it in around her shoulders and arms, making sure she was covered.

'I saw Brantwood Road, on Sky News,' said Sarah. 'When I was downstairs on the sofa. I was channel-hopping when I could keep my eyes open.'

'Oh, yes?' he said breezily, but in his mind he was back in the old lady's room, an open locket on the dresser, the faces of two children, a lock of hair; and a corpse, unmissed and unmourned, in the bed just behind him.

'I had a thought, about this Herod. It's more specific. He hates his mother. He hates his mother with a vengeance but – turn the light out, David.'

The room was full of textured darkness, corrugations of shadow. Sarah curled into Rosen.

45

'I'll pick you up from school tomorrow. Five-ish?'

'Full governors' meeting, I'm afraid,' she replied.

'Then I'll see you at ten o'clock tomorrow night. I wish you hadn't taken on that teacher-governor's job.' He backtracked to what she'd just said about Herod. 'He hates his mother. The forensic psychs said as much.'

'But somewhere,' said Sarah, 'beneath the depths of hatred he has for the woman who gave birth to him, he hates himself much more. Yes, he's murdering these poor women, but what he's doing with the babies is ritual self-destruction. He's removing himself from the face of the earth.'

'If he's removing himself from the face of the earth, then what's the reverse side of the action?'

'What do you mean?' Her voice was sleepy.

'What's he replacing himself with?'

'Maybe that's the scariest thing. Something inhuman.'

'Mind if I pass that off as my idea at the next team briefing?'

'Haven't the forensic psychologists said as much?'

'No.'

'No?'

Within moments, her breathing changed and she was on the descent into sleep. Rosen, his body aching and tired, his mind wide awake, craved sleep but grew accustomed to the darkness, wondering what Herod was aspiring to and hoping that somehow the morning would bring a better day.

11

The memory of all those childhood autumns spent on that flat land brought with it a sense of shame and anger. Before the Kent farms all became fully mechanized, the work of picking hops was light and well paid. His mum had sold it to him and his brothers and sisters as an annual holiday, but as Rosen grew older, it had to become another thing to resent.

The work was monotonous, the stuff of dead ends, not of dreams. And, each year, he was thrust into the company of the same migrant families, a protracted reminder of the hand-to-mouth world he longed to escape.

Aged thirteen, he knew for a fact that football and music were never going to be his way out. Hard, meaningful work with a solid education were the key to a better life. But, each year, in September and October, he missed the first half-term of school, and from November through to the following July he felt he never quite caught up.

The weather had improved a little and the sun coaxed a dreamy mist over the flatlands. St Mark's was a turn in the road away. Rosen switched on the radio, Classic FM. Vaughan Williams's take on 'Greensleeves'. He turned it off and stopped the car at the mouth of the entrance of

St Mark's, invaded by the strangest urge. *Turn round, go home, resign from the case, give in to Baxter and straighten paper clips until you retire or die, whichever comes first.*

He drove down the lane and parked at the front entrance of the monastery. There was no one there to greet him and, as he got out of his car, he imagined for a moment he was in some place deserted by all humankind.

He thought he could smell hops but it was the wrong time of year. Then, he heard a voice.

'Can I help you?' It belonged to a fat, bald man, sweating through exertion. He wiped his fingers on his dungarees and extended a wet hand that was still caked in dirt. Rosen recognized the voice from his answering machine.

'Brother Aidan?'

'Yes?' The monk sounded mildly surprised to be identified. 'Who are you?'

'You left a message on my answering machine. I'm DCI David Rosen from the Met.' Rosen showed his warrant card and Brother Aidan took a half-step backwards.

Mild surprise gave way to something more uneasy. 'You didn't reply,' Aidan answered, defensively. Grey stubble dotted his face and scalp, and there was something rubbery about his features that made Rosen think of a cheap Hallowe'en disguise.

'I did. What were you doing at nine o'clock last night?'

'We were in evening prayer.'

'That's when I called you back, Brother Aidan.'

'But who answered?'

'Father Sebastian. I've travelled from London to meet him.'

'Well, I—'

Aidan looked as if he was casting around in his mind for excuses, as if the suddenness of Rosen's arrival made the meeting somehow a non-starter.

The prospect of yet another disappointment overtook Rosen.

'We arranged it last night as you were praying.'

'Yeah, yes, I'm sure you did. I'll take you to him.'

———

WHEN ROSEN FOLLOWED Aidan across the threshold of St Mark's, he felt the urge to remove his shoes and was glad he'd forgotten his mobile phone, leaving it in the car.

'There are seven men permanently here, including myself and Father Sebastian,' Aidan replied to a question Rosen hadn't posed.

Above the staircase, a Victorian oil painting of St Dominic, unsmiling and solitary, cast his eyes on Rosen as he made his way up to the upstairs landing and a dark windowless corridor.

'I was surprised by his asking me to call you.' Aidan smiled but didn't look happy. 'You should listen to him closely. He's – the word *blessed* seems inappropriate. He's insightful.'

Aidan stopped at a door with the number eleven painted onto its dark surface. There was a single scratch mark that cut through the white digits, along with a network of cracks, and made Rosen think of a DNA helix.

'There are more rooms than men,' said Aidan, tapping on the door, nervously it seemed to Rosen. Silence. He knocked again, a little more firmly and said, 'Father Sebastian? You have a visitor. Father, are you there?'

In the space of a breath, Rosen recollected the grey acres of his childhood. The central image was of a thin man, his own absent father, with a few possessions stuffed into two carrier bags, walking away from the front door of the flat, along the landing of the tenement block, never looking back as he turned onto the staircase, never to be seen again.

'He mightn't be in his room.' Aidan banged on the door with the palm of his hand. 'He has hearing difficulties. After Kenya.'

Slowly, Aidan turned the handle and pushed the door open. Inside the room, a match was struck on a coarse surface, its red tip flaring. The door opened wider.

His back turned to the opening door, Father Sebastian was lighting an incense stick. A sliver of smoke rose from its tip. He killed the match with dampened finger and thumb.

It was a small room, with a single bed, one closed window, a small row of books, and a porcelain sink with a mirror above in which Rosen glimpsed Father Sebastian's face. His eyes were blue, his face ageing but model handsome, his hair black and slick with sweat or water. Their eyes connected in the glass.

'It's an upside-down and back-to-front world,' said the priest, smiling and turning. 'Chief Inspector David Rosen?'

'Father Sebastian.'

'Thank you for coming to see me. Would you like to – please, come in.'

Sebastian turned back to the sink, ran hot water over a white flannel and placed the plug in the plughole. His white T-shirt was grey with age and clung to his back with a circle of sweat. There was a hole in the side, the size of a fifty-pence piece, just above the hip where the elasticized band of his shapeless jogging bottoms hugged his narrow waist. *Lean and poor*, thought Rosen, *poor and lean*.

Rosen moved into the room, the smell of incense rising above the salt of the priest's body and the fading sulphur of the match.

'Aidan, thank you so much for calling Detective Rosen.'

'You spoke with him yourself, last night.'

'A ringing phone in an empty room. In the silence of the evening, the sound could have pierced the walls and disturbed your prayers. I picked up and spoke to Detective Rosen. Serendipity.'

He dipped his head and wiped his face with the flannel.

So why weren't you praying with them?, thought Rosen, but asked, 'You a keen runner, Father?'

'Just a couple of hours each morning.'

'Would you like some tea, Detective Rosen?' asked Aidan. 'Coffee, perhaps?'

'Aidan, we'll join you in the kitchen, in a few minutes,' said the priest, and Rosen wondered who the most senior member of the community was.

'No problem, Sebastian.'

Aidan closed the door and walked away with brisk footsteps; the sounds of someone keen to be elsewhere.

There were deep white marks, fierce lines on the priest's skin, scar tissue, showing through the wet patch on his T-shirt. Rosen ran his eyes up and down his muscular arms. Nothing. Only unmatching sweatbands, oddly old-fashioned, around each wrist, and on his feet trainers that didn't belong to the same pair.

'I hope you don't mind the holy smoke. It's a small room and it becomes unpleasant if I don't. Someone, some clever soul, painted over the woodwork on the window and it's stuck, it won't open.'

Sebastian dried his face on a hand towel and sat down on the bed.

'I haven't got a chair.'

The bed was the only alternative then, to standing awkwardly and trying not to stare down at the priest's face.

Rosen sat on the bed. On the floor, at his feet, face down, lay a sheet of glossy paper, A4, with blu-tak in each corner. A picture for the bare walls? There were blu-tak marks on the wall between the bed and the sink, and the discolorations made Rosen think of the remains of the old lady at 24 Brantwood Road; chemical stains left behind by a neglected life.

'You look pensive, Detective.' Rosen felt pensive. 'Mind if I call you David?'

'Not at all.'

'Did your mother name you after the great Hebrew king?'

'I come from a long line of secular Jews, Father. But I am married to a Catholic.'

He appeared not to hear.

'You didn't do Hebrew at your school?'

'We didn't do a great deal of English at my school, Father.'

'I'm younger than you, David. Drop the "Father", and call me Sebastian, if you like.'

'You said you had some information.'

'What a world we live in.'

Rosen gave him time, but he said nothing further for what soon felt like too long. Monastic time and real time collided in Rosen's head and his patience frayed. He pulled a dictaphone from his pocket.

'Mind if I record this chat of ours?'

Nothing. Not a flicker.

Rosen pressed 'record'.

'Date, fourteenth of March. Time of interview, eight-fifteen. DCI David Rosen interviewing Father Sebastian, in his room, room number eleven, at St Mark's Monastery, near Faversham in Kent. No other witnesses present.'

Amusement danced in the priest's eyes.

'Would you please state your name? For the tape.'

'Father Sebastian.'

'Father, you told me on the telephone last night that you knew the motive for the killings of four women and the abduction of Julia Caton. Is that correct?'

'That is correct.'

'You also told me how the killer gained access to the home of his fifth victim.' Flint nodded at Rosen's words. 'That detail is known only to the police and to the killer. Given that knowledge, and your claim to knowing the motive for the abduction and killings, then, logically, as I stated on the phone last night, this means you either know the killer or are the killer.'

'I do not know the killer. I am not the killer.'

'Then how do you know the motive?'

'I also told you, on the phone last night, I was once the pope's adviser on all matters relating to the occult.'

'That is indeed what you told me.' Rosen made a mental note to check the claim.

Silence, broken only by the drone of a tractor in the distant countryside.

'How does your former occupation give you an insight into the motive for the murders? How does your expertise in the occult allow you to know how the killer got into Julia Caton's home?'

A battered gathering of hardback and paperback books by the bedside. *The Holy Bible NIV*. *Malleus Maleficarum*. St Augustine's *Confessions*. St Julian of Norwich's *Revelations of Divine Love*. *Thomas à Kempis*. *Songs of Innocence and Experience* by William Blake.

Rosen touched his throat.

'Insight, Father Sebastian – what is your insight into the killer's motive?'

'These are copycat killings, I suspect. Does the name Alessio Capaneus mean anything to you?'

'Should it?'

'Not really. He's a fairly obscure figure, remembered by few. It's my belief, I'm afraid, that he's at the root of these abductions and killings.'

'Who is Alessio Capaneus?'

'Was. He's dead.'

'Who was Alessio Capaneus?'

'He was alive somewhere around 1265; his date of birth is not certain but he died for sure in 1291. There's no doubt about his demise.'

Rosen was suddenly visited by the notion that he'd seen the priest before, that he knew his face, but couldn't fix it in a time or place.

'Who was he?'

'He was a necromancer, one who conjures up the dead to learn the secrets of heaven and hell. He lived in Florence.'

'In the thirteenth century?'

Because it was officially his day off, Rosen couldn't charge the priest with wasting police time, but he couldn't help his desperate disappointment showing in his slowly sinking shoulders.

'David, you're looking at me as if I should be in a psychiatric unit, not a monastery.'

'No, I'm . . . I'm sure I've seen you before.'

Was he one of those vague rambling men who used to haunt the day room when Sarah was ill in hospital? *If so,* thought Rosen, *I must be kind to the priest, and patient, not let my disappointment show.*

'I'm sorry, Father, you were saying.'

'Very little is known about him. He abducted and killed six Florentine women and removed their babies from their wombs.'

'That's why you said he'd take one more woman after Julia Caton?'

'Exactly. There is one telling detail: the audacious manner of abducting his fifth victim from her home by breaking into the house next door. It's my view that Capaneus was pouring contempt on the Florentine authorities and cranking up the terror. But so little else is known. It's as if the human race made a decision long ago to wipe the memory of Capaneus from the face of the earth. A fragment here, a mention there in a footnote. Some scholars – the ones who have heard of him – even deny his existence, claiming it as a medieval myth, one of many designed to control and suppress women.'

'If there's any information about him, it's bound to be on the internet,' observed Rosen.

'We don't have the internet here. Or TV. We do have a radio. This is how I learned of the murders in the capital.'

'I have a laptop. We could look him up on the internet, before I leave.'

'We'd have to OK it with Aidan, he's in charge.'

Rosen searched Sebastian's face for a smile, a flicker of irony, but he was deadpan.

Sebastian picked up the picture that had fallen onto the floor and looked at the image, showing only the blank side to Rosen. He placed it face downwards on the pillow.

'Aren't you going to put the picture back on the wall?' suggested Rosen.

'This afternoon perhaps.'

Rosen wanted to know which single image the priest would exhibit in the confines of his cell and said, 'No time like the present.'

'Then I'll have nothing to do later on today.'

'Coffee. Let's have a coffee.'

Rosen suspended the interview, shut down the dictaphone and followed the priest out of the poverty of his narrow room.

12

The kitchen at St Mark's was stone-built but warm from the iron ovens, and full of the aroma of bread and coffee. *A great hideout from the world*, thought Rosen.

Aidan stood at a distance that professed a lack of interest in the internet but at an angle that allowed him to see the screen.

'There was a time,' said Sebastian, 'when you had to get into the British Library to see anything like this. Have you been to the British Library, Aidan?'

'I've never been, Sebastian.'

'OK! We're in business.' Rosen ran his index finger over the mouse pad as Aidan placed two mugs of coffee on the plain wooden table on which sat the laptop.

'Thanks, Aidan.' Sebastian moved the cups to a safe distance from Rosen's laptop and asked, 'Not joining us?'

Aidan raised a glass of water to his lips and shook his head.

'Type the name of the person in the box,' said Rosen, an unconfident speller.

With one finger, Sebastian typed the words *Alessio Capaneus* and asked, 'What now?'

Rosen rolled the cursor onto the search button and clicked. Just 0.73 seconds later 1,400,000 matches had been found.

'Wow!' A sigh of heartfelt wonder escaped Sebastian.

'Don't get too excited. They aren't all actually about the man we're investigating.'

Rosen scrolled down the first page and, after the sixth reference, direct references to Alessio Capaneus went cold. He skipped to page two and found a reference that replicated one from the first page. Page three, nothing. Four, five, six, seven, blank. Nothing.

He came back to the first page.

'You're going too fast for me,' said Sebastian.

'You were right. He is obscure.'

Of the six sites found, three were one and the same. The fourth and fifth site contained a one-line reference to 'Alessio Capaneus, thirteenth-century witch'.

'But he wasn't a witch,' said Sebastian.

'Which gives you a clue as to how reliable information on the internet can be.'

'You mean there's no editorial control on the internet?' Sebastian sounded astonished.

Rosen didn't know what to say, or where to begin explaining, so he just said, 'That's correct, Father Sebastian. There is no editorial control on the internet. It would be like trying to create order in grains of desert sand when a windstorm was raging. Didn't you use the internet when you were at the Vatican?'

'Grains of sand?' replied the priest. The sixth site merely listed Alessio Capaneus among other known Florentines of the period. 'The internet was just about coming in when I left Rome for Kenya.'

'What were you doing in Kenya?' asked Rosen.

'The Lord's work. What about these three at the top?' asked Sebastian.

'It's . . . the same three.' Rosen clicked onto the top site. 'It's a directory of the occult. Look.' He scrolled so that the single paragraph referring to Alessio Capaneus was visible on screen.

> Alessio Capaneus, thirteenth century, precise birth date and parentage unknown, Florentine street child, taken into the home of Filippo Capaneus, White Guelph (who gave him his family name), as penance for pederastic abuse.

'Tshhh!' The sound escaped from Rosen's lips, steam from the valves of his heart. 'Brilliant. Punish a paedophile by making him take in a vulnerable child.'

'You have a child, David?' asked the priest.

Rosen looked at the priest and then back at the laptop screen.

'No,' he replied. 'No, no . . .'

'I thought you were going to say, "Yes" and then you said "No" . . . three times.'

Rosen tapped the screen and began reading aloud, 'Alessio began having religious visions, which became more and more disturbing, evoking violent reactions from the teenager.' The almost invisible footprint of someone from the depths of history started mattering to him. The boy who was Alessio Capaneus was no doubt driven mad by the attentions of a sexually perverted stepfather. He continued to read:

> Exiled from Florence, he returned – incognito – with esoteric texts from the Middle East and Africa. He was arrested, tried and hanged for the abduction and murder of six pregnant women, notably Beatrice Ciacco, fifth victim, a neighbour of the Capaneus family. Capaneus broke into his family home and into the Ciacco house to abduct Beatrice. Foetuses were removed for an obscure Satanic rite. Under torture, Capaneus refused to testify. Following moral

panic, his execution sparked a riot in which his body was torn down from the gallows and ripped asunder so that no vestige of his earthly existence remained.

'That's why I asked Aidan to contact you. That's why I told you he'd take another woman after he'd destroyed Julia Caton and her child.'

'What else do you know about Capaneus?' Rosen tried to hide the hunger in his voice.

'To be honest, I've learned a great deal simply from looking at this account on the internet. This is positively encyclopaedic. I didn't know he was a street child, I assumed he was a blood member of the Capaneus family. His name and his crime and the time and place he lived in: that's the sum of my knowledge.'

'There must be other information about him out there.'

'I haven't seen anything other than two references in articles about the Florentine legal system.'

'Can you recall what the references to Capaneus stated?' asked Rosen, without much hope.

'Something about a book he's alleged to have written, or a pamphlet.'

'What's the book called, Father Sebastian?'

'It's speculation, hearsay from the trial.' He shook his head. 'I don't think such a book exists.'

'No one's going to copycat on such meagre pickings. There's got to be more meat on the bone to inspire a copycat.' Rosen moved up a gear.

'Then it's down to you to find it, Detective Rosen. The meat and the bone.'

Outside, a blackbird gave up her song and an ascending plane made the sky moan.

'If you don't mind me asking, Father Sebastian, how did you get to be a papal adviser on the occult?'

'I gained a PhD in Anthropolgy from Cambridge. My thesis, "Beyond *The Golden Bough*", required me to research magic and ritual.'

That's how, thought Rosen, with the ache of a boy who'd never quite caught up in class.

'Is there anything else you'd like to add, Father Sebastian?'

Sebastian shook his head. Across the length of the kitchen, Rosen read the crease in Aidan's brow.

'Nothing at all?' Rosen pushed the priest but looked directly at Aidan.

'I've told you everything I know.' A flicker of thought made the priest's expression quizzical.

'What is it, Father?' asked Rosen.

'Can you look up anyone on the internet?'

'Just Google the name. Want me to do you?'

The priest laughed and looked at Brother Aidan, who said, 'Why not?'

Rosen typed in 'Father Sebastian' and within a second an ocean of matches came up but none, it seemed, immediately to match Father + Sebastian + Flint. He scrolled. Nothing. He turned to page two. In the middle, a page of obituaries for Roman Catholic priests. The priest's name was there.

Rosen opened the site and scrolled through the brief nutshells of the lives of dead priests.

'Well, it can't be you, obviously,' said Rosen. 'There are other people who share the same name, of course.'

'Let me see . . .' said the priest. He read out, 'Father Sebastian, born Bolton, England, 1969, missionary to Kenya, died near Lake Victoria in a road traffic accident, 1998.'

Rosen watched the priest closely.

He looked back at the police officer.

'You can't believe everything you see on the internet, I guess,' said Father Sebastian.

From Rosen's laptop, two loud sudden notes. Aidan dropped his glass, shards scattering across the stone floor, water spreading across the smooth surface. Sebastian didn't seem to notice the accident, his attention fixed on the laptop.

'What was that?' Sebastian asked, then added, 'Here, Aidan, let me help you.'

'I've got an email,' Rosen replied, but Sebastian was busy on his hands and knees, picking up pieces of jagged glass.

Rosen opened it.

From: Carol Bellwood
Subject: Urgent!
   David, I've tried your phone several times. Get back asap. Call me as soon as you can. Development! Carol

Rosen thanked the priests for their time and apologized for the suddenness of his departure.

'God bless you, David Rosen!' Father Sebastian's voice followed Rosen as he swept out of the kitchen.

Aidan turned to Sebastian.

'You said you'd tell me why you wanted to speak to the police officer.'

'Detective Rosen's arrival reminded me of something. Of what the world does and doesn't do, Aidan. It just doesn't do faith. You saw the way he looked when he was searching out that information about Capaneus. He was humouring me, almost as if I'd committed an act of indecent exposure of the spirit. I wanted to help, that was all. But the world doesn't believe in what it cannot see, own, eat or fornicate with. You know that. I know that.'

Father Sebastian fell silent. Brother Aidan drew breath to speak but said nothing as the priest held up his index finger.

'Aidan, I'll tell you what I'm going to do. I'm going to rack my brain, and I'm going to pray for inspiration, and I'm going to sit in quiet contemplation of what those poor women and children have suffered and what their families are suffering. Is that good enough for you?'

Sebastian stood up and dropped broken glass into the bin. He spread his fingers and stared into the lines on his hands.

'You always try to make me feel that I'm not quite good enough,' said the priest. Something faceless, yet with a strong pulse, raced along Aidan's spine.

'You think essentially that I'm a bad man, Aidan; you think I'm a bad man and a bad priest, don't you?'

He moved to the door.

'Sebastian, please—'

'I'm glad, Brother Aidan,' said Sebastian, without turning, 'that you haven't lived through my life, my suffering. That's all.'

As Father Sebastian walked out, Brother Aidan stooped to pick up the finer shards of glass from the cold stone floor.

———

SIX MISSED MESSAGES. All from Carol Bellwood. Rosen returned the call as he turned on the ignition.

'Hello, David, where are you?' She was outdoors and in a hurry.

'St Mark's, Faversham, Kent.'

'You've got to get back here.'

'I got your email . . . what's the development?'

'The old lady from 24 Brantwood Road. The pathologist says—'

'Which pathologist?'

'Dr Sweeney.'

She said something else but the line wasn't good and her voice broke up. 'I missed that, Carol. Again?'

'The old lady was murdered. Eighteen months ago.'

13

In life, the old lady at 24 Brantwood Road had the name Isobel Swift. In the fluorescent glare of the mortuary, there was something birdlike about her skeleton, a lightness and vulnerability that reminded Rosen – if a reminder was needed – how fragile life was.

Dr Sweeney hummed an improvised melody and rinsed his hands under the tap, the sound of running water reminding Rosen of Father Sebastian and his impoverished room. But instead of aromatic incense and the undertone of sweat, the mortuary smelled of chemical cold and the ultimate transience of the flesh.

Sweeney snapped on his gloves, his fingers, much travelled into the dark spaces of the human body, flexing in the harsh overhead light. Of all the rooms and places Rosen had had to enter in his capacity as a detective, the mortuary was the one he always wanted to be out of fastest.

'Detective Rosen.'

Rosen raised his eyes from Isobel Swift to meet Sweeney's.

'Cadavers can't bite.' Sweeney may have sounded happy, but his face was frozen behind an impassive mask. 'She died of asphyxiation and the person who killed her knew what he was doing. I wouldn't even rule out an advanced knowledge of medicine or the human body. There are five separate and deliberate blows to the ribcage. The five ribs have penetrated inwards, two to the left, three to the right. Within her chest, blood had flooded both lungs. Look at the top ribs: they're short and chunky and hardly ever break. He's picked the middle ribs, dainty and long. Why? Because it takes a long time to die of a haemothorax. If you were speculating about her death, she drowned in the thin air around her, so to speak, her own blood filling up her lungs from within.'

Rosen considered. In a bungled burglary, he'd once seen an old lady's ribcage smashed in a panic of blows. But the breaks before his eyes were precise and had a sinister symmetry.

'Sadistic,' whispered Rosen. 'Only five broken ribs, so it took the longest possible time to die. This man wanted to observe.' He stopped thinking aloud when he saw the smile in Sweeney's eyes evolve into a smirk.

'What is it, Dr Sweeney?'

'Why do you insist on tormenting yourself over the victims?'

Rosen was lost for words. Bellwood stepped closer to the slab. She said 'Whoever did this wanted to savour and enjoy it.'

Sweeney's forehead shone in the overhead light of the windowless room.

A string of possibilities occurred to Rosen, which he kept to himself. *The person who killed Mrs Swift, eighteen months ago, is Herod. Herod doesn't appear to know his more recent victims, but I'd bet my last pound he knew Mrs Swift. What's the link here? How do the pieces connect?*

'Anything else to add, Dr Sweeney?'

'Do you mean, was there any sexual interference, Detective Rosen?'

Rosen wished hard for a 'no'.

'It's hard to tell from a skeleton but I've had an initial report from the forensics lab and there was no semen on her bedsheets and nothing alien came out of the pubic comb-through.' Sweeney spoke to Rosen as if he was a child, and a rather stupid one at that.

'Let's go, Carol.'

Although grateful for Sweeney's information, Rosen resisted the urge to thank him or even say farewell to a man who thought compassion was a sign of weakness.

———

'YOU THINK THERE'S a link between Mrs Swift's murder and the murder of our pregnant mothers?' he asked Bellwood.

'The proximity between numbers 22 and 24 could be a coincidence. What do you think, David?'

'It's too much of a coincidence. We know Herod was in 24 Brantwood Road recently. We know there was a murder there eighteen months ago. We know he abducted a woman from number 22 in the last few days. Running parallel with this is a medical background. He knew which ribs to break, he knows how to perform a Caesarean section. That's the only certain link.'

Rosen hung on to Flint's connection to Alessio Capaneus, sticking to hard facts.

'As a link it's a useful one,' said Bellwood. 'But as a line of inquiry it's going to be hard to progress.'

'Granted.' Rosen considered for a moment. 'You know what we need to do, Carol?'

He went back in his mind's eye to Mrs Swift's bedroom, stopped at the dresser and scanned the surface, settling on one item.

'We need to meet the children in the golden locket, the little boy and the teenage girl. And the girl whose bedroom was a museum.'

'But the girl in the locket was the girl in the bedroom—'

'No,' said Rosen. 'Two different girls. There was a picture of the girl in her bedroom. The girl in the locket had dark hair. The bedroom girl was blonde. We'll go there now. And, Carol, as soon as we're done at

Brantwood Road, I need you to dig out contact details for the Roman Catholic diocese of Southwark.'

'Sure,' she replied, with a mild twist of bewilderment.

As they walked, Bellwood's phone beeped, signalling the arrival of a text, which she opened without breaking her stride.

'What is it?' asked Rosen.

'It's good timing. Text message from Parker and Willis at the Catons' house. They want us to get over there now. Good news and bad.'

'Tell them we're on our way.'

14

'You wanna see some dirty pictures?' asked Parker, leading Rosen and Bellwood into Julia and Phillip Caton's brand-new fitted kitchen.

Sitting on a black marble-effect work surface was a laptop computer, turned on and casting a blue light onto the polished surface.

'Where's Willis?' asked Bellwood. Parker pointed at Willis who was seated on the floor, back against the cooker, head slumped and asleep, hands folded in her lap.

'We worked through the night,' explained Parker.

Bellwood tapped Willis on the shoulder and she got to her feet instantly.

'Do you want the good news or the bad?' asked Parker.

'The bad,' said Rosen.

'The bricks that he handled in the loft,' said Parker. 'Not a single fingerprint on any of them. OK, disappointing to say the least, but have a look at this.'

Parker indicated the laptop. Onscreen, there was an image of a square wooden frame. 'What's this?' asked Rosen.

'It's the frame around the loft entrance,' said Willis. 'Watch closely.' She moved on to the next image, a close-up of a section of the frame. 'He's left us a present.'

'Yes!' Rosen saw a small, wet-looking stain on the wood.

'What is it?' Bellwood peered at the image, her view distorted by standing at an oblique angle to the screen.

'It's a fresh ear print. It's the outside edge of his right ear. When he's been doing his peeping Tom thing through the hole in the loft door, he's printed his ear onto the wooden frame.' Willis moved on to the next image, a large close-up of the print. She drew her finger over the shape. It was an almost perfect outline.

Rosen picked up the laptop and held it close to his face, his eyes digging into the shell-like image of the place where all sound entered Herod's head, the sounds made by the mothers, their breathing, their pleas, their screams.

'He's a Satanist.' Rosen dropped the statement casually. The power in the fridge's motor shifted up a gear, its steady hum higher pitched.

'Hang on, David,' responded Bellwood. 'We've had several forensic psychologists, some paid, some offering their advice gratis, but they all came to the same conclusion. *This is not an occult thing.* None of the usual supernatural gibberish – you told me this yourself when I joined the team last month.'

'Let's assume he's a Satanist,' Rosen repeated, slightly more quietly. 'OK. There's no Satanic graffiti on the victims; we've taken expert advice and there's no ritualistic precedent; there's no significance in the murder dates and try as we might we can't detect a pattern in the body drop-offs.'

'Satanism's got something in common with Christianity, David,' replied Bellwood. 'It's a social activity. The sheer lack of forensic evidence shouts out that this is the work of one man, not the collective action of a gang of counter-culture weirdos.'

Rosen suddenly heard Harrison's voice in another room, coming closer.

'Bear with me. Put the occult idea on the back burner. What have we got here and now?' he asked, changing the subject.

'About the potential of this ear print,' said Bellwood. 'It's clearly the most significant clue he's left—'

'Not necessarily,' said Willis. She handed a small evidence bag to Parker, one he clearly hadn't seen before. 'I just went up for one more look; I had a feeling, you know.' Parker looked back at Willis, perplexed. 'I fell asleep while I was waiting for you to tell you about it.'

It was short and black and looked greasy, almost wet.

'Where'd you find it?'

'It was jammed between the loft entrance and the flooring, right above the Catons' bathroom. Near the ear print on the frame. He lost a hair in the process of spying on them.'

Rosen gazed at the hair, transfixed. The ear print was one thing but the sight of Herod's hair sent a surge of electricity through his body.

'It was hard to get hold of the hair with the tweezers, as there was just a small piece poking out through the join between the entrance and the flooring. It felt coated in oil. To be honest, even though I went over and over the loft entrance, I nearly missed it. What are we going to do with it?' Willis asked.

Rosen knew exactly what he was going to do.

'You remember that guy John Mason, the forensic artist who reconstructed the head and face of the first victim in the Black Box case? He had just one section of skull to work from.'

'Yes,' said Bellwood. 'Mason Forensic Images.'

'Fingers crossed he's available. Every constabulary in the country queues up for his help. We'll copy him in on the hair and ear print. He did the Black Box job in twenty-four hours.'

Rosen noticed that Harrison, who had now joined them in the kitchen, was positioning himself just out of his eyeline.

'Any news, Robert?' asked Rosen. 'On the door to door?'

'Yeah, actually. The old lady at number 35, she hasn't answered her door. Until now. Says she's got something to tell us.'

'What did she say exactly, Robert?' Rosen turned his head to look Harrison in the eye.

'She said, *I want to speak to the nice young woman.* She's been watching the comings and goings and she described you, Carol. She wants to talk to you, *the black girl*, she said.'

'OK, Robert,' said Rosen. 'Thanks for that. Now I've got a job for you.' Rosen handed him a piece of paper on which Harrison silently read the words, 'Alessio Capaneus'.

'Internet search. Go back to Isaac Street and find out as much as you can about this guy. There won't be much but just keep going. Go as far as two hundred pages. Print off every page. Show me you've been there. Go into any sites that throw up a meaningful match, print those sites off.'

'Who is Alessio Capaneus?'

'That's what I want you to find out. While you're looking, I want you to focus on any reference at all to a book or a pamphlet this Capaneus may possibly have written.'

Rosen recalled the one detail that stood out from Harrison's skills profile. He could speak Italian. He'd followed Sebastian's pronunciation of the surname but Harrison had turned 'Cap-a-nay-us' into 'Cap-a-knee-us'.

'And make a note of this name. Father Sebastian. I want you to get in touch with the Vatican and find out what his working history was in Rome. Was he or was he not a papal adviser, mid to late nineties?'

Harrison reiterated, 'Father Sebastian? The Vatican?'

'Two tasks, Robert. Try to come up with the goods as quickly as you can.'

Harrison shrugged as he walked out of the kitchen into the adjoining room. As Rosen followed him, Harrison stopped, turned.

'Yes?'

'If you see Baxter, tell him I'm coming in to see him.'

'Sure.'

Rosen stared at Harrison. Harrison looked away.

'When you've finished on the internet and with the Vatican, leave everything you find on my desk.' Satisfied that Harrison was aware that he was on to him, Rosen said, 'OK, Robert, off you go.'

Harrison left and Rosen returned to the kitchen, bringing back the sour aura of the exchange in the other room.

Rosen smiled but said nothing. He could feel a cold twitch between his shoulder blades, a tender place for a long knife.

'Where did you get this Capaneus thing?' Parker said.

'A Roman Catholic priest called Father Sebastian.'

'Who's this Capaneus? I've never heard of him,' said Bellwood.

'He's pretty obscure. A thirteenth-century necromancer, who abducted and murdered six pregnant women, and cut them up for the foetuses.'

There was a dense silence in the kitchen.

'I know what you're all thinking,' said Rosen. 'That this is desperate. I don't care if it makes me look stupid.'

He turned to Parker and Willis. 'Call Gold or Feldman. If they can, get them to bring John Mason here to look at the hair and the print, but don't let the originals go. If they can't get him, we'll have to cast around for other forensic artists.' He smiled at Bellwood. 'OK, Carol, let's go and see the old lady at number 35.'

15

At 35 Brantwood Road, Rosen positioned himself just out of the old lady's line of vision and pressed record on his dictaphone.

'Well, I was her best friend as far as neighbours go but that was a long time ago and it was all very tragic and, well . . . it was heartbreaking.'

In the brief journey from the front door to the living room, Rosen had learned, though Bellwood had not asked for the information, that the old lady was ninety-seven years old and that for forty years she had been a primary-school teacher.

Bellwood, on a low sofa, looked up and smiled at Mrs Nicholas seated on the high armchair opposite as she folded her arthritic hands in her lap, cleared her throat with a genteel cough and fixed her attention on her.

'Are you ready?' asked Mrs Nicholas. 'If you have any questions could you please save them until the end.'

'Of course.'

And put your hand up first, thought Rosen, with the faintest yet clearest sensation that their luck was turning.

'Isobel Swift was the kind of neighbour anyone in their right mind would wish for. Nothing was too much trouble for her. She kept herself to herself but when you needed a helping hand she had an uncanny knack of being there in the right place, at the right time. She was married to Harold and they had one daughter whom they simply doted on, Gwen . . .' She paused in her delivery and sighed under the weight of memory.

'I'll come to that later on. Isobel wasn't just a woman who had an eye to help those immediately around her, oh no, she had a much broader social conscience than that. After she had Gwen, she found she couldn't have any more children because something went wrong at the birth. I don't know the details, we didn't dwell on such matters in those days, but I suspect she had a hysterectomy. But after she'd had Gwen, Isobel and Harold – he was a lovely man, a true gentleman – decided they were going to foster abandoned children from London orphanages. I kept count. Twelve long-term foster-children . . .'

Rosen made a mental note to pull the Social Services records. Twelve long-term foster-children, and yet Isobel Swift had lain dead and undiscovered in her bed for eighteen months. His focus returned to the old lady.

'. . . and my goodness, they were so good to those children, so good that the council used to send them short-term emergency cases, so many I couldn't possibly keep count. Taxis used to roll up at all hours with social workers carrying little bundles of life to Isobel's door. You know, if a single mum got ill and had to go to hospital or a parent was arrested, it was always the children who suffered.'

Mrs Nicholas took a couple of puffs on an inhaler. Rosen guessed her days, like her weeks, were largely silent and so talking was akin to vigorous exercise.

'But their suffering was alleviated by Isobel.' The old lady fell silent, long enough to warrant a question in spite of the retired teacher's terms and conditions.

'All those foster-children, Mrs Nicholas, and yet no one ever visited her? Why did she lie undisturbed all that time?' Rosen asked, as if speaking a thought out loud.

'It was 1973 or 1974. Everything changed then. Gwen was murdered just before Christmas, on her way home from school in the dark, a dreadful, dreadful time. December, it was 1973, yes. Harold never got over it, of course. He ended up, you know, in a hospital.' She indicated her left temple. 'As for Isobel, she changed overnight. The big light inside her went out. She had three foster-children with her at the time, one long term, two short termers. The last time I was over there, January 1974, just after New Year it was, three foster-children were lined up in the kitchen and she was screaming at them, *Why couldn't it have been you? Why are you still alive? Why aren't you in the ground?* The children were crying, hysterical. I tried to calm things down but she turned on me then, and slapped me in the face, called me an interfering – well, I can't repeat it. They were lovely children. They were forever in and out of here, passing a message for Isobel or seeing if they could earn a little pocket money by doing jobs for me. I even helped the ones that, you know, were a bit slow; I gave them help with their reading.'

Mrs Nicholas leaned forward, staring at a point in space as if eyeballing the past. She came back to Bellwood. 'I don't want to speak ill of the dead,' she said.

'The truth, however unpleasant, is the truth and must be told.'

'She sent the children packing back to Social Services. She stopped speaking to all the neighbours. You want to know what happened to all the other foster-children, the ones that had grown up and used to knock on her door with flowers? She wouldn't answer the door to them. One girl, Susie Armitage, she was eighteen or thereabouts, came over the road to me with some flowers, asked me to mind them, to hand them over to Isobel. Susie broke down on the doorstep. I brought her inside and she showed me this letter that Isobel had sent to her. Poor Susie.'

Mrs Nicholas produced a piece of folded white paper from the pocket of her cardigan and offered it to Bellwood.

'What is this, Mrs Nicholas?'

'Susie asked me to throw it away as she left. I don't know why, but I couldn't do it. It's the letter Isobel sent to Susie.'

Bellwood took the paper and unfolded it.

> *You are not to visit, telephone, write or communicate with*
> *me in any way, shape or form. I wash my hands of you.*
> *Mrs I. Swift*

'Can I hang on to this?'

Mrs Nicholas nodded. 'That's why no one called, not even Susie, who was the favourite of them all. The police never caught Gwen's killer; they seemed to think at the time it was a schoolboy who did it. Some schoolboys were questioned by the police but no one was ever charged with Gwen's murder. I think that just drove Isobel deeper underground.'

Mrs Nicholas fell silent.

'Did Gwen have a middle name?' asked Bellwood.

'Just Gwen Swift.'

'You've been an enormous help, Mrs Nicholas. Thank you.' Bellwood handed Mrs Nicholas her card. 'If anything else occurs to you, please call me straight away on this number.'

'Make sure you shut the door properly on your way out. This road, you know, is a magnet for murderers.'

In the hall on the way out, Rosen took out his mobile phone and Bellwood closed the front door behind them with a reassuring slam.

On the step, Rosen dialled.

'Who are you calling?' she asked.

'Archives, Gwen Swift's cold case file,' replied Rosen.

Walking down the path, Bellwood took out her mobile.

'Who are you calling?' asked Rosen.

'Social Services. We need to track down the foster-children.'

'I was just about to ask you to do that.'

'I guessed you would,' said Bellwood.

Rosen's phone rang and he waited.

'I think this is the worst case I've ever tackled in my life,' he said.

The phone kept ringing as the clouds thickened against the sun.

'Carol?'

'Yes?'

'It's good to have you on board.'

She nodded and, turning away from Rosen, could do nothing to stop the brief smile blossoming on her face.

16

It took several phone calls and two and a half hours for Social Services to come up with the list of the twelve long-term foster-children on Isobel Swift's books. Along with the names, an email arrived with the last known contact details of the twelve and a resolute promise to find the names of the short-term foster-children. Contact details for the twelve went back as far as the mid-1970s and continued up to the early 1980s.

Bellwood looked around the incident room and saw Harrison, staring at his laptop screen, sullen to the marrow, with a pile of printouts from the internet following his search for Alessio Capaneus.

As she began the obligatory task of ringing round the last known numbers, Bellwood watched Harrison make his way to Rosen's desk to drop off the Capaneus printouts. Harrison hovered there, scanning its surface.

He picked up the one framed picture of Rosen's wife and smirked at the image. Bellwood watched, resisting the urge to tell Harrison to put it down.

'Is it true she lost her marbles?' asked Harrison.

'Who?'

'Rosen's wife. I overheard some talk in the canteen when I first came to this nick.'

Bellwood didn't want to have the conversation with Harrison but he already had a little information, so she decided to appeal to any semblance of a better nature in him.

'I don't know the details, Robert, but yes, she did suffer with her nerves though she's well now. Did you hear why she became ill?'

'Nah.'

'They had a baby; this is going back years. Hannah, they named her. She died of cot death.'

'Oh.' He looked completely untouched and Bellwood wished she'd kept her mouth shut.

Harrison passed Bellwood on the way back to his desk. Her face was set, her eyes lowered, her attention locked onto the phone.

'Tough-looking bitch, that old Mrs Rosen,' said Harrison. 'Wouldn't like to get on the wrong side of her in a darkened corner.'

Bellwood said nothing, but committed every word and action to memory.

17

Memory.

Herod sat on the cold stone floor of his basement. The dim blue light gave him the sense that he was hundreds of metres below the surface of the water and the silence that filled his head was like the pressure of a whole ocean bearing down on him.

He surveyed the basement, its doors and fortified walls. If he'd designed it himself, he couldn't have come up with a more user-friendly suite of rooms.

The estate agent who'd sold it to him had been reluctant to fill him in on the background to the basement. But the property had been growing stale on the books and so he had decided to spice things up with a little house history.

'Mr Graham, the farmer who lived here, was in the RAF during World War II. He was an observer when the bomb was dropped on Nagasaki. He never got over it. He'd seen what a little bomb could do at first hand. Actions have consequences. He believed he was going to be paid back. Hence the underground bunker.'

The squalor of the living space above the basement had been in stark contrast to the minimalist perfection below. It was the perfect house. A basement with three rooms. He had asked the estate agent about the door in the basement wall. There was no mention of it in the particulars, or in his sales pitch. The agent had shrugged, opening the half-door to reveal a gouge of darkness.

'It's a tunnel. It's well constructed and it leads to a manhole in the farmyard. Built by Mr Graham in case the radiated survivors out there got down here.'

He had stuck his head into the mouth of the tunnel, breathing in the damp, stale air.

Herod had offered the asking price there and then.

He blitzed the house with two tranches of ten thousand pounds. One pot of money went to a gang of Serbian builders who ripped the place to shreds and restored it to a structurally sound, plastered skeleton. The second pot went to an overfed interior designer who – on his instruction – made the whole place neutral in fixtures, fittings and decor. And with a third pot of five thousand pounds he bought a flotation tank and paid a plumber to install the tank in the basement, along with the oxygen pump. A plumber who insisted on talking about his recent wedding and who, without asking first, had showed a photograph of his bride.

But all that seemed long ago.

The time for the fifth unbirthing was drawing near.

18

It didn't take long for the foster-child trail to go cold on Bellwood.

She managed to trace a Jean White to Perth in Australia where she had moved with her husband and two children. There was a temporary address in Perth but no phone number.

Bellwood replaced the receiver and, as she did so, the phone rang.

'Is that you, Carol?'

It took her a second to work out who the caller was.

'Mrs Nicholas, how are you?'

'I've got your card here, that card you gave me, remember?'

'Yes, of course . . .'

'But you've been engaged an awfully long time: I had to use ringback in the end and that's expensive, but this is important so never mind.'

The old lady went from virtual jabbering to utterly silent in a solitary beat.

'Is there something you've recalled?' probed Bellwood.

'No.'

Bellwood could hear another voice. There was someone in the room with Mrs Nicholas.

'Are you alone, Mrs Nicholas?'

'No. Her name's not Armitage any more because she got married. She's Mrs Cooper now, aren't you, Susie?' In the background, someone replied in the affirmative. 'Carol, guess who I've got here? In the very chair in which you were sitting?'

'I don't know.' Bellwood played along and made a fist of delight beneath her desk. Hope danced on the horizon.

'I've been trying to call you all day but your line's been busy.'

'I do apologize for that, Mrs Nicholas.' Playing to the old lady's sense of theatre, she asked, 'Who are you sitting with, Mrs Nicholas?'

'Susie, Isobel's favourite. Would you like to meet her?'

'I'll be there in half an hour. Please can I speak to her now, briefly?' Seconds passed.

'Hello?' Susie Cooper sounded anxious and upset. 'I've never spoken to a police officer before, regarding, you know, an investigation into *murder*.'

'Susie, my name's Carol, DS Carol Bellwood. Can you wait where you are? You have nothing to worry about, but I would like to speak with you.'

Susie agreed and Bellwood grabbed her coat, anxious to get there quickly in case Susie changed her mind about talking.

19

'As soon as I read about . . .' Susie struggled for the next words. 'Your old foster-mother,' said Mrs Nicholas. 'That's who she was.'

'Yes. I had to come back. All that time, lying dead, no one calling.'

'Don't blame yourself, Susie. She sent you away, after she changed.'

Both Susie and Mrs Nicholas looked directly at Bellwood.

'My parents didn't abandon me. I want you to know that. They didn't not want me. Dad died and Mum had health problems, you know, with her nerves.'

Bellwood felt a welling-up of compassion for the woman in her fifties who spoke of her parents with the defensiveness and uncertainty of a twelve-year-old girl.

'I believe you were the "head girl" in Mrs Swift's house.'

'I was, yes. What's this police business you want me for?'

'Maybe you could help me. I need to know the whereabouts of the other foster-children.'

Susie was quiet, blank faced, and Bellwood feared she was about to dismiss the idea because she, too, was in the dark.

'Then you've come to the right place. I'm in touch with nine of the twelve. I'll talk to them. I know they'll help if they can.'

She reeled off a list of names and, as Bellwood ticked off those in her notepad, she found it strange how the sound of words could make a taste like butter on her tongue.

'I know that Jean went down under in the early nineties,' said Bellwood. 'But what about John Price?'

'Johnny died in the Falklands War.'

'I'm sorry to hear that. There's one last name then. Paul Dwyer?'

'Poor little Paul. I don't know where he is or what he's doing now but I pray to God for him each day. He was the baby.'

'Did he die?'

'No!' Susie looked uncomfortable, began to shift in her seat. 'It was worse than that. On his seventh birthday, on his party day, the doorbell rang, just as he was blowing out the candles and making a wish. Some wish.'

'A fate worse than death, Susie?' prompted Mrs. Nicholas.

'Almost. He'd been with Isobel since he was just days old.'

'Who rang the doorbell that day?'

'His real mother. She called to collect him, to take him back.'

'And that was a fate worse than death?' Bellwood asked.

'My foster-mother tried to fight it but it was no good. He didn't come back, Paul. It was the last we saw of him.'

Bellwood held back, giving Susie room to elaborate.

'That's about all I can think of for now.' she concluded.

Bellwood thanked her for the information and wanted nothing more than to jump up from her seat, call Rosen and hit the HOLMES laptop. Instead, she stayed where she was, and counted to thirty to avoid the appearance of indecent haste. As she sat there, she stripped the years away from Susie's face. It wasn't definite but Bellwood would have wagered a month's salary on her observation.

Susie Cooper was the girl in the gold locket.

20

Baxter didn't announce his intention of attending the five o'clock team briefing, and his silence, when Rosen passed him on his way to address the troops, was loaded. Rosen guessed Baxter was going to hit him with details of the peer review of the case. The peer review was a useful tool when used fairly; it was an extra set of eyes in the dense thickets of casework, but it would be applied by Baxter to humiliate Rosen while giving himself distance in a high-profile case where progress was slow and painful.

'Oh, David . . .' said Baxter, making him stop and have to turn back. 'One of the deputy CCs, Hargreaves, made a good point this morning. He was a beat bobby in West Yorkshire back in the eighties. He hasn't known an atmosphere like this since the West Yorkshire Constabulary made a balls-up of the Peter Sutcliffe debacle. Funny how history repeats itself, huh?'

Rosen didn't respond. He made his way to the head of the room and called for silence. Registering the faces of those present, he noted the absence of Bellwood.

'Mrs Isobel Swift, the body in 24 Brantwood Road, has been

confirmed as a murder victim, eighteen months previously. Is this murder linked to the abduction next door? I'm pretty certain that it is. I'm pursuing a line of enquiry at the moment that should confirm this in more concrete terms, but there is a degree of competence at work in the murder of Mrs Swift that's reflected in the Herod killings. More on that as things develop.

'Second up, we've had a fairly speculative offer of help from a Roman Catholic priest, Father Sebastian, an expert social anthropologist. It could be something, it may be nothing, but that's a very fresh item and we're still ascertaining the authenticity of the volunteer.'

Harrison held up a hand.

'Yes, Robert?'

'I'm sorry I didn't have time to catch you before the meeting. I've had a call back from *L'Osservatore Romano*.' Harrison paused, savouring the silence. 'It's the Vatican's official newspaper. I spoke with the editor, Gianni Giuntti. Father Sebastian was based at the Vatican between February and September 1996. He was a special adviser to the pope.'

'Thanks for that, Robert.'

'*Di niente, ma era un spreco di tempo.* My father's English, my mother's Italian, which is just as well, as Giuntti's English was primitive, to say the least,' explained Harrison.

'Good job, well done!' Baxter chipped in across the floor.

Rosen seized control again 'The good news on the hair from the loft in 22 Brantwood Road is that it's fresh; it belongs to whoever was in that loft, whoever took Julia Caton. It's gone to the DNA database, so keep your fingers crossed. It's the one piece of good luck we've had. John Mason of Mason Forensic Images has also come on board. He's worked hard and fast. You have something to show us, John?'

Mason, a shy man, stepped forward with a small plastic stacker box.

'For those of you who haven't had the pleasure of meeting John, he's worked for constabularies across the country for years, putting together reconstructions of victims and perpetrators. John, would you like to tell everyone what you've done?'

John Mason looked around and spoke quietly.

'Based on the ear print on the loft door of 22 Brantwood Road, I made a cast of Herod's ear. Based on the measurements of the ear, I constructed this model of his head.'

He placed the box on the floor and sank both hands inside, pulling out a raw clay model of a little head, with two shrimp-like ears on either side of a narrow face. On top, a wig of greasy black hair. The face was blank, a smooth, sinister sweep of clay. It was a labour of love.

'John, thank you so much for that. How did you go about creating this?' asked Rosen.

'The hair length of the wig is based on the single hair found in the loft space, assuming it came from the temple. I reckon he wears his hair cropped, but, based on the jagged edge, I guess he cuts it himself. Maybe he's funny about being touched, can't stand the barber's hands.'

'Or the hairdresser, a female with a sharp instrument close to his head,' speculated Rosen.

The hard edge in the room softened with a ripple of approval and positive comments for the forensic artist.

'Thank you,' said Rosen and, turning to the assembly, 'When we've got so little, this means so much.' He turned back to Mason. 'I owe you one.'

'OK!' Baxter's voice cut through the air. 'This is all well and good but . . .' – when he was sure he had the quantity and quality of attention that he felt his point of view deserved, he carried on – 'we can't release images of this, it's too vague and would only serve to confuse the public. It could even lead to innocent people being attacked by vigilante individuals and groups. So, let's keep it in context. It's OK for the office as a useful focus.' Baxter looked directly at the forensic artist. 'Leave your invoice with Rosen and—'

'Oh, no!' said Mason, the shyness leaving him. 'I don't charge law enforcement agencies for this work. If you look on my website, it'll tell you.' And he quoted with pride, '*Mason Forensic Images seeks to support police forces everywhere in the pursuit of finding missing persons and solving outstanding murder investigations.* You see, I value what you people do.'

The full room was quiet.

Mason placed the clay model back inside the stacker box. Rosen looked at Baxter.

'John, can I have the box, please?'

Mason handed it to Rosen who took out the model and showed the back of the head to the room.

'Potentially, we have a rear view of our target that we didn't have before.'

He carried the model to his desk and put it down there.

'This is staying on my desk, this is a focus, until we nail Herod.'

Baxter had gone – the door of his room closed with a bad-tempered slam.

'I guess that's it for now,' said Rosen. 'Does anyone know where Carol Bellwood went?'

———

THERE WAS A note on Rosen's desk from Bellwood.

> *David, the HQ for the Roman Catholic Diocese of*
> *Southwark is based at Archbishop's House, 150 St George's*
> *Road, London SE1 6HX*
> *Good luck, Carol*

At a quarter to six, in the relative quiet of the office, he dialled the number for Archbishop's House.

'Hello.' A friendly but androgynous voice.

'My name is Detective Chief Inspector David Rosen, I'm with the

Metropolitan Police. I was wondering if I could talk to somebody about a priest who lives in your diocese.'

'OK . . . Who would that priest be?'

'Father Sebastian.'

There was a dense silence. Rosen waited.

'Can you hold the line, please?'

Rosen waited, staring at the blank mask on the clay model that was Herod's face and wishing Mason could have given him a nose, eyes, a mouth.

'Detective Chief Inspector Rosen?'

'Who am I speaking to?'

'Father Luke Frazer. I'm personal secretary to the archbishop. I gather you want to talk about Father Sebastian?'

'That's correct.'

'Is there a problem?'

'No.'

'Then how can we help you?'

'I need some background information.'

'He's not in trouble, is he?'

'Not at all.'

'Why do you require background information on him?'

'Father Frazer, I'd like to meet personally with you, rather than go into detail on the phone. When are you, or the archbishop, available?'

'The archbishop's out of the country. One moment.'

While he waited, Rosen turned the model of Herod's head to gain a rear view.

'Detective Rosen?' It was Father Frazer again.

'Yes.'

'I can see you at Archbishop's House in an hour.'

'I look forward to seeing you then, Father Frazer.'

He replaced the receiver, wondering why Father Frazer had been nervous when he had mentioned Father Sebastian's name.

21

At six o'clock, Sarah Rosen entered Boots the Chemist to buy paracetamol for the headache that was building at the back of her skull. As she waited in the queue, she wished she was at home and thought to herself, *David's right, this teacher-governor job's too much.*

She shifted up a place in the queue and looked past the smiling woman serving the customer in front of her, taking in the range of products available behind the counter. She picked out the painkillers she wanted among medication for colds and coughs, seeing a section of stock that made her pause.

Pregnancy testing kits.

Her stomach turned over. The shop and the people around her seemed to dissolve. As if she had tunnel vision, all she could see were the boxes of testing kits.

A strange idea crept into her head. The idea repeated itself, almost a voice in her ear now. She focussed on the ClearView Digital Pregnancy Testing Kit.

She could feel her heart rate rising, her nerves jangling in excitement and fear.

'That's ridiculous,' she whispered, as the voice repeated itself over and over. She felt the smallest smile form on her lips, but suppressed it because with happiness came the fear of tempting fate.

What if you're not sick? What if you're pregnant? The voice was inside her head, loud and clear. The coins she had ready to pay for the paracetamol were back in her pocket and her credit card was out of her purse.

It's not beyond the realms of possibility, she thought, recalling the rain-drenched weekend away in the Cotswolds some two and a half months earlier. But, then again, after her troubled pregnancy with Hannah all those years ago, she'd been told it was highly unlikely she could conceive.

ClearView Digital Pregnancy Testing Kit. She could even see the box she wanted, the one that the smiling woman behind the counter would reach up for, take from the shelf and hand over to her.

Her mouth was dry and she was trembling. She clasped the credit card in both hands, knitting them together to stop her shaking.

She would do the test in secret, of course, not wanting to raise David's long-dead hopes only to see them dashed by a negative result. And if the result was negative, the secret would remain hers and only hers. If she dared to dream a reckless dream, then she'd better bear the disappointment alone.

'Madam! Excuse me, madam!'

In an instant, the smiling woman's voice brought everything back into place.

'Oh, I'm sorry,' said Sarah. 'Can I have Boots own paracetamol, a box of sixteen, please.' As the woman fetched them, Sarah's eyes darted back to the ClearView Digital Pregnancy Testing Kit.

The woman scanned the painkillers through the till.

A long pause.

'Will that be everything?' The woman smiled, patiently.

'Yes, that's everything,' replied Sarah. 'Sorry, daydreaming.'

'That'll be just thirty-nine pence, please.'

Sarah again took a coin from her pocket, but just as she was about to hand it to the woman, she added, 'And a ClearView pregnancy testing kit.'

'Sure.'

The sales assistant took down the kit, scanned it and placed it in a carrier bag. 'That'll be eleven pounds and thirty-eight pence altogether.'

Sarah paid with her card. The woman handed over the bag, glancing around, and said softly, kindly, 'Good luck!'

'I'll need it,' responded Sarah.

Outside the shop, she transferred the items to her shoulder bag and headed back to the school for the governors' meeting at seven.

Hope lay heavy and, even heavier still, the dashed hopes of a lifetime. She remembered her daughter Hannah as a weight in her arms and her death as an emptiness that had consumed her. Hannah's face, her eyes as she breastfed her, that unerasable image of love stamped on her memory and marbled through her bones. How many times had they tried to have another child? How many times had they been told her cervix wasn't 'fit for purpose'?

As she walked through the rain, tears rolled down her face.

22

Halfway between Westminster Bridge and the Elephant and Castle, the façade of Archbishop's House looked strangely out of place, like a castle with turrets and arched windows on a busy urban street with modern grey paving stones. The crest of the diocese of Southwark above the imposing double door told DCI Rosen that he was in the right place. He rang the bell and waited.

A young priest opened the door and asked, 'DCI Rosen?'

He showed the priest his warrant card and the young man moved aside to allow Rosen in.

'Father Frazer is waiting for you. Follow me, please.'

The priest stopped at a door on the ground floor with a brass nameplate – FR L. FRAZER – and knocked.

In his office, Frazer sat at a broad wooden desk, on the telephone, and smiled as the priest introduced Rosen. In the moment it took Frazer to put down the receiver, Rosen heard the engaged tone.

You've been trying to get through to St Mark's, he thought, shaking Frazer's outstretched hand across the desk.

As the young priest closed the door behind him, Father Frazer indicated the chair across the desk from where he sat.

'Thank you for agreeing to see me at such short notice,' said Rosen.

'Father Sebastian?' replied Father Frazer, his expression deadpan.

'I'd just like some background information on him.'

'Yes, sure. What do you want to know?'

'A brief biography would be helpful.'

Father Frazer typed something into his laptop.

'We used to have cabinets full of files on the priests living and working in the diocese, now it's all held on computer.' After the program loaded, he said, 'Father Sebastian,' as he typed in the name.

Frazer looked at Rosen, waiting for the details to materialize onscreen.

'I looked on the internet,' said Rosen, deciding to jump in feet first. 'According to the net, he died in a road traffic accident in Kenya.'

'Which shows you how unreliable the internet can be. He's alive and living in this diocese,' confirmed Frazer. 'Here we go. Born in Bolton, academic high flyer, Cambridge, top of his class in the seminary, chose to do missionary work. Around the mid-nineties, in his mid- to late twenties, he was posted to Kenya.'

Frazer stopped talking and read the rest of the information in silence. Rosen watched his face but it was an impassive mask. After a minute, Frazer logged off and closed the laptop.

'He did much good work out there but the amount of work affected him and he was returned to this country after suffering a severe nervous breakdown. He was sent to St Mark's after his discharge from hospital and he's been there ever since. He performs mass there each day and lives a quiet reflective life. It's hoped that, one day, he'll be able to return to full active life in a parish, perhaps, or even serving as assistant to one of the archbishops in England or Wales, thus fulfilling his vast potential. But until he is well enough to do so, at St Mark's he stays, following his vocation through administering the Holy Sacrament to that community and praying for the life and works of the Church.'

'He's still not well?' asked Rosen. Flint had looked a model of good health.

'Apparently not.'

'And there's no more information in his file?'

Frazer shook his head and leaned back, stretching a little as he did so.

Well done, mused Rosen. *All those words and not a single mention of the Vatican, the pope or the occult.*

'Now, Detective Rosen, I've divulged information to you about Father Sebastian. Don't you think you should tell me why you're asking about him?' Frazer had skirted around the truth effortlessly. Rosen picked out one detail and joined in the game, keeping it vague but loaded.

'We're holding a Kenyan national on suspicion of a serious crime.' For a moment, a cloud crossed Frazer's eyes. 'That's all I can tell you.'

'I'm sure Father Sebastian would be happy to help you,' said Father Frazer.

Sharp blasts of sound suddenly pumped from the phone on the desk. The ringback tone. Father Frazer looked at the instrument and the noise carried on.

'Don't let me stop you,' said Rosen.

Father Frazer glanced at Rosen and the ringback tone continued. He picked up the receiver to hear the dialling tone. Two tones in, the receiver at the other end was lifted and Rosen heard, 'Hello.'

Soft and far away, it was Brother Aidan.

'It's Father Luke Frazer from Archbishop's House. I'm busy now. I shall call you later. Keep your line free.'

He replaced the receiver, a little too hard.

'The archbishop will be back in two days. I'd be grateful if you could keep His Grace informed of any developments and, in his absence, if you could keep me abreast of any if you involve Father Sebastian in your investigation.'

'Of course.'

'In the Catholic Church, Detective Rosen, we're all members of Christ's body on earth. What happens to one impacts on all of us, you understand?'

'I understand. Nobody likes it when the police show up.'

'This Kenyan—?' asked Father Frazer.

'I can't say another thing about that. It's an ongoing investigation.'

Rosen stood and shook hands with Father Frazer, feeling a film of perspiration on the man's palm.

As he left the building, Rosen had the clearest sense that he'd just stumbled across something deeply hidden and equally nasty.

23

Rosen walked briskly from Archbishop's House, back the way he had come, towards Westminster Bridge. He stopped at the pelican crossing on the corner of Morley Street and waited for the green man to illuminate.

'Detective Chief Inspector Rosen?' A voice came from behind him, which Rosen recognized straight away. It was the androgynous voice at the end of the line when he had first phoned Archbishop's House. He turned to see a masculine-looking woman in her late fifties. He turned back to face the traffic.

'Yes?'

'Do you have some time to spare?'

'Yes. You have something you'd like to share with me?' asked Rosen.

'Buy me a drink, and I'll fill you in on Father Sebastian.'

———

IN THE DRAGON, a small pub near St George's Road, Rosen bought Alice Stanley a large glass of red wine and himself a sparkling mineral water. He sat facing her across a small rickety table.

'How long have you worked for the diocese, Alice?'

'Thirty years, as a secretary, receptionist, all-round dogsbody.'

Thirty years. Long enough to inspire undying loyalty or undiminished resentment.

'Why do you want to tell me about Father Sebastian, Alice?' probed Rosen.

'Because Father Frazer isn't in a position to be exactly . . . generous with the truth, and if it's a police matter it must be serious. It's the least I can do with the information I have.'

In Rosen's book, she went up four divisions in one leap.

'Let me guess what Father Frazer told you about Flint.' She repeated Frazer's brief notes almost to the letter.

'Are you ready, Detective Rosen?'

'I'm listening.'

'Father Frazer already told you Flint was a bit of a star student. He didn't mention the Vatican, did he? After Cambridge, Flint went to the Vatican seminary: that's where he was top of the class, that's how brilliant he was. He was ordained, spent six weeks in a regular parish on what amounted to a perfunctory work experience and then went back to the Vatican. He was twenty-six, twenty-seven years old, tipped for greatness. Then, after twelve months in the corridors of power, he puts in a request for missionary service in East Africa. A request, mind, from the most high to the most low. It was not well-received.' Alice sipped her wine.

'I'd have thought that marked him down as a genuine priest,' said Rosen.

'Genuine but not best-serving the interests of the Church. To draw a sporting analogy, it was like a high-scoring premiership striker asking for a transfer to a pub team. Flint was under all kinds of pressure from all kinds of people to make him withdraw his request but nothing moved him, and then there was a meeting with the Holy Father. Private, behind closed doors, one on one. It was due to last ten minutes, but it went on for an hour and, when he came out, the Holy Father apparently said, *Permission granted, request approved.* Flint went to Kenya.'

Outside, rain ground against the windows.

'So, Father Sebastian went to Kenya. What happened to him out there?'

'He got lynched by a hysterical mob,' said Alice, without emotion.

'Pardon?' Rosen sat up a little in his seat. 'Why?'

'Flint was an exorcist.'

David Rosen, a lifelong sceptic, kept his mouth firmly shut, reminding himself that the woman opposite had made her central life choices based on a faith that made little or no sense to him.

'I know what you must be thinking,' said Alice. 'Demonic possession in any context adds up to mental illness by any other name.'

'Why did he get lynched?' asked David.

'Flint went to Kenya, in his late twenties and in perfect health, but came back twelve months later as if he'd been smashed on death's door. He was based in a rural district, in the highlands of south-western Kenya, north of Lake Victoria. It began with one case, one fifteen-year-old boy from a small band of nomadic farmers. The boy started with convulsive fits, then went into a catatonic state. His grandmother – she was the family doctor, lawyer, soothsayer – tried everything but the boy was out of it. Until . . . the sun comes up one morning. The boy's gone. They went looking for him. No sign. He'd upped and left in the night. One night, two nights, three nights. On the third night, the hammer fell.

'He came back and attacked his family in their beds. The other families got it when they heard the screams and came to intervene. The boy escaped from the mob but, as he did so, he took a machete. He came across a goatherd, a young boy. Then he came across the goats. They found what was left of the boy in twelve separate places. The news spread, and there was a panic. Sebastian was twelve miles away. Hundreds of men gathered to hunt down the demon-possessed child.

They caught up with him and, just after that, Sebastian arrived.

'This boy, he was on a rock, surrounded, raving at the crowd, machete swinging. No one would go near him but Sebastian. He commanded the spirit out of the boy. The spirit knew Sebastian. *We've been waiting for you*, it said through the boy. Then it left the boy. And everything went quiet. For a few days. Then, ten miles north, another case of child possession, another massacre.'

'Grimly reassuring, isn't it?' said David Rosen.

'What?'

'It's not just the developed countries that cop it when a teenager flips out.'

Rosen considered the contrast. If they'd been in Milwaukee, these 'possessed' children, armed with subautomatics, there'd have been a much bigger body count. They'd have gone into the school dining room and blasted indiscriminately. *We blame TV and video games; they blame the devil*, he concluded.

He asked, 'How come Father Sebastian ended up being lynched?'

'He had a powerful gift. Devils recognized him, just as they recognized Christ in the Gospels. They were scared of him. He cast out ten devils in three months, and each time the spirit was different, stronger. How did he end up getting lynched? The tenth devil took up residence in Sebastian, the tenth devil was the devil, Satan himself, according to the Kenyan first-hand accounts.'

'Are you saying—' Rosen chose his words as carefully as if he'd been picking nettles with his bare hands. 'Are you saying that Father Sebastian followed the pattern of those other murderous, possessed men and women, and actually massacred people under the influence of an evil spirit?'

'The story goes cold there. He was attacked by the mob, subjected to a brutal beating and left for dead. I can see your scepticism, Detective Rosen, it's written all over your face.'

'No, Alice, I believe you. I believe the surface of this history. I just don't know how Sebastian Flint could survive that.'

She pulled out a placebo cigarette from her handbag and sucked hard on it. There was a lengthy silence.

'So, he survived the lynch mob. What happened next?' Rosen encouraged her to go on.

'He was found three days later by a safari bus and was taken to the nearest medical centre. When his identity became clear, he was collected by a local diocesan representative.' She paused. 'I need to pay a visit,' said Alice, standing. 'Stay there.' She wandered off to the ladies.

From a dirt road in Kenya to a monastery in Kent? It was the stuff of legends and Rosen hoped it wasn't true. He spiralled quickly through a grim chain of thought. If it *was* true and Father Sebastian had acted like all the other demon-possessed people he had exorcised, that made him a mass murderer. And if that was the case, he should be extradited back to Kenya and the Kenyan police needed to reopen some cold cases.

Rosen ran through the logic of the detail in Alice's story. How could a man at death's door survive the heat of the African day and the cold of the tropical night with no water or shelter?

The wind pummelled the darkened windows. Alice returned and sat down.

'If they find out I've told you all this, I could lose my job,' she said.

'They'll never know.'

'Anyway, he's tucked away in St Mark's now, safe and sound.'

'I know,' said Rosen. 'I've been to see him.'

'Really?' She sounded amazed.

'When I went there, I showed him my laptop because they don't have computers at St Mark's. I Googled his name. There was very little about him. There were brief replicated accounts of him dying in a road traffic accident in Kenya, but there was absolutely nothing about the story you've told me, Alice.'

'I'm only telling you what I heard at the time, in the nineties.'

'I'm not doubting you,' said Rosen. 'It's just . . . How is it that he's been reported as having died in a road traffic accident? The internet thrives on events such as you've recounted: devils, possession, murder, lynch mobs, miraculous survival . . . Yet there's nothing on the net.'

'This happened during the infancy of the internet and it happened a long way from here.' She paused, waiting for Rosen to speak. Easily irritated by half-baked speculation about police corruption and manipulation of the truth, he remained silent about his conclusions on the behaviour of the Roman Catholic Church.

'What do you think happened, David?' asked Alice.

'From what you're saying,' – Rosen spoke as if he found it hard to believe the words coming from his mouth – 'the Catholic Church got Father Sebastian out of Kenya as quickly as possible.'

Alice nodded. 'And?'

'And stories about his death in an RTA were manufactured and posted on the internet during the early days of the World Wide Web to kill off the version you've told me.'

'That's about the top and bottom of it. We've covered up tens of thousands of child abuse cases, why not this?'

Why not a handful of dead Africans? thought Rosen. Especially as Flint had received summary justice from the mob. Especially as he had gone to Kenya with the pope's blessing.

'Is there anything else?' he asked.

Alice shook her head. 'No. Nothing else to add.'

Rosen thanked her sincerely and reassured her that he would protect her as a source of information.

He stood up. 'Are you sure there's nothing else?'

'Yes. I'll have another large glass of red wine before you leave. And will you be seeing Father Sebastian again?'

'Almost certainly.'

'Then be very, very careful. You don't know what you're dealing with. No one does.'

24

The idea for the hoist came from a TV medical documentary that Herod had taped and watched whenever he needed a distraction. He'd had the tape for years and, although he wasn't keeping count, he knew he must have watched it from beginning to end at least two hundred times.

'Saving Dannie' detailed a day in the life of Laura Ashe, a single mother from Glasgow, and her daughter Dannie, a paraplegic eight-year-old with profound and multiple learning difficulties. Dannie, whose range of independent abilities extended to blinking, swallowing, filling her nappy and – sometimes – smiling at the sound of her mother's voice when she sang, made Herod feel better.

To bath Dannie, Laura used a Faboorgliften hoist, a merciful wonder of Norwegian engineering. The Faboorgliften was strong and sturdy. It was a gift for carers too old, too young or too ill to handle heavy equipment and the heavier bodies that the hoist made manageable.

The documentary was tastefully filmed with no specific nudity. The Faboorgliften hoist acted much like a claw in an amusement arcade 'Grab-a-Gift' game. When the arm of the hoist descended, Laura fitted the sling, which was hooked to the arm by four clips, beneath Dannie's body. With the aid of the hoist, Dannie could be lifted by her sciatic mother from wheelchair to bath to mobile bed.

When the will of Satan was made known to him, his first step on the path of faith was to order a Faboorgliften hoist, just like the one used by Dannie's self-deprecating mother.

Long distance and direct to Faboorg Medical Suppliers in Oslo, he gave his Mastercard number and was asked, for the purposes of market research, 'Is the sling for an elderly relative? Your mother, maybe?'

Now, he wheeled the hoist alongside the flotation tank and flicked open the locks on the side of the lid, wondering if the vibration caused would alert the carrier inside the tank.

On the sling, he'd placed a hypodermic needle, its chamber filled with Pentothal, an insurance policy against futile but tiresome resistance.

He waited a moment, to see if there would be some idle, worn-out attempt to raise the lid of the tank but there was nothing, absolutely no sign, and he was assailed by a moment of blind terror: *Carrier dead, baby's soul departed.*

He raised the lid quickly and something snapped.

One of the locks had not opened fully. The snapping seemed to echo. The body of the lock buckled and a piece of the catch flew away, clinking as it landed on the ground.

He lifted the lid and looked down on her.

One hand covered the curve of her womb, one hand reached out. *For what?* he wondered. The fingers of her outstretched hand curled in the stillness and her mouth moved but was soundless.

Her lips continued to move but the probing hand sank back into the saline. She was so removed from the reality of where she was and what was happening, more so than the others, that he wondered if the part of her brain that computed language had already started to decay, a process of living death inside the carrier.

Each time, he was getting better at piping in less oxygen to the tank: just enough to sustain the body and blow the mind.

She didn't need all the functions of her brain to sustain the soul of the life inside her. As soon as she was dead, he had minutes to remove the child, minutes in which the retained soul – still unblemished by original sin – swam in the flesh of the infant.

Herod unhooked the cloth catches of the sling and fed it beneath Julia's body.

'Bh-rhh!' It was just a mental sneeze from her battered brain, but she had been the first to utter anything, whether consciously or not. She was further into her pregnancy than the others and it was difficult to weave the sling underneath her distended belly.

He hooked the sling's catches to the arm of the hoist.

Beneath her skin, the infant moved, blunt fumblings under her belly, waves in the womb.

He depressed the lift button and with a comforting, Norwegian-engineering-standard whirr, Julia's body rose from the sensory deprivation chamber, hanging in the air like a cow being transferred from ship to shore, swinging slightly, her arms and feet dangling down.

He looked at the sensory deprivation chamber, feeling a weight settle on his shoulders. He was used to cleaning it out because they all fouled it. Eighty kilos of salt and gallons of fresh water were easy to come by. But the broken lock? He was useless at DIY but would have to try to mend the lock somehow.

A surge of hot anger shot up inside him.

She stared at him with empty eyes.

'You know that greedy, money-grabbing plumber that you were married to, Julia?' He paused, rubbing the side of his neck. 'Do you want to know something? It's quite ironic or maybe just a coincidence but your husband . . .'

And just as quickly as the anger surged within him, a coldness replaced it.

There was no need to speak to the carrier, so why speak? There was no need to have feelings, so why feel? There was no need for opinion, so why think? All he needed to do was act.

So he acted.

Julia Caton's body descended onto the table at 4.13 a.m. Times and dates were irrelevant in Satanic worship but he couldn't escape his compulsion to pay attention to detail. He then produced the oldest piece of surgical equipment, the first piece of kit he'd ever owned, from the battered doctor's case he'd carried and loved since his two years as a medical student attached to St Thomas's.

No other doctor, no other medical student had one of these, but he was special.

Memory. Act. Ritual. Worship.

It was a thin piece of metal, three millimetres in diameter at the base, one at the sharpened tip; cut down from its original thirty-eight centimetres in length, it was now twenty centimetres long. It was his childhood in a single artefact.

He had a mental snapshot of a bicycle, its wheel turning, a broken spoke pointing out at the sky, and he heard himself as he lay on the ground, a crying child.

Julia's eyes rolled and her lips made a single smacking noise, as if blowing a kiss.

He adjusted her position, swung the sling over the table and pressed the 'down' button. She touched the table feet first, followed by her backside and spine. She seemed to squirm in the sling and said, 'Garld!'

Her eyes stopped rolling, became still, as he unhooked the straps from the hoist and the rest of her body slammed on the table like something dead. She shivered, and the surface of her skin was raised in goosebumps.

He straightened her legs and placed at her side the arm that flopped over the table's edge, as he surveyed her swollen form. She was dehydrated so that the bladder wouldn't get in the way of the womb.

He drew a straight line with his finger from her right hip to her left hip. Once open, the womb could not be missed.

And he held the tip of the spoke against her chest cavity.

Julia Caton let out a cry that froze him, and then there was a noise of running liquid.

Fluid poured across the table and dripped onto the floor. Her waters had broken.

He plunged the spoke into her heart.

At 4.17 a.m., Julia Caton let out a long sigh and died.

He raised his sharpened scalpel and gave thanks to Alessio Capaneus, Satanic prophet, before turning his attention to the unborn.

And the last of her oxygen passed to a little boy who would have been called Jamie.

25

Rosen was drifting into what felt like a deep but troubled sleep when he felt Sarah getting out of their bed and heard her walking through the darkness of their room.

'You OK, love?'

'Yeah, just going to the loo. Go to sleep . . .' Her voice tailed off as she moved in the direction of the bathroom.

He felt himself rise from the tug of sleep. Since he'd picked her up from school, he'd noticed she'd seemed unsettled, distracted, a bit unhappy, even. He'd asked her as gently as he could if there was anything wrong but she'd insisted she was fine, just a little tired, and he'd told her she ought to quit as teacher-governor: it was a thankless and time-consuming role, when her life was already cluttered enough.

He opened his eyes wide and blinked, growing accustomed to the darkness around the digital display on his bedside clock. Halfway between midnight and one o'clock in the morning, he wondered how Julia was, whether she was alive still; alive and terrified or just plain dead.

Sarah was taking her time in the bathroom.

Rosen waited, rolled over into her space to keep it warm for her and saw the curtains twitched by a stray March breeze. Original windows were Sarah's passion; he'd have to press the case for double glazing sometime. As he waited, he was seized by acute anxiety.

Unsettled, distracted: was she on the downward curve? Was this the first step towards illness, a recurrence of the depression that had crippled her?

He got out of bed, walked to the bathroom and tapped on the door.

'Are you OK, love?'

She didn't reply.

'OK if I come inside?'

She didn't reply, and his apprehension rocketed.

He pushed the door open, slowly so as not to alarm her.

'Sarah, is everything—?'

She stood between the door and the toilet, with something white in her hand, plastic, her face streaming with tears.

'Sarah, what's wrong?'

By way of answer, she held out her hand, the one with the device in it, and Rosen recognized it for what it was. This was confirmed by the rectangular box in the sink with the words 'ClearView digital pregnancy testing kit' printed across it.

'Sarah, what is this?'

She opened her mouth to speak, but all that came out was a sob from the heart that cut him in two. A massive heat rose up behind his eyes and the weight of their grief and despair pressed down inside him.

'Sarah, we have to accept the truth, we can't have a child. I thought we'd accepted that—'

'Look!'

He looked, not quite understanding what he should be looking for in the device in his wife's hand. A small grey rectangular screen at one end read: *Pregnant.*

'Sarah, love, listen to me. It looks like the kit is saying you are but let's not run away with ourselves. It could be faulty, it could be a mistake . . .' He was about to say *you* but stamped it down. 'We can't have children, Sarah. We haven't got the ability.'

'I'll tell you what I haven't got, David. I haven't got a peptic ulcer. I'm pregnant. Aren't you happy about it?'

He looked at the screen and then snatched up the box because he just couldn't answer his wife's question in the affirmative. He scanned the instructions. They stated that the digital kit would deny or confirm pregnancy. They also advised that a confirmation should be sought from a health practitioner.

He laid the box back down in the sink, looked at Sarah and then at the screen on the kit.

'You know I want a baby as much as you, of course I do.' *But*, he thought, *I don't want the despair that I can feel just around the corner.*

When he saw her break into a smile, he did the only thing that seemed right.

He put his arms around her and said, 'I love you.'

26

The advantage of driving around in a vehicle that looked exactly like a paramedic ambulance was that everyone noticed but no one saw. It was a thing of despair, and other people – motorists, passengers and pedestrians – consciously or unconsciously pushed the thing of despair to the margins. It was all right to drive a little too fast, and acceptable to be a bit too slow, but most of all it was OK to hit a steady 35mph, as Herod did when he was gathering in the carriers and disposing of their remains.

The one thing he never did was turn on the flashing light or blare the siren. He had disabled both features. A light and a siren made the almost invisible screamingly obvious, and works of faith required discretion.

Julia Caton was in the back wrapped in a thick black plastic sheet, her womb filled with a smooth-surfaced rock: five kilos of ballast to keep her where she needed to be at the drop-off point.

She was foetal in pose, and balanced on a four-wheeled scissor stretcher.

It was to be a river drop-off, this time near Albert Bridge Road. As he negotiated the streets of SW11, the night was clear and the traffic was light, for which he gave praise and thanks in abundance.

He backed up the ambulance. Two unskippered boats bobbed on the swell, the sound and the sight of the water restorative to his ears and eyes.

He grew impatient with having to wait He got out and stood at the back, conscious of the cold through his green paramedic's uniform.

He could hear the traffic but not see it, which meant no one could see him. He opened the back of the ambulance and had a good look around.

A tramp wandered near the water's edge, along the river's westward curve, and dissolved into the darkness. If some unfortunate soul happened to disturb him as he wheeled the stretcher to the water, he was ready with a story: 'I'm retrieving the body from the water. It looks like suicide. Could you just come a little closer, my partner's down there, see, if you could just – come here . . .'

So far, the work had been undisturbed – his prayers had been answered.

He untied the plastic sheet and tipped her into the water. It lapped over her and would ebb to reveal her as night gave way to dawn.

If he complied with instructions, he would succeed where Alessio Capaneus had failed.

He lingered a moment, observing the form beneath the water. She'd been the prettiest of the unbirthed and, now that she was no longer under his influence, he was surprised by a feeling that had swamped him in childhood, something he believed he'd long overcome.

In the ambulance, he slipped through the light traffic that surfed the dead of night, but couldn't shake off the feeling.

In an attempt to drown it out, he thought about the detective who was running round in a circle after his own tail. David Rosen.

He turned on the radio to hear the sound of human voices and kill the unfathomable depths of his loneliness.

27

A bank of cloud fell away from the moon and a beam of pale light picked out the face of Jesus Christ. His eyes were closed and the upper half of his face covered by a length of gauze.

Eyes wide open, sleepless, Father Sebastian stared up at the wall and the picture of the Messiah above his bed.

Dawn was an ocean away. He turned his eyes to the window and the night sky. Judging by the position of the stars, Aidan and the others would be filing into the chapel for Matins -- prayers at two in the morning – and it was there, at the door of the chapel, that Sebastian was going to address the leader of the community.

He closed the door of his room and walked through darkness.

Even at the height of summer, the corridors of St Mark's were cold, and in March there was a bitterness seemingly designed to turn a man against his own body, creating enough discomfort to make him yearn to cast off his skin, so that the death and decay of flesh and bone would be a thing to look forward to.

There was a window seat, cut into the wall, and it was here that Sebastian waited, unnoticed by the thin trail of men who filed past him into the chapel. He counted them in like sheep.

Aidan's footsteps stopped in the corridor as he looked around.

'I'm here, Aidan. I'm here.'

Aidan stared into the darkness.

Sebastian stood up from the window seat, separating from the shadows in the moonlit corridor.

'You're joining us for prayers, Sebastian?'

'I'd like to make a request.'

Aidan's eyes flicked from the chapel door to Sebastian's face, settling uneasily on the priest.

'And your request is?'

'I want to go to London.'

'Why?'

'To visit Detective David Rosen.'

'If you want to see Rosen, surely he would come here as he did last time.'

'I've recalled something that could prove useful to Detective Rosen.'

'Perhaps you could phone him in the morning.'

'Perhaps, or perhaps I could go and see him in person, as he did with me.'

'What is it you've remembered?'

'A memory. I've recalled something, Aidan. Are you listening to me?'

'I'm late for prayers.'

'This is important, Aidan.'

'You've never asked to leave before . . .'

'I'll get the seven-thirty-seven to Charing Cross. I'll return on the five-fifteen.'

'Maybe you'll arrive in London and it's Detective Rosen's day off, or he's otherwise occupied?'

'Is this my prison?' asked Sebastian.

'Whatever do you mean?'

'I haven't been found guilty of a crime. Can you say the same?'

'No.'

'Dizzy days, weren't they, on the London Stock Exchange?'

Aidan looked away.

'All that money. Exhilarating, risky business, and then Pentonville. The place where you rediscovered the God of your childhood, and that's how you came to know me. The Lord surely moves in mysterious ways. I'll ask again. Is this my prison? Are you my gaoler? I need an answer now.'

'I'll open the safe in the morning. You'll need money for your rail fare, to travel on the tube, to eat.'

Aidan moved to go into the chapel for prayer but was held back when Sebastian said, 'Don't wait until the morning. I know, tell me the safe's combination number now and I can be on the seven-thirty-seven to Charing Cross and no further trouble to you.'

'Please stay, Father.'

'You should go and pray, Aidan.' Sebastian moved his face a little closer to Aidan, pinning his eyes with a look. 'You're trembling, Aidan. Are you cold?' Sebastian smiled. 'Don't be scared, Aidan, just give me the combination and you can go and pray.'

Aidan remained still.

'You're keeping God waiting, Aidan. Tell me the combination.'

'One-two-three-four . . .'

'Thank you, Aidan. Now, go on,' said Father Sebastian. 'Go, go worship God.'

28

At eight-forty-five in the morning, Bella Dunne, a practice nurse in the Rosens' GP's surgery, turned away from Sarah's onscreen notes and said, 'These things happen.' Bella looked from Rosen to Sarah, focussed on her and smiled. 'You're definitely pregnant.'

Sarah's fingers squeezed Rosen's tightly. She glanced at her husband, knowing that the nurse's confirmation hadn't prompted in him the same unequivocal surge of joy that it had in her.

'There could be complications. Your age, of course, is an issue, but with your medical history this could well be an ectopic pregnancy and, as you know – and I don't want to alarm you – ectopic pregnancies don't succeed to full term. They're dangerous. I have to be totally honest with you, as I appreciate all you've been through . . . When was your last period?'

'I've missed two, I think.'

'So at least eight weeks – perhaps more?'

'Does that add up?'

They'd had a few days away in the Cotswolds, a Christmas break to escape the pressure of the case. Away from London and home, and given the terrible weather, in that short time they'd had more sex than in the previous few months put together. It was one of the few recent memories that automatically made Sarah smile to herself.

'Yes, yes, that sounds right.'

'And do you want—?'

'Yes!' Sarah almost shouted.

'In which case we have to get a move on,' said the nurse. She picked up a phone. 'Given the circumstances,' she said as she dialled, 'I'm going to pull strings.' She spoke to three people in the course of two calls before reaching her ultimate target. She turned to Sarah and David Rosen.

'OK, you're booked in for an ultrasound, this afternoon, three o'clock at St Thomas's Hospital.'

'Three o'clock, thank you,' said Sarah.

'Mrs Rosen? I'm aware of your medical history. Your notes indicate the gynaecological complications you've been through, the death of your daughter, your depression. Please be careful with how you approach this . . . unforeseen development.'

'Be careful?' Sarah almost whispered. The nurse nodded.

Sarah turned to her husband, who spoke so low as to be almost inaudible. 'Hope can be a terrible thing.'

As they headed out of the surgery, Rosen felt the vibration of his phone inside his jacket. He closed the door and answered the call. It was Bellwood, and she was driving at speed.

'David, Julia Caton's body has turned up.'

'Same MO?'

'Herod.'

'Where?'

'Bank of the Thames, just beyond Albert Bridge Road.'

'If you're there before me, take charge of the scene, Carol.'

As he ended the call, Sarah said, 'Go on, David, go now.'

29

When DCI David Rosen arrived, a small crowd had already formed at the scene-of-crime tape at the junction of Albert Bridge Road and Oakley Gardens. The white tent erected over Julia Caton's body by Parker and Willis was more to do with salvaging what was left of her dignity than protecting forensic evidence: given the action of the Thames and the length of time she'd been there, it was unlikely there would be much left in the way of it.

When Rosen arrived at the tent, the first face he saw was Harrison's, white protective suit, muddy overshoes, eyes fixed on the middle distance.

Rosen pulled a white suit from the back of the van and started hauling himself into it.

'It was a jogger who found her,' said Harrison. 'She thought it was a sheet of plastic embedded in the mud at first but when she took a closer look—'

'Is it definitely Julia?'

'It's definitely the Caton woman, sir.'

'She had a name.'

'I'm trying to remain detached.'

'Got your digital camera with you?'

Harrison nodded.

'Then go and take pictures of the ghouls at the SOC tape.'

Inside the white tent, Julia lay on her back, arms at her side, eyes shut as if she were in a deep sleep.

And Rosen found he just couldn't look.

'Water's washed away anything that may have been here.' Parker sounded the way Rosen felt: picked on by the universal engine, bullied by the stars. Rosen's gaze dropped to the mud and he reminded himself of the true victim. Sixty years hence, she should have been passing away peacefully, medicated to ease the journey, her children and grandchildren in attendance.

Parker shone his hand-held torch below Julia's collarbone and slowly tracked the light to the point between her ribs where an almost imperceptible red dot nestled.

'Cause of death, same as the other ladies,' said Parker.

'Cardiac tamponade. I wonder where he got the idea from?'

'Could be the killer's a Kenyan,' suggested Bellwood, at her first body recovery.

Willis stopped taking pictures. 'I hadn't thought of that, but, yeah!' Willis turned her attention to Bellwood and Rosen suddenly felt as if he were tuning in to a foreign language

'What do you mean, Carol?' asked Rosen.

'It was a popular murder method in the gang wars in Nairobi back in the nineties. The hoodies would pull a spoke off a bicycle wheel, sharpen it and puncture the heart of their opposite number in the other gang. Look at the size of the hole. It's minute. On black skins, the puncture was usually overlooked at first and the doctors in casualty were at a loss to know how come this fit young kid's had a massive cardiac arrest.'

A moment of quiet passed, then Eleanor Willis said, 'It's how that Australian guy, Steve Irwin, died. The stingray penetrated the pericardium, into the heart; blood from the heart floods the pericardial space, stops the heart pumping; he was dead in seconds flat.'

'Cheaper and easier to find than a gun,' concluded Bellwood.

'Murder weapon easy to dispose of,' added Willis.

Parker flicked the light onto Julia's hands. There were no apparent signs of damage to the fingers or nails, as there had been with the first four victims.

'Maybe he didn't lock Julia up in the same box, like the others. Maybe she was killed before she had a chance to—'

The mental image left a foul taste in Rosen's mouth and he wondered if he was merely making noise to fend off the moment when he had to follow Parker's light to the extensive wounds around Julia's abdomen. He forced himself to look.

The sight of the stone in her womb, the deadness of the rock in the seat of life, dried Rosen's mouth and throat. He'd considered in depth the ritual significance of the stone in place of the carved-out womb; he had taken the advice of anthropological experts and found no precedent for it. It was, it seemed, a practical device, a deadweight to anchor the body to the spot.

The idea made Rosen want to scream out loud, long and hard at the top of his range. He left the tent.

'Can I have the map?' Rosen called to Bellwood. 'The map, please.'

Bellwood came outside and handed him a clear plastic wallet with a map of London. He unfolded it and marked the location of Chelsea Embankment and Albert Bridge Road with a blue cross and a circled number five. The blue crosses for the first body in the lake at St James's Park, and the third body at the corner of Victoria Street and Vauxhall Bridge Road, connected with Julia's site to form a crooked diagonal trajectory.

'The odds form one line,' said Rosen, tracing it with his finger down to St James's Park. 'The evens form another line, coming down. Second body drop-off, Alison Todd, just under Lambeth Bridge; fourth body,

Sylvia Green, outside the Oval cricket ground. Carol, can you see? Can you see what this is?'

'A crooked triangle without a base.'

'No, not a crooked triangle; in fact, not a triangle at all. This is a letter, the letter A. A for Alessio.' His voice dropped both in volume and octave. A dark and private thought crept out into the morning light. 'I need to speak to Father Sebastian. A for Alessio. He's marking the earth with the initial letter of the name that mankind tried to obliterate.'

Rosen placed his finger on the centre of Vauxhall Bridge Road, the space at the heart of the A where the dash would go to link the two diagonal sides, and felt a frisson of certainty about the future. Father Sebastian was right – Herod would kill again, and soon.

———

AT THE JUNCTION of Oakley Gardens and Albert Bridge Road, a thickening band of pedestrians gathered at the SOC tape. A sergeant refused to answer their questions while, a little further up the road, a constable made sure the traffic followed the diversion sign.

Two police cars, one marked, one unmarked, parked at the tape but Harrison didn't notice who got out because his attention was drawn to a single figure at the back of the gathering crowd.

Black suit, black coat, face turned to the sky, he appeared to be gazing in accusation at the clouds. One of many unhinged wanderers on the streets of London, albeit well-dressed and physically fit-looking, head tilted upwards, his features not visible for a separate shot on the digital camera.

Harrison took pictures of individuals and groups, couples, people arriving and departing, forced to leave by other commitments. The black suit was still looking skywards, but his head was slowly sinking, his face clearly visible now. Harrison took a snap of the man. He checked the picture. The glare was horrible and all he could see was a blurred shape. Delete? Harrison pressed OK. Image gone.

He noticed that all eyes were fixed on the white tent on the banks of the Thames. All except for one pair.

The man in the black suit was looking directly at him. Or was the man staring into the space that he just happened to occupy? The man's gaze hardened and Harrison knew the man was watching him. The man smiled but the smile faded almost at once. He half held up a hand in salutation, pointed at Harrison and then at himself, making a connection between them. Then, he pointed to an area a little way from the crowd and walked to it. Harrison followed.

'Yeah?' said Harrison.

'Why are you here?'

'What do you mean?'

'DCI Rosen, your boss, is an idiot. That's why you're here, taking photographs, when you should be down there analysing the evidence.'

'Who are you?' asked Harrison.

'I'll show you my warrant card if you show me yours.'

A voice, passing in the middle distance, called, 'Harrison!' Harrison turned in its direction. It was Feldman. 'Boss wants us all together in five!'

'Who are you?' Harrison repeated, facing the man once more.

'Who am I? I'm very angry with Rosen, that's who I am. See you soon.'

The man turned and walked away. Harrison resisted the urge to call him back and instead watched him as he receded, blending into the milling horde in the busy London street for whom ordinary life rolled on.

Harrison raised his camera to take more shots of the faces in the growing crowd at the SOC tape and, behind the lens, he smiled.

———

THE WATER LAPPED at Rosen's feet, the points of a crooked letter A etched on his mind's eye. He glanced over his shoulder to where

Bellwood and Corrigan were talking over the map, discussing some permutation or other.

Rosen felt his phone vibrate in his pocket.

The display registered an inner London landline number.

'David Rosen?'

He knew the voice immediately.

'Father Sebastian. I was just thinking about you.'

'I'm flattered. And I'm happy to say I can repay the compliment, with sincerity. I've been thinking about you, too.'

'You're – where are you?'

'I'm in London today. I'm calling from a phone box. Can I see you sometime?'

'Yes. Where are you exactly?'

'Are you busy?'

'Yes, I am busy but I can—'

'That sounds like bad news. Is that water I can hear?'

'Why are you in London, Father?'

'Something that came out of our little chat. I've never been to London before. I'm curious. You know, not to see the sights. I want to go and check something, at the British Library.'

'What would that be?' Silence. 'What are you checking at the British Library?'

'Books.'

Rosen returned the silent treatment while the water behind him churned.

'I think, if my research goes well today, I can help you out some more.'

'Put a place and a time on it, Father.'

'Charing Cross Station, the concourse, five . . .'

And with that the line went dead.

Bellwood approached him, asking, 'Who was that?'

'Father Sebastian. He's never seen you, has he?'

'No.'

'If he's planning on making a journey back to St Mark's this afternoon, I want you to tail him. From Charing Cross to Canterbury East, the nearest station; it's miles away, but it's the closest to St Mark's.'

'Why?' Bellwood sounded perplexed but, more than this, she looked concerned.

'There's a possibility he's a killer.'

'A killer or our killer?'

'I'm not certain yet. He may have killed during his time in Kenya.' Rosen held up his hands. 'Get to Charing Cross for five. For now, you stay here, Carol; you're in charge of the scene. I want you to phone the Kenyan police. Start with Nairobi but work out from there into the south-western regions, north of Lake Victoria. Contact the regional police HQ and ask them about Flint's involvement in some unsolved killings in the nineties. I don't know how far you'll get but do your best. I'm taking Mike Feldman with me to the British Library.'

Rosen walked towards the cordon and, as he did so, he dialled the public phone box that Father Sebastian had just called from. The line was busy. Rosen wondered, *Who are you talking to now, Flint?*

30

It was Rosen's first time in the new British Library at St Pancras, and he was immediately struck with the contrast to the old one, which he'd visited twice in his lifetime. As the old British Library was a celebration of the circle, with curve and dome; so the new one was a monument to symmetry, the clean line, the square and the rectangle.

On the way over, Feldman had used his iPhone to check the website of the British Library.

'There are eleven reading rooms. How are we going to know which one he's in?' asked Feldman. 'I don't even know what the guy looks like.'

'Stay here,' said Rosen, indicating the main entrance. 'When I find him, I'll take a picture of his face on my phone. I'll send it to your phone. If he leaves here, you're to follow him.'

'How do we know he's here yet?'

'We don't. We only have his say-so.'

'What's he done, boss?'

'He's turned up at the wrong place and the wrong time: London on the morning of a body drop-off. Between you and me, Mike, he's starting to make my skin crawl. While you're waiting here, two things to do. Ask to see the head of security; we need all their CCTV from now: entrances, exits, all their interior stuff. Also, check the locale of this public phone box.' He showed Feldman the number on his phone.

'Excuse me.' A tall, unsmiling librarian said, 'Put your phones away, please; turn them off and put them away.'

Rosen flashed his warrant card.

'Oh! It's not a terrorist threat, is it? I mean, the books, we have some very old books and manuscripts; the Sir John Ritblat Gallery—'

'Please assist my colleague DC Mike Feldman in every way you can. We'll alert your security that we're here. Otherwise, please keep your mouth closed about our presence here today.'

Stacked high with books and teeming with life, the first reading room that Rosen entered surprised him. He'd half expected something scholarly and churchlike. It was more like an elegant shopping mall with only one main product for consumers: the printed word.

As Rosen wandered past the wide oak and green-leather-topped tables, he felt the weight of his phone in his pocket, knowing he'd have to call in support, knowing that he should phone Sarah, but also that he must focus on locating Father Sebastian. He felt the sting of conflicted priorities.

Am I going to be a father? he thought, for the first time since leaving the GP's surgery. *Am I going to be a father? Again?*

The sheer scale and number of books available was intimidating, and he mourned those autumns spent picking hops when he could have been reading. If all went well, education was going to be the number one priority for their child.

Uncertain that he hadn't missed Flint in the first reading room, Rosen made his way into the second; and knew he'd have to call for that back-up sooner rather than later.

He stopped behind a young woman logging on to the internet on her laptop. *If I bring people in, how will they know what Flint looks like? I'm the only one who does*, he thought. *If I can't find him, how will they know?*

'Excuse me,' said Rosen to the young woman. 'Can I check something on Google Images?' *It's a long, long shot.*

'Well, I was just—'

Rosen showed his warrant card. 'It's important.'

She stood up and Rosen thanked her as he sat at her place. He typed 'Father Sebastian' into the Google search engine and clicked on Images. There were hundreds of thousands of results but, as he scrolled desperately through the first ten pages, absolutely nothing like the man he was after. All kinds of fathers, all kinds of people called Sebastian and so many Flints, but not the one combination of the three that Rosen needed.

'I'm sorry to have—' Rosen looked up at the young woman, who made a bad job of looking uninterested, glancing away to the other side of the room.

Blind! Rosen accused himself, silently. *Blind! Blind! Blind!*

Five rows of desks away, with his back turned to Rosen, a lean, dark-haired man sat alone, reading. Rosen went back in his mind to the first time he'd seen Flint, his sweat-stained back, his worn running shirt riddled with holes. He couldn't be certain it was Flint, but from behind it looked a whole lot like him.

Rosen got up and picked out a stack of book-laden shelves a metre ahead of the mark, from which he could get a clear view of the man's face. Casually, he walked to the widest point in the space between reading desks and stacks. He waited and, as a lone and obese man passed him, Rosen slipped into the man's wake, his bulk shielding Rosen as he passed the dark-haired man. He reached the stack and turned the corner, facing the spines of books.

Father Sebastian sat alone with a small heap of books in front of him, the reading light turned on because of the dull morning, dressed in a smart black suit and a black overcoat, an inverse image of the shabby priest Rosen had encountered on their meeting at St Mark's.

Rosen took a picture and another and another and, of the three, one was a clear shot of Flint's face.

He concealed himself behind the stack and quietly called Feldman.

Rosen told him to expect a photo, along with a description and the location where the priest was sitting.

'He doesn't know what you look like, Mike, so you're to tail him and get photographs, particularly of anyone he speaks to or of anyone who sits next to him or near him.'

Rosen sent the photo of Flint to Feldman and then to Carol Bellwood. He followed the photo with a call to Bellwood.

'Carol, send Dave Gold to the British Library immediately to cover Feldman at the entrance. Send Dave this image of Flint. Mike's tailing Flint. I want Dave here as back-up. I'm coming back to Albert Bridge Road, but I've got to go somewhere else en route.'

'Where to, David?'

'I'm going to Brantwood Avenue, to speak to Phillip Caton. Have you called the Kenyan police yet?'

'Yes. Nairobi gave me a number for the police HQ in a town called Eldoret. I'm going to call Eldoret next, see what comes up.'

'Thanks, Carol.'

———

IN THE SPACE of twenty-five minutes, Gold arrived to cover the front of the building and Feldman came to the reading room to relieve Rosen. During that time Father Sebastian sat at the table, his only movement that of his eyes as he read and his hands turning pages, but nothing more.

While Rosen watched him, Flint's stillness was so complete that there were times when he wondered whether he had fallen asleep as he studied the book in front of him. And then slowly he'd move his hands and his eyes a little, subtle motions that filled Rosen with such an inexplicable nausea that a primal part of himself wanted to find the nearest blunt object and bury it in Flint's skull.

He thought about Phillip Caton and how he was feeling at that moment. But the image at the core of Rosen's brain was that of Father Sebastian, his eyes raking the text and his hands manipulating pages, otherwise a waxwork dummy in a fancy library.

31

O n the surface, everything appeared to be back to normal in Brantwood Road. But as Rosen walked down the path, images invaded his mind of Julia Caton, beached in the mud on the banks of the Thames, her baby ripped out and replaced with a stone – the sudden reversals of the natural order. He could not help but think of his wife Sarah, her womb, dismissed by experts as too damaged by her one full-term pregnancy, suddenly blossoming with their child. It was almost too much to fathom.

As he pressed the bell, he tried to replace the image of Julia with the thought of Father Sebastian in his monastic cell, sweating; in the monastery kitchen, in awe of the wonders of the internet; in the British Library, wrapped up in study.

The door of number 22 opened slowly.

A middle-aged woman stood there, a version of what Julia should one day have been. 'Yes?'

'I'm Detective Chief Inspector David Rosen.'

'Yes, I know, Victim Liaison have already been here. You've found my daughter's body.' She shut her eyes tightly, as if trying to block out the world, and hung on to the door frame with the fingers of one hand, her knuckles white. To Rosen's eyes, it looked as if the door was all that stood between her and total collapse.

'Yes.'

'How can I help you?'

'I've come to offer my condolences.'

'Come inside then.'

On the arm of the sofa in the front room, a tall bald man – Julia's father Rosen supposed – sat slumped forward, head down, staring at a picture in his hand. He wasn't crying but he looked as if he'd only just stopped, after hours and hours of weeping, his face scarlet, his nose shining and wet.

'Dan, this is David Rosen, he's a police officer.'

Rosen was grateful that no one invited him to sit down. He wondered where Phillip Caton was.

'Was she wearing any clothes?' asked Julia's dad, abruptly.

'No.'

'Is it the same as the other women?'

'I'm afraid so, yes.'

Her father held his hand out to Rosen and said, 'Here.'

Rosen took the picture from him. It was a scan photograph of Julia's baby.

'Our first grandchild.'

'And our last,' added Julia's mother. 'She was an only child, Julia.'

As Rosen looked at the photo, he felt the return of the old weight of his own grief over Hannah. He remembered the compulsion to scream and never stop. And he recognized the hollowness in the eyes of Julia's mother and father. He handed the photograph back to Julia's mother.

'Are you any closer to catching him?' asked her father.

'There have been some significant developments—'

'Yes, but are you any closer to catching this . . . thing?'

'We know more than we did four days ago. We have forensic evidence.

We have a clearer understanding of the killer's modus operandi. Things are moving forward.'

'But do you know who did it?' In a nanosecond, Julia Caton's father shifted from first to fourth gear, his voice rising in anger. 'And are you in the process of arresting and charging the fucking bastard?'

'OK, Dan, please don't shout—'

'No,' said Rosen. 'We aren't.'

A silence, dense and ugly.

Julia's father stood up and looked directly at Rosen. As quickly as his anger had gained momentum and volume, it diminished into a chilling softness.

'Then what is the point of you? Get out, just get out.'

At the front door, Rosen turned and faced Julia's mother in the hallway.

'I'm very sorry,' said Rosen. 'We're doing all we can.'

Julia's mother said nothing.

'You have the details for Victim Liaison?'

'We don't want them, thank you.'

'If there's anything we can do . . .'

'Catch the person who's done this to her, to us.'

'Is Phillip around?'

'He's upstairs.'

'Can I talk to him?'

'He's asleep, and I don't want to wake him up. Don't worry, Mr Rosen, as soon as he's awake and in a position to understand, we'll tell him the news.'

'I'm deeply sorry.'

She looked as if she was searching for the right words. Rosen stayed where he was, waiting.

'One second, I wish I was blind and deaf,' she said, 'so that I couldn't see or hear any of this. But then, the next second, I wish I could go to sleep and never wake up again. I want that to happen so badly. I don't think you will ever understand what it's like to be in my shoes.'

Rosen nodded and dropped his eyes. There was simply nothing he could say, though he wished there were.

As she opened the front door to let him out, Rosen's eyes fixed on a patch of darkness on the hall carpet, just beneath the wedding photo of Phillip and Julia. It was the scan photograph of their baby that must have fallen from his grandmother's hand.

Rosen stooped, picked it up and handed it to Julia's mother.

She looked at the image and turned her eyes on Rosen.

'I guess that's the end of us, then.'

As soon as he stepped outside the house, Rosen heard the door closing behind him. As he paused at the gate of 22 Brantwood Road, he noticed a small tag of blue and white scene-of-crime tape, a fragment of the recent police presence. Although Julia's home was no longer a crime scene under investigation, for those left behind it would always be a place of tragedy – where something unbearable had happened, something they must always endure.

He got into his car, but didn't drive away immediately. Instead, he did the thing he'd been aching to do all day. He called Sarah on his phone.

'Hi, David?'

'Sarah, where are you?'

'I'm in school.' He was pleased. It was a safe place to be. 'Where are you?'

'I've just been to visit Julia Caton's parents.'

'I'm sorry.'

'Are you all right, Sarah?'

'I'm not all right. I'm amazed, I'm overjoyed, and I'm frantic with worry. You?'

'All of those things.'

'Will you be able to make it this afternoon for the ultrasound?'

Her words seemed to stream around his head.

'David, are you still there?'

'Yes, I am, I'm here.'

'Will you make the scan this afternoon?'

'Yes,' he said, with a certainty he didn't feel. His copper's instinct told him something foul lay close by, something he could not ignore. 'I love you,' he said, guilt making his entire scalp crawl.

In the background, a bell rang harshly and Sarah said, 'I'll meet you in reception, St Thomas's, at three. Got to go!'

And with that she was gone.

32

At a little after two-fifteen, as Rosen drove away from Albert Bridge Road towards St Thomas's Hospital, his hands-free mobile rang on the dashboard. He flicked it on to speakerphone, expecting it to be another bulletin from the British Library, telling him that Father Sebastian still hadn't moved from his reading station.

'DCI Rosen speaking.'

'Hello?' Clear, tentative, African, by the sound of the masculine voice on the other end of the line, and then an uneasy silence. 'Is that Detective Chief Inspector David Rosen, Metropolitan Police, England?'

'Yes, it is. Who am I speaking to?'

'I was speaking with your assistant an hour or so ago, Detective Sergeant Carol Bellwood. I am Sergeant Joseph Kimurer, Kenyan police.'

Rosen hit the tail end of a short queue at a red light.

'Your assistant gave me your number.'

'Thank you for getting back to us, Sergeant Kimurer.'

'I'd like to say it's a pleasure.'

'No doubt Detective Sergeant Bellwood asked you about Father Sebastian. You have some information you'd like to share?'

'Can we speak in confidence?'

'We can speak in confidence.'

'Father Sebastian is a well-known name in the Uasin Gishu District.'

Rosen shifted into first gear and joined the trickle of traffic through the junction.

'Fame comes for many reasons, Sergeant Kimurer. What's Father Sebastian's claim to fame in your part of the world?'

'He came in the name of Christ and left with the name of Satan.'

'How do you mean?' asked Rosen.

'Detective, Father Sebastian is a man who must be treated with great caution. He is a man to be feared. During his time in Uasin Gishu, he cast out many demons but, in the end, became possessed by the chief demon he exorcised. He killed six children and six mothers.'

'Do you think he was possessed by the devil, Sergeant Kimurer?'

Kimurer laughed across the distance of seas and continents, but there was no joy in that sound.

'Not at all. I'm a rationalist, an atheist. I have a master's degree in Psychology. Sebastian Flint is a paranoid sociopath. The problem is not his soul. It is his conscience or, rather, his lack of one. He came to my country for fun, perverse fun.'

'When you say he killed six women and their children, were the children *in utero* or had they been born?'

'They had been born already.'

'Why wasn't he arrested?'

'The people got to him first. They tried to kill him, though he survived. Then the Catholic Church found him and smuggled him from the Rift Valley province and back to England. Do you have problems in England with dishonest policemen? Bribes?'

'Indeed we do.'

'We share a burden. High-ranking officers were given money and the case was made to disappear. Do you have Flint in your custody?'

'Not at the moment.'

'Who is being bribed by the Church?'

'No one. He hasn't been charged with a crime at present.'

'Do you have him in your sights?'

'I have him in my sights.'

'Has he committed a crime?' asked Sergeant Kimurer.

'It's my growing belief that he is connected to a series of unsolved crimes, though I have yet to prove it. Sergeant Kimurer?'

'Yes?'

'How positive are you that Flint killed six women and children? How certain?'

'I am one hundred per cent certain.'

'How can you be so sure?'

'I was a boy at the time of these killings. I lived twenty miles away.'

'So you didn't see Flint kill anyone with your own eyes?'

'No, but I know people who were there, eyewitnesses, reliable people. One man told me that he saw Flint enter the house of his first victim. It was his neighbour's house. Flint went in and a minute later there were screams, a woman and a child screaming. He hurried over to see what was wrong. There was blood everywhere. Two mutilated bodies on the floor, an innocent woman and her young daughter hacked to pieces. He saw Flint leaving by the back door as calmly as if he'd just paid a social call. Other people saw him get into his car and drive away. He was at the wheel, covered in blood. One man tried to make Flint stop the car but Flint drove at him at speed so he had to throw himself out of the way.'

Rosen felt cold but wiped a film of perspiration from his brow.

'I went looking for evidence in the archive but couldn't find it. It had all been destroyed years ago. For money.' The anger in Kimurer's voice was fresh. 'So I went looking for people. In my own time, I tracked down eyewitnesses and have detailed statements from the other five attacks. There were twelve victims in all, before the people caught up with Flint.'

'Sergeant Kimurer, with respect, there must be many cold cases on your files. You feel strongly about this one. Why?'

'It had a profound effect on me as a child – on all of us children. Flint became the stuff of nightmares. The world stopped being innocent. But that's not all, Detective Rosen. I dream of the day Flint comes back to Kenya to pay for his crimes. I will be there with the evidence I recorded before those witnesses died.'

You're a good man, thought Rosen, and wished Kimurer was on his team.

'Detective Rosen, when you were a child, was there a murderer in your country who terrified you?'

A grim, iconic, black and white mugshot sprang to mind.

'Yes. He terrified a generation.'

'What was his name?'

'Ian Brady.'

'You must understand, Father Sebastian is our Ian Brady. He is a bogeyman, his name is used to scare young children even to this day.'

Rosen pulled his car into a pay and display grid.

'Thank you, Sergeant Kimurer. You've been most helpful.'

'Detective Rosen, if you go near this man, please remember, he has no remorse, so don't turn your back on him for one second. You understand?'

'I understand,' said Rosen.

As Sergeant Kimurer hung up, the knot in Rosen's stomach tightened.

In a matter of hours, he would come face to face with Flint.

33

'I don't think I've ever been this nervous in my life,' said Sarah.

He wanted to say, 'You'll be fine,' but the best he could come up with was, 'Let's just take this one step at a time.'

They approached reception at the antenatal clinic in St Thomas's Hospital.

'I'm here for an ultrasound scan,' explained Sarah.

'Name, please?' asked the receptionist, not looking up from her screen.

'Sarah Rosen.'

The receptionist scrolled down her onscreen list.

'You're not here.'

Sarah tried to explain but her words became tangled.

'We're an emergency case—' tried Rosen.

'Well, your case notes aren't here, either.'

At that moment, another woman arrived carrying a thick folder of case notes with a yellow Post-it attached to the front, and threw it down.

'They're my notes!' said Sarah, seeing her name in block capitals across the top of the battered file.

'OK, take a seat, please.'

Sarah picked up a leaflet from the low table before them while Rosen looked around without connecting with anyone's eye.

Although there were around thirty mothers with partners, parents and friends in support, the waiting room was curiously quiet, as if even a little speech was somehow a dangerous thing.

'What's that you're reading, Sarah?'

'Just a leaflet.'

She handed it to Rosen. A smiling mum, T-shirt riding above her bump, hands cupped above her pubic bone. The model was a young woman whose pregnancy was no doubt going to be a walk in the park given the healthy glow she radiated – a wellness of being she no doubt took for granted.

'What are you thinking?' asked Sarah.

'I think we have to be utterly realistic,' said Rosen.

'Could you be a little more precise?'

He didn't want to say the words, he didn't even know how to, but he tried. 'We might not make it.'

'Yes,' she said, her voice fracturing with fear. 'I know.' She looked at her husband. 'It's just so unfair.' Her eyes brimmed but she took in a deep breath, her spirit fighting back.

Their eyes locked in tenderness and, in a single moment, there was a deep connection. To lose a child again would be unbearable.

'We'll just have to help each other,' said Rosen. 'Day by day, if things don't go our way.'

'I know you'll help me, whatever happens.'

Suddenly, the weight of their shared history hit Rosen hard and he found to his shame he couldn't look at his wife. In that unforgiving public space, he needed to separate himself from the moment.

Across the aisle, he noticed a young man staring hard at him and automatically wondered what he'd arrested him for and when. He quickly reviewed his mental list and decided that he hadn't. The young man and his girlfriend, both aged about seventeen, in matching tracksuits, caught the hardness of Rosen's stare and looked away.

'What's up with them?' asked Sarah.

'It's the concept of us, at our age, having a sexual relationship and making a baby. That's my guess, anyway.'

He watched the hands of the plain white clock shift from a minute after three to a quarter past, and felt the uneasy tugging of conscience, the anxiety of having to be in one place when another called to him.

'Excuse me,' he said to a passing nurse, 'is there a delay on appointments?'

'Yeah, we've had extras thrown in at the drop of a hat.'

'If you have to go, go,' said Sarah.

'Sarah Rosen!' a sonographer called.

They followed the woman to a plain room with a scan machine and a green vinyl bed. Rosen closed the door after himself as the sonographer invited Sarah to lie down. He sat on a chair next to Sarah.

Sarah squeezed Rosen's fingers as the sonographer, whose face looked elderly but whose movements belonged to a young person, squeezed cold gel on her stomach. She smiled and asked, 'Ready, Mrs Rosen?'

Laying the ultrasound transducer on the curve of Sarah's womb, exploring and examining, the sonographer said, 'Listen.'

'Ectopic?' asked Sarah.

'Not at all. The baby's in your womb. Absolutely normal place and position.'

There was silence for what felt like an age and then the rapid beating of a tiny heart registered onscreen as a soundwave. Sarah laughed and Rosen felt as if a bolted door inside him had unlocked.

'Look.'

A head. Two arms. Two legs. A body. The pathway of the baby's spine.

'It's for real, then,' said Rosen, withdrawing his eyes from the screen to Sarah's smile, then returning them to the screen. The baby was still there, arm rising, thumb to lips.

'He's sucking his thumb.' Such a small action, such a huge event.

'Could be a girl,' said Sarah.

'Could be, but I didn't know babies did that in the womb.' As he spoke, Rosen realized how much he might have to relearn. 'Didn't know that.' Calming the awe in his voice, he looked more closely at the screen. Still there. The baby was still there.

'They do all kinds of wonderful things in the womb. When you've done as many scans as I have, you get to know something about babies. Their different personalities are stamped on them already. From the jolly to the grumpy and all the places in between. Look at the face. Can you see?'

Rosen tried to focus on the tiny features but didn't quite know where he was supposed to be looking.

'This is a calm baby. The calm ones usually have an inborn sense that they're wanted and loved.'

'Can you tell if it's a boy or a girl?' asked Rosen.

'I'm not sure,' said Sarah, quickly.

Rosen wondered whether future Saturdays would be spent at White Hart Lane or reading the papers at some dance studio or other, though the only thing that really mattered was that there would be future Saturdays to share with his son or daughter.

'Some people want to know so they can plan ahead,' the radiographer explained. 'Painting the room, buying clothes, that sort of thing. We can't be sure about the sex at this stage, but I can try and tell you.'

'Do you want to know, David?'

'If you do.'

'Is it a boy or a girl?'

'Look at the screen; we'll wait till the baby turns a little this way.'

The sonographer focussed on the screen, then on Sarah, finally on David.

'I can see the parents' features in the facial shape. If you look at the shape of the baby's nose, well, that's you, Mrs Rosen, but the jawline is definitely dad's. The baby's got elements of both of you but my hunch is, this baby's going to be a ringer for you, Mr Rosen.'

Time and space collapsed and the jagged memory of his father leaving came into focus once more but, for the first time, without the ever-present pain that accompanied it.

'I'll never do that to you,' murmured Rosen.

'What was that, Mr Rosen?' asked the sonographer. Sarah's hand tightened around his.

'I think he's apologizing to the baby for inflicting his face on him, or her.'

'I'm eighty percent sure it's a boy,' said the sonographer. 'Silly question time. Would you care for a picture of your child? I'm afraid a small charge is incurred.'

They asked for six. As the printer issued the images, Rosen picked up the first, looked at his son, and handed it to Sarah.

'Is that a smile on his face?' she asked.

'They experience pleasure, the sound of mum's voice, familiar music . . .'

And pain? Rosen pushed the thought away but it pushed back harder.

The sonographer glanced at her watch and said, 'You need to get back to your GP to make an appointment at Mr Gilling-Smith's clinic.'

The sonographer took another furtive look at her watch as Sarah wiped the rest of the gel from her abdomen before sitting up and fixing her top. They thanked the sonographer who smiled, wished them luck and held the door open for them to leave.

'I'll phone the surgery and make an appointment,' said Sarah. 'Do you want to come along?'

'I want to come with you, Sarah.'

'But you can't?'

'I can't, I'm sorry.'

'Going anywhere nice?' she asked.

'Charing Cross Station.'

'What are you doing there?'

'Meeting a suspected murderer.'

They passed a clock on the wall on the way to the lifts. He wasn't desperately short of time for his scheduled appointment at the station, and wished he could stop feeling torn, forced into two races at the same time.

'Let me walk you to your car . . .'

'Is it Herod?' she asked.

'It's the priest, the ever-so helpful priest, Father Sebastian.'

'Is he a murderer?'

They arrived at the lifts and, within a matter of moments, were joined by a very young and heavily pregnant woman with her mother.

David and Sarah Rosen exchanged a glance.

'Could be – looks as if he could well be.'

34

Father Sebastian was sitting, drinking mineral water from a plastic bottle and watching the mating ritual of two pigeons when Rosen first spotted him on the concourse at Charing Cross Station.

In the same few seconds, Rosen saw Carol Bellwood in the middle distance, eyeing the destination and arrivals board. She glanced back at Rosen as she turned her head, looking right through him.

It was rush hour and the place had the feeling of a besieged city about to fall into enemy hands, with a continuous flow of single-minded commuters in flight.

'Father?'

Rosen was struck by the stillness of the priest, the same stillness he'd observed that morning in the British Library. Did he have hearing problems? After Kenya? After they'd lynched him?

'Father Sebastian?' This time a little louder.

'Hello, David. Glad you could make it.' The priest didn't look up at the detective.

In a single moment, dozens of copies of the *Evening Standard* seemed to fly past Rosen, clutched by commuters, the headline pronouncing the discovery of Julia Caton's body.

Father Sebastian looked up at Rosen and said, 'Poor Julia. It's a tragedy.'

'What time's your train?'

'You've got me for about ten minutes.'

'What are you doing in London, Father Sebastian?'

'The connection between Herod and Alessio Capaneus woke me up in the middle of the night. To be honest with you, I'm more than a little disappointed in myself for not seeing it sooner in the broad light of day, but in my own defence I have to confess that it's not a hotbed of intellectual activity at St Mark's, and I've become a somewhat dull shadow of my former self. But you don't want to know about me, do you? You want to know about Alessio Capaneus. He's not on the internet, but I found him in some very interesting books today.'

Rosen saw time dripping away on a digital clock.

'Alessio Capaneus? What did you discover?' asked Rosen.

'Erzurum, it's a rather beautiful city, ever heard of it? No. Why should you? It's centuries old, at the foot of the Palandöken Mountains in the eastern Anatolian region of modern-day Turkey. It's the place where Capaneus had his Satanic visions, where he travelled to after he was banished from Florence. It's where he wrote his book.'

'Alessio Capaneus wrote a book? You said the book was hearsay, that it didn't exist.'

'I said at the time, *I think* it doesn't exist, *I think* it was hearsay. Well, I did some digging today in an effort to help you and, guess what, I thought wrong. There is a book. It's made up of two distinct parts. An Old Testament and a New Testament, if you like. The first part's an account of creation, the ascent of man, the war in heaven and the creation of hell. Ever heard the expression, "History is written by the victors"?'

'Yes, I have.'

'Well, Capaneus's book, you see, is history written by the so-called losers. It's Satan's reply to the Holy Bible. It's Satan's side of the story. Some of the individual books that make up the whole piece even have the same names as the books in the Holy Bible. There's a Book of Genesis, Exodus, Job – they're all in there.'

'The Capaneusian Bible, then,' said Rosen.

'Oh, very good,' replied Flint, bringing his hands together in a single clap. 'The Capaneusian Bible, what a neat title you've come up with, David.'

Rosen eyed the clock, ignored Flint's patronizing tone and asked, 'What about the second part?'

'The New Testament of Capaneus? In part it's a prophetic vision, in part a guidebook. The prophetic vision tells the future story of what will happen when Satan comes to earth in spirit to take on human form. You look perplexed, David. Think Jesus Christ in first-century Judea, now flip it on its head and think Satan Morningstar in the twenty-first century, right here. The guidebook's there for anyone willing to conjure up the Satanic spirit and act as host. That's where this killer comes in. He's had access to the information in the Capaneusian Bible. Your killer's been out there gathering in carriers – that's Capaneus's specific term for pregnant mothers and souls, unborn babies not corrupted by original sin. In Capaneus's view, when the child is born it draws in original sin with its first breath, gets contaminated by the air around it at the moment it becomes an independent human. If it is taken from the womb, the soul remains in the body untouched by original sin. It's partly written in Latin, the language of the empire that subjugated Jesus and his people, and it's partly written in first-century Aramaic, the language that would have been spoken by the Messiah. It's part mockery, part blasphemy.'

I want to go home, thought Rosen. *I want to go away, far, far away.*

'Are you all right, David?'

'For the killer to know all this . . . is it a widely circulated book in occult circles?'

Father Sebastian laughed. 'No. Not at all. I believe there's only one copy in the whole world.'

'And that's in the British Library?' Rosen spoke his thought aloud.

'No. The Vatican.'

'You had access to it when you were at the Vatican?'

'No. The Holy Father's the only human being allowed to look at it and, if the account I read today is accurate, Pope Pius XII was the last pope to do so. Besides, I had absolutely no interest in Capaneus at that time. He was barely a footnote.'

'Today, then, today you've found out all this information?'

'Today, but not from the book itself, of course. Secondary sources – second-hand accounts if you like – in a whole range of antiquarian books. Some are in the British Library, others will probably be in the Bodleian, the Carnegie, all the major libraries of the world. That's why I went to the British Library today, to refresh my memory from a range of other sources. You've got to understand, David, this book's been buried by the Church, absolutely suppressed for centuries. Just as the Florentines suppressed the name of Alessio Capaneus, and tried to wipe his memory from the face of the earth, so the Church has tried to wipe out his account of the dawn of time and this manifesto for the overturning of the universe.'

'What if he succeeds?'

'Who, David? What if who succeeds?'

'Julia Caton's killer.'

'If he follows the Capaneusian Bible, there'll be six dead mothers and six dead babies. I don't need to tell you the religious significance of the number six. You don't strike me as a believer. You don't believe, do you?'

'No, I don't believe in the possibility of a Satanic revolution.'

'You know, for a clever man, that's a rather dim point of view.'

'I'm an equal-opportunities sceptic. I don't believe in God, either.'

'Sadistic rabbi, was it? Turned you against the Lord?'

'No.'

'Or are you the kind of atheist who thinks nothing so bad's ever going to befall them so they don't need a little heavenly help?'

'I'm a policeman. I do evidence, hard evidence; stuff that will stand up in court.'

'I see. This scepticism, did it come from your father?'

'How's the killer accessing this information if it's so buried, if it's so scattered?'

'Time's marching on, David. I shall miss my train if I don't go now.'

'Wait a minute, Father Sebastian. Let me get this straight. The killer thinks that by killing six women and hacking out their foetuses, he's going to unleash a force of evil in the universe and he's going to come out as king in this newly Satanized world – ?'

Sebastian smiled. 'Crazy, absolutely crazy. Right? You know it's nuts. But he's a believer and those beliefs, however you view them, have resulted in five dead women, five dead foetuses, so far. Just as Hitler believed he could wipe out your tribe. Like emptying the sea with a thimble. A deluded and idiotic belief. However, the end result was the end result. If you've got a problem computing this in terms of theology and Satanism, then think of what's going on in London as a . . . as a mini Holocaust. I hope I've been of some help to you, David. And I wish you well with the ongoing investigation.'

Sebastian placed the empty water bottle on the ground, smiled at Rosen and said, 'I guess we're done.'

'How can an individual get access to a book that's buried in the Vatican and is written in first-century Aramaic?'

'The same way I saw much of it this afternoon. That's where your visit to St Mark's came in so handy. The Church can suppress a book until the College of Cardinals is collectively blue in the face. The problem is that suppression of information's a thing of the past. The internet, Detective Rosen. My guess is, your killer's getting it all off the World Wide Web. I checked the computers at the British Library this afternoon. I wish we had one at St Mark's. The Capaneusian Bible is largely but not completely online.'

'How can that be?' asked Rosen. 'We put his name into the search engine back at St Mark's and nothing came up. We did an in-depth search at Isaac Street and nothing came up there, either.'

'The book isn't really called the Capaneusian Bible or the Book of Alessio Capaneus,' explained Flint. 'It's called something else entirely different.' He glanced up at the clock. 'I need to board my train.'

'What is it called? This book?'

'Oh, it's very simple. It's called *A*. Does that speak of significance in your case, David? A for Alessio, maybe . . .'

Rosen pictured five dead women, their faces, their bodies, at the points where they were dropped off. An image formed of the map with those five places marked, and the shape that was emerging.

'A,' said Flint. 'Maybe an initial from a name or maybe A for alpha. Alpha, David: the first letter, the opening sound, the beginning, the brand-new beginning heralded by the Satanic revolution. I have to tell you, there is no omega to this alpha. I'm convinced there is no concept of an end to the torments that this brand-new world promises. Alpha, it's the opening word of A's Book of Genesis. Alpha, just that, just that. Goodbye, David. Brother Aidan awaits me.'

'Body drop-off number six – it'll be at the midpoint of Vauxhall Bridge Road. That'll form a nice crooked bridge between body drop-offs two and three. I think you're right about the "A"; I think you're right because I've seen a pattern.'

Rosen felt the satisfaction of having slapped someone in the face.

'I don't know what you mean, David.'

'Next time you're in London, buy a map and visit an internet café. Google the case. Check it out.'

Rosen fixed his gaze in neutral.

'Maybe I should,' said the priest.

You're an arrogant bastard, thought Rosen.

'God bless you, David Rosen. You'll need His blessing one day, even if you don't believe in Him.'

Father Sebastian turned away and made for the barrier. Rosen kept his eyes clamped onto the priest's back but also kept the water bottle firmly in his field of vision.

Bellwood, armed with a commuter's briefcase and a copy of a glossy magazine, appeared and melted into the tide following the priest.

Father Sebastian walked past the barrier, blending into a stream of people heading for the same platform.

In the moment that Flint was no longer distinguishable from the flowing mass of humanity, a station cleaner stepped in front of David and stooped to pick up the bottle.

'Stop! Don't you touch that!' The cleaner froze, shock and fear on his face at Rosen's sharp command. 'Don't touch the bottle.' Rosen flashed his warrant card and picked up the bottle at the base, using his thumb and forefinger. The neck of the bottle had something on it that was of particular interest to him.

He returned the way he had come, careful to sidestep people coming the other way who might brush against his prize.

He was consumed with purpose, and grateful for the sense of direction that went with it. He would need to bring in civilian IT support.

In his car, he snatched an evidence bag from the glove compartment and secured the water bottle.

Taking out his mobile, he scrolled through his contacts and came to Karen Jones of ICT, a civilian computer specialist and the soul of discretion. He called her.

'Karen?'

'David? You don't sound too good.'

'I'm OK. Listen, it's probably a cinch to find . . .' He explained the bare bones of what Flint had told him. 'Can you find anything about this thing, this *A*, this Capaneusian Bible? Dig as deep as you can.'

'I take it mum's the word?' said Karen.

'Mum is indeed the word,' said Rosen, as he turned on the ignition and shifted into gear.

35

On the platform, the station guard slammed shut the last open door of the train and raised his whistle to his mouth.

On the 17.15 train from London Charing Cross to Ramsgate, Carol Bellwood sat seven seats behind Father Sebastian. There was standing room only for the commuters and the journey promised to be short of fresh air.

He was sitting next to the aisle, two seats away from the door. She'd picked a seat that gave her the best unobstructed view of her mark. A heavy inward surge of passengers at Chatham Station, the next along, and a shuffling of bodies up the aisle would be enough to completely obstruct her view of him.

She stood up to gain a better view of the priest.

Just before the train doors closed at Chatham Station, she felt a tightening in her stomach, expecting him to rise and calmly get off at the last moment, leaving her behind. But he didn't. He remained where he was, and she was struck by his stillness in the milling of bodies around the doors. Even the woman sitting next to him, and the people opposite, seemed over-animated as they sat staring at newspapers and into space.

A newspaper unfolded just in front of him. There was a photograph on the front page of the *Evening Standard* of the white tent around Julia Caton's corpse and, next to this, a picture of Julia from her wedding day. It was close to Sebastian, just diagonally across the aisle from him. Still, his head was set like stone.

At Gillingham, Bellwood's adrenalin pumped. A handful of people left the train but many more boarded, forcing door-hangers further down the aisle and making the carriage uncomfortably full.

In the jostling of bodies, a lone mother, tired and stressed to the point of tears, double buggy in tow with two crying children under the age of three, struggled to find a space between the doors and the aisle. As the doors slid shut and the train pulled out of Gillingham, no one moved a muscle to help her.

Then Father Sebastian stood up. He was taller than he'd appeared at Charing Cross. He caught the woman's attention and spoke to her, but it was clear she didn't follow his English. He spoke again. Bellwood struggled to hear but couldn't make it out through the din of the moving train, but the woman's expression shifted to one of understanding.

Father Sebastian reached out and, in a single motion, took the buggy from the woman, folded it and stored it in the coat rack above. He indicated the seat he'd occupied and with her children in tow, she edged past the passengers to take it.

Flint half turned to smile down at the woman and Bellwood caught his profile. He would be handsome when he was an old man – his bone structure was good; his immense good looks were not the fleeting gift of time.

The woman spoke to him and he listened. There was clearly a problem with the wriggling children in the space-to-adult ratio of the double-facing seats.

Flint made a suggestion, waited a moment and then leaned down to pick up the older of the two children, a boy of about two and a half years.

In his arms, the fractious child settled, smiled and raised a hand towards Flint's face. Then, Flint turned slowly, slowly, his profile clear once more.

Bellwood felt her spine stiffen. The boy's fingers were inside Flint's mouth. The mother's voice cut across the carriage as she ordered her child to remove them in a language Bellwood didn't understand.

Flint tugged the boy's hand away as he turned his back on Bellwood. He replied to the mother in a calm voice, in her own language, telling her, Bellwood guessed, not to worry, children will be children . . .

By Sittingbourne, the passengers thinned out, but Flint still stood, his body rocking slightly, his head now moving with the motion of a nursery rhyme or some song for bedtime. The boy laid his head on Flint's shoulder and by Sheerness-on-Sea was fast asleep.

At Faversham, Flint reclaimed a seat, with the sleeping child on his lap, and returned to the stillness of his former self, the complete, unassailable self-possession that was as remarkable as it was enviable.

The automated voice and the electronic noticeboard told the passengers that Canterbury East was the next stop. Tenderly, Flint handed the child to his mother and made his way to the door.

Bellwood tried to imagine what it would be like to utterly dismiss the prospect of tenderness, intimacy and sex, as he had done by pledging himself to God and the Church.

She stood up and shuffled down the aisle, her magazine open. *Cosmopolitan*. 'How to Have First-Time Sex Every Time.'

The train slowed.

He glanced back not at her but at the magazine, and she shut it fast, suddenly blushing to the roots of her hair, embarrassed by what she was apparently reading.

Handsome, calm, a natural with children. It was a waste of a man.

The train stopped but the doors remained closed. As he reached to press 'open', between his coat sleeve and the hem of his glove, she caught sight of a wound on his wrist. The white scar looked like the result of a blow from a heavy blade, the edge of a machete perhaps. She looked up. He was gazing back at her. The doors opened.

'After you?' he said.

'Thank you,' she replied, and stepped off the train. Bodies flowed past on either side of her but he was not among them. She stopped.

She turned slightly and almost bumped into him as he came the other way. His hand grasped her shoulder and slid down a few inches. He said, 'I beg your pardon.'

She nodded. And on he went.

She followed him. As he headed for the taxi rank outside the station, she waved as if saying goodbye to a friend still on board the train. When she waved, DS Corrigan, in the private hire car he'd occupied at the head of the taxi rank since half past five, caught sight of Father Sebastian approaching his passenger door.

'St Mark's,' said the priest.

'Get in,' Bellwood heard Corrigan reply.

Bellwood watched the car go and, reaching in her bag for a cigarette, remembered she'd quit many years ago.

She called Rosen. 'He's in the car with Corrigan.'

'Any incident?'

'None.'

'Good job, Carol, well done.'

Bellwood didn't agree with Rosen, but said nothing.

In the space of a single train journey from Charing Cross to Canterbury East, station by station, she had grown steadily and more deeply attracted to the man she'd been tailing. And, as she made her way to the meeting point with Corrigan, who would drive her back to London once he'd dropped off Flint, she wished her mother had been there. She wished her mother had been there to give her a damn good slap in the face.

36

At just after half past eight, Corrigan and Bellwood arrived back at the incident room. Feldman and Gold had already begun the eye-watering task of viewing a combination of over twenty-four hours of footage from the British Library's CCTV, both interior and exterior.

Rosen called them all together.

'Let's do it chronologically.' He turned to Feldman. 'Take it from the point where I passed over to you, Mike, in the reading room at the British Library.'

Feldman held his hands up. 'He read, he got up and stretched his legs, he visited the toilet, he read . . .'

'How long was he in the toilet?'

'Half a minute to a minute. Time to pee and wash his hands. He went to the café and had lunch.'

'Which was?'

'Tap water and an apple. He went back and read. At four o'clock, he went to the John Ritblat Gallery and looked at the old manuscripts.'

'Did he talk to anyone?'

'No.'

'Did anyone sit with him in the reading room?'

'Lots of people sat near and around him, coming and going, but no one engaged with him and he didn't engage with any of the other readers. Then he made his way to the front entrance.'

Gold picked up the baton.

'Feldman joined me in the entrance and, separately, we followed him on the tube to Charing Cross. We waited on the concourse until you met up with him.'

'He got the train to Canterbury East,' said Bellwood. 'He has a way with small children, he's very good with little kids. He engaged with a mother struggling with her little ones, but that was all.'

Corrigan continued, 'I took him by car to St Mark's. He went inside.'

'Have you looked at the footage inside the Ritblat Gallery?' asked Rosen.

'No, not yet,' Feldman replied.

'Look at that footage next.'

Gold and Feldman exchanged glances.

'Because I want to see how he is around the things of antiquity, the ancient and the sacred . . .'

'Why?' asked Bellwood.

'Humour me. There's background on this character Flint. He opted to leave a plum job in the Vatican to go and work in Kenya. Flint hits the outback at a time of a plague of demonic possession, with people running around "possessed" by devils, but also, more to the point, lots of brutal murders. No one else on the team needs to know this, so keep it close, OK? Flint the exorcist himself becomes "possessed". He ends up getting lynched. Why? Did the saviour turned into the scourge? I spoke to a Kenyan police officer today, Sergeant Kimurer. He said he's talked to reliable eyewitnesses who saw Flint enter and leave a house. A mother and her child were butchered while Flint was inside that house. Kimurer said there were twelve victims in total. The Catholic Church whisked Flint out of Kenya before you could say boohoo. If Kimurer's right, Flint's a serial killer. I found out only a few hours ago, just before I met up with him at Charing Cross.'

The door to Baxter's office opened and Baxter walked into the middle of the incident room.

'OK, troops, that'll do for now.'

'David!' called Baxter, disappearing back into his office. Rosen followed.

'Shut the door.'

Rosen closed the door. 'Yes?' he asked.

'Where did you disappear to mid-afternoon?'

'Hospital appointment.'

'What's up with you?'

'Plenty.'

'What medical reason can you give for walking away on the day a body is discovered?'

'I can't. The appointment wasn't mine. It was Sarah's.'

'Is it her nerves again?'

'No, her nerves are fine; they have been for a long time. I think I've explained to you on more than one occasion, mental illness isn't permanent.'

Rosen regretted having to mention Sarah's name in Baxter's presence, let alone discuss her former illness. It felt like an enforced act of betrayal.

'What else did you do, when you weren't otherwise occupied?'

'I went to pursue a lead.'

'Which was?'

'At the British Library.' Rosen considered telling Baxter about Father Sebastian and dismissed the notion in the same instant.

'What was at the British Library that you had to deploy officers there?' The colour purple shot up from Baxter's throat. 'And what's with all this fucking off up and down to Kent?'

'Robert really has been doing a good job. He wasn't in on the Kent loop.'

'At least DC Harrison has the communication skills to inform his superior officers about what is going on, unlike you.'

'Do you believe in God, Inspector Baxter? The devil?'

Baxter looked as if he'd just bitten into a shiny red apple that was rotten to the core.

'The Herod murders could be – could be – copycat killings. Herod, it appears, is basing his MO on a thirteenth-century Florentine Satanist.'

'Alessio Capaneus.'

'Robert again,' said Rosen.

'Do you know what, David, I just wanted to hear it from your own mouth because I can't believe the way you've wasted the time of officers on your team. I've heard enough from you. I'm not even going to ask you any more. I can wait a couple of days, because on Tuesday morning you can explain it all in the initial peer review meeting, which will take place at nine o'clock. Everyone who is or has been involved in this investigation on any level whatsoever has been invited and is strongly advised to attend. The guys from Islington can ask you where and why because, frankly, I'm sick to death of trying to talk to you.'

Rosen closed Baxter's door behind him and looked around the incident room.

Gold and Feldman stared at CCTV footage. Bellwood was on the phone.

Corrigan entered through the main door.

'Peer review, Tuesday,' said Rosen.

'Crock of shit, Wednesday,' said Corrigan.

37

The morning brought cold daylight and the arrival, at last, of Gwen Swift's cold case file.

Baxter's door was shut tight and there had been no sign of him all morning.

Flint's water bottle had been sent by DHL to the DNA database and had been signed for at nine, with an urgent request to process the sample.

Bellwood watched Rosen as he took the cold case file from the clerk who delivered it to his desk.

'Sorry it took so long,' said the clerk. 'It was misfiled under G and not S.'

The thinness of the brown card file told Rosen, at a glance, that the detectives investigating back in the early 1970s had laboured in a desert, chasing phantoms. How he sympathized as he opened it.

Inside lay a deeper tale of frustration. There was no order. The last person to handle it must have thrown back the papers and pictures in anger or despair.

Rosen now sorted it. Three fruitless interviews with three schoolboys who had the misfortune of being short, thin and dark haired; a description in a witness statement given by a driver, of a boy of this type, seen following – or maybe just walking behind – Gwen when she got off the bus.

The photographs of Gwen at the scene of the murder were black and white and grainy. It hadn't been a ferocious attack. There was no blood evident and, had the attack not occurred on a lonely footpath, she could have been sleeping. He lingered on her face, going back in his mind to the discovery of her mother's body, and the picture of her in her shrine of a bedroom. Then his thoughts turned to the children in the heart-shaped locket on the dressing table, the picture of a girl and a little boy.

Most murder victims know their killer: the words spun around his head as if on a carousel. He turned his attention to the coroner's report, scanning it until he came to cause of death. As he read the uneven typewritten findings, the blurred and speckled print seemed to dance off the page. He felt a sensation like a pair of steel talons bearing down hard on his skull. Abruptly he was on his feet, the report gripped in both hands.

He looked around the incident room. Seven of the team in. The door to Baxter's office still closed. Harrison on his way back from the water fountain. Bellwood working on the computer at her time-shared desk. Gold and Feldman bug-eyed at their laptops. Others coming and going. He sat down, having caught Harrison's eye, but Harrison looked away. Rosen stared at the coroner's report again and said, 'Carol, got a minute?'

Bellwood strolled over. 'Still no word back on Flint's DNA?'

Rosen pointed at the file on his desk. 'Look at that,' he whispered. 'Look at that, Carol, look at the cause of death but don't react.'

Harrison glanced up from his laptop, looked across and back at the screen.

She focussed on the coroner's report and read silently: 'Gwen Swift died of cardiac tamponade after being stabbed in the chest cavity by a thin, sharp piece of metal, possibly the spoke of a bicycle wheel or a section of a wire coat-hanger.'

'Just like Jenny Maguire, Alison Todd, Jane Wise, Sylvia Green and Julia Caton. We've got a connection from 1973 to today. Who have we got from 1973?' His mind raced and he whispered, 'Susie Armitage', in the same moment that Bellwood said her name. An image crossed his mind: a girl and a little boy – Paul Dwyer – trapped in a locket with a lock of black hair on a dressing table at 24 Brantwood Road.

'Get hold of Susie. We need her to look at the locket from Mrs Swift's dressing table.' Rosen looked up at her 'OK, Carol. Stand right there. If anyone comes this way, you act as a shield between the screen and their eyes.'

'Anyone being Harrison?'

'Anyone.'

Rosen scrolled into the Police National Computer.

He typed in the name Paul Dwyer.

'How old?'

'He was seven in the late sixties.'

'Let's stay safe with either side of the low forties.' He typed in 'Age forty to fifty-five'.

Four names appeared on the screen; three were deceased, one had been a resident of Broadmoor since the eighties.

'Shit.' Rosen wanted to bang the table. 'He won't be operating under that name, though. Let's try the HOLMES reader.'

Bellwood fetched her HOLMES laptop from her desk and took over Rosen's seat as he blocked the view of the rest of the office. She logged on to the system and said, 'If there's one specific commonality between any single detail in two separate cases, this computer system's going to match them and throw it up. I've been up and down the highways and byways on HOLMES with all the information we have and nothing's chimed so far. What do you want me to try next?'

He considered. Rosen picked up Harrison's internet printout, of Alessio Capaneus's brief and bloody biography.

'Capaneus. Have you ever typed that into the system?'

She shook her head. 'I stuck to forensics, time, logistical details, places . . . that's what HOLMES sorts. In terms of HOLMES, Capaneus is ancient history.'

'Let's imagine Capaneus's crimes have just been reported to us. Put them in the system, Carol. We'll take some antiquated maybes and see how they square up with some modern definites.'

He took the scant internet information from the in-tray on his desk and summarized.

'Alessio, precise birth date and parents unknown, thirteenth century, adopted by Filippo Capaneus and given the family name. Exiled from Florence, he returns from the Middle East and Africa with esoteric texts. Arrested, hanged for the murder of six pregnant women, notably Beatrice Ciacco, fifth victim, neighbour of the Capaneus family . . .' Rosen paused. 'Let's try that. Type in Capaneus *and* fifth victim *and* adoptive family *and* neighbour *and* Beatrice Ciacco.'

As she typed, Rosen asked, 'Have you recorded everything about the murder of Julia Caton?'

'Yes.'

'OK?'

'Done,' said Bellwood.

She pressed 'enter' and within seconds a match showed onscreen.

Capaneus, fifth victim, adoptive family, pregnant neighbour,
Beatrice Ciacco

        fifth victim,   pregnant neighbour

'Look at the gaps,' said Rosen. 'Whose names go in the gaps?'

'Dwyer and Julia Caton.'

'And he was fostered, not adopted, which for our purposes amounts to the same thing.'

'As copycats go,' said Bellwood, 'that's a pretty compelling match.'

'We need to talk with Susie Armitage. We'll meet her at 24 Brantwood Road. We need to pump her on Dwyer, take her back in time. We need to mine her memory. You've got her number?'

Bellwood dialled Susie's number and within a minute she had agreed to meet them at 24 Brantwood Road.

Rosen called Craig Parker.

'The old lady's bedroom had been mostly emptied, David.'

'What's been left?'

'The dressing table and the wardrobe,' said Parker.

'Can you bring me the gold locket from the dressing table?' asked Rosen.

'The heart-shaped one with the kids' picture and the lock of hair?'

'Get it here pronto, Craig. I need to place it back at the scene.'

————

HARRISON WATCHED ROSEN and Bellwood leave the office, noting their sudden departure and the nervous energy around them, without a word to anyone. The others, the London officers who looked down their collective noses at him because he dared to come from outside the capital city, were busy at their computers. Harrison strolled casually across the office to Rosen's desk and almost laughed out loud. The dope had walked out leaving his mobile phone squarely on his desk for all to see.

Harrison looked around. No one was watching. It was a Motorola, a crap phone for a crap detective, a has-been, resting on laurels grown brown and grey with age, a joke detective who hadn't even locked his phone. He put the mobile in his pocket and went back to his own desk, the one he shared with three other people he couldn't stand and who couldn't stand him because they knew he was a threat, a high flyer, the sharpest blade in the box but the one most blunted by Rosen and his lack of imagination.

The weight of Rosen's phone felt strange in Harrison's pocket. How he looked forward to seeing who was in the address book and intercepting any texts and voicemail messages intended for Rosen, the idiot in the eye of a storm.

38

In Isobel Swift's bedroom at 24 Brantwood Road, Susie Armitage looked like a child locked in the body of a middle-aged woman.

'Mrs Armitage,' said Rosen, 'I'm very grateful to you for coming here so promptly, so willingly.'

'I feel like I'm on another planet, in some other world.'

'Most people go through a whole lifetime and don't go near the scene of a serious crime,' Rosen said, to encourage her. 'You're not only at the scene of a murder, you're in a place that was once a childhood home. Thank you for helping us today.'

It felt as though Mrs Swift's bedroom had been shrink-wrapped in silence. Susie hovered just inside the doorway and Rosen judged correctly that she was scared to the point of panic.

He drew a line in the air that showed her a path from the place she was standing to the place he wanted her to go; her former foster-mother's dressing table, where the only item remaining was a gold locket. Bellwood gave Susie's elbow the merest of touches to send her over.

'Where is everything? Where's the bed?'

'Detective Sergeant Parker has had to remove the bed for our forensic scientists to study.'

'Oh.'

'If you wouldn't mind, the thing we'd like you to look at is the locket on the dressing table. See.' Automatically, she reached for the object. 'But, please don't touch.' She snatched her hand back.

It was open, made of worn-out gold, the lock of hair on one side, the picture of the young girl and a small boy on the other. Susie squinted.

'Would you like some more light?' asked Bellwood.

'Yes, please.'

'Not a problem.' She flicked her torch onto the locket and Susie let out an incoherent sound that spoke of a lifetime of unresolved sorrow. Bellwood held Susie in her arms and, for the time being, the questioning was suspended as the woman sobbed from the depths of her soul.

Rosen drifted to the window and looked down at the path next door along which the killer had managed to take Julia Caton, and put her into some sort of vehicle, without anyone seeing him. The reason dawned on Rosen as he gazed up and down the tree-lined road. The only person who could have had a clear view of the front path of 22 Brantwood Road was the neighbour at 24 Brantwood Road and, it was his conviction, the killer had murdered that witness some eighteen months earlier.

'Cunning bastard,' Rosen spoke quietly, his breath misting on the window.

'I'm sorry.' Susie was calming down, and Rosen returned to join them at the dressing table. 'That's a picture of me, and the little boy with me, that's Paul Dwyer. I've been talking to the others since I last saw you. I can tell you more, much more about what happened.'

'Thank you for that, Susie,' said Bellwood, softly.

She pointed at the image of herself and Paul Dwyer in the locket. 'She must have still cared for me, deep down, to keep my picture like this.'

'It wasn't you she rejected, Susie; it was the whole world she pushed away.'

'And the lock of hair?'

'It's not Gwen's hair. Wrong colour.'

'Her husband?'

'He was fair haired.'

The beam of the torch played on the sleek black hair, the same colour as the single hair recovered by DC Willis from the loft of 22 Brantwood Road.

'It's the same colour as Paul's hair. See.' She pointed at the hair, then at the image of the little boy.

'Why would she have taken and kept a lock of Paul's hair?'

'She was lovely to all the children, but especially to Paul, as he was . . . vulnerable.'

'Vulnerable? Did he have learning difficulties? A physical disability?'

'He wasn't an attractive child. I think she viewed him with great compassion and that compassion turned to love for the son she could never have herself. You've got to remember she had him from a baby and he was just snatched away seven years later. You know, she went strange after what happened to Gwen, but it wasn't an overnight change. Things took a turn for the worse after Paul's birth mother arrived. I was sixteen when Paul was taken away, and I left shortly afterwards. I visited but . . . after Gwen, well, you know what happened with Gwen and the foster-children, don't you, Carol?'

'Yes, I know.'

'I think that hair is Paul's. He's not in trouble, is he?'

'We're not sure.'

'I hope and pray not.'

'If he is in trouble,' said Rosen, 'we'll do what we can to help him.'

But as he spoke, Rosen thought about the guns of CO19 – Central Operations Firearms Control – at one extreme and, at the other end of the spectrum, the folk who took care of the criminally insane in Broadmoor in the south and at Maghull up north.

'What happened when Paul was taken away by his birth mother?'

'His real mother turned up at his seventh birthday party. She was dressed formally but you could tell by her face, she looked harrowed. Drugs, a former drug addict, now wearing this huge cross around her neck. She was with a man in a dog collar who called himself Pastor Jim. He tried to calm Isobel down. Paul's mum was a member of the Church of the Living Light. The old ways were over, she said. She'd seen the light and she'd found Jesus. It sounded good but there was something that just felt bizarre and horrible about the whole thing. Paul was clutching on to Isobel, crying, "Mum, don't let them take me!"'

'Where was the social worker?' asked Rosen.

'Standing behind the pastor, saying, "We did notify you, Mrs Swift, we did tell you this was going to happen but you ignored us. As an experienced foster-parent, you know the birth mother has this right."'

'What do you know about Paul's mother?'

'She came from a wealthy family. As long as she stayed clean from the drugs, they paid her an allowance.'

'What was her name?'

'Kate, Kate Dwyer. That's all I know. I've been interrogating my memory, interrogating myself for detail, but that's all I can honestly remember.'

Susie looked around the room, at the space where the bed used to be, and seemed completely wrung out.

'Can I go now?'

'Thank you, Mrs Armitage. If you think of anything else, please call me or DS Bellwood.'

Bellwood said, 'Let's go and get some fresh air.'

She took Susie by her elbow and left Rosen alone in Isobel Swift's bedroom.

Rosen considered his available manpower. Harrison was the least busy. He wanted some background on the Church of the Living Light.

Harrison could do the digging. He reached into his pocket where his phone should have been and cursed quietly.

Rosen rebagged the locket and, as he left the room, felt Isobel Swift's pain at the snatching away of a much-loved child and the gaping absence that followed the theft of love.

39

On the way back to Isaac Street, Rosen pulled away sharply at a green light.

'We'll get a confirmation from the DNA database one way or the other, if the hair in the locket's a match for the loft sample,' he observed, accelerating.

'Hopefully this side of Christmas,' said Bellwood.

The speedo on the dashboard said forty-five and the sign on the pavement thirty.

'David?'

'Yes?'

'Do you think Flint did commit those murders in Kenya?'

'I don't know. But I do know Flint's been resident in this country since his run-in with the Kenyans, and I know there are unsolved crimes in this country since he came home that he's got the inside track on. That's why I want a result on his water bottle from the database.'

Bellwood's mobile went off and she said to the caller, 'Hi, Goldie, what's up?' She switched to speakerphone.

'The DNA?' Rosen said hopefully.

'Carol, where are you?' Gold's voice echoed from her mobile.

'On the way back to the station.'

'You with the boss?'

'Yeah, I'm here,' confirmed Rosen.

'David, great news maybe. We think we've got something on the CCTV from the British Library.'

'Flint?'

'Flint and A. N. Other. It might be something, it might be nothing. Two brief sequences, but there's definitely a connection between them.'

'We won't be long!' said Rosen, the speedo rising to fifty, fifty-five.

'David, David, slow down, let's get there alive, please.'

———

HARRISON WAS ON the pavement, smoking his fifth of ten cigarettes that day, when Rosen's phone rang. The display read 'Sarah', and Harrison knew from what he'd heard that this was the bow-wow wife from the picture on Rosen's desk. It rang for an awfully long time before she gave up.

As his cigarette burned down past the halfway stage, sending up a thin stream of smoke to the sky, the phone rang again briefly. This time, it was a voicemail message.

Harrison called it and listened.

'Hi, David, it's me. I've been back to the GP. Just to let you know, St Thomas's Hospital clinical appointments are open and I've got an antenatal appointment with the consultant gynaecologist, Mr Gilling-Smith, tomorrow morning at ten. I know, I know, I can hardly believe I've just said those words.' She laughed. 'Can you believe it, David? You and me, parents? I know you're busy but please try to make the appointment with me. I'll tell you the rest when I see you. I love you, David. Bye.'

He listened again, and again, and again. He entered Sarah Rosen's mobile number onto his own mobile, saved it under SR and deleted her voicemail message on Rosen's mobile with the same dexterous thumb.

He crushed the cigarette beneath the sole of his foot and hurried back to the incident room.

———

'WE'VE COME UP with two interior sequences,' said Gold, slipping the first of two 'British Library'-stamped pen drives into his laptop's USB port. 'You know when you said, look at how the priest acts in the John Ritblat Gallery . . . ?'

Gold and Feldman stood on either side of Bellwood and Rosen, their eyes on the laptop they'd been staring at for hours on end.

'I'll narrate,' said Gold. 'This is the entrance to the gents' toilet on the first floor of the library. People come and go. Then, watch this. Five minutes before the priest arrives, watch. We don't see much of his face, but this guy with black hair goes into the toilet. People come and go, but the little guy stays inside, doesn't come out. Here comes the priest. He goes into the toilet. We catch a glimpse of Feldman who doesn't enter the toilet but backs away from the door. Half a minute to a minute later, out comes the priest and away he goes. Two minutes later, out comes the black-haired guy.' Gold paused the image and pointed across the office at the sculpture on Rosen's desk. 'Scale-wise, colourwise, Mason hit the nail on the head, if this is the guy.'

'If this is Paul Dwyer . . .' It was a clear, full-on shot of the man.

'He's crying,' said Bellwood.

'I wonder what's upset him?' said Gold.

Bellwood leaned in closer to the screen. 'Go back.' Gold obliged. 'Pause.' She drank in the image of Dwyer and said, 'My God. He's not upset. He's crying with absolute joy, as if he's just had a religious experience.'

'Take us to the Ritblat Gallery,' said Rosen. 'What have you got?'

As Feldman changed pen drives, Harrison breezed past. Rosen glanced across the room. Harrison was hanging around at Rosen's desk, blocking the view of Mason's clay bust of the killer.

'Do you need me, Robert?' asked Rosen.

Harrison shook his head and headed slowly in Rosen's direction.

'Here he is, Father Sebastian entering the gallery, staring into the cases at the old books and such, then he pauses at this centrally placed display cabinet. It's three-forty-three, he doesn't move. Around him, people are coming, going, glancing at the things of antiquity rather than really looking, most of them. Then in comes . . . shall we call him Herod?'

'Let's call him Paul,' said Rosen.

'Paul edges himself close to the case Flint's staring into. See Feldman in the background, out of Flint's eyeline?' Gold paused the footage. 'Watch this. I apologize, I totally missed this on the day.'

Harrison joined the group at the laptop.

The paused onscreen image showed Flint's back and Paul's face peering at Flint through the glass cabinet from the opposite side.

'Hi, Robert,' said Bellwood.

'Robert, I've got a job for you' said Rosen smoothly. 'Internet search, Church of the Living Light, early to mid-seventies, London.'

'Church of the Living Light? No problem, sir.'

Harrison headed for his desk, the hint of a smile just lurking beneath the surface of his face, as persistent as it was irritating to Rosen.

'Here's Paul, now watch his face.'

Paul stared through the cabinet with a look of adoration directly at Flint. Paul's lips moved.

'It can't be the Capaneusian Bible that they're looking at, can it?' Rosen wondered aloud.

'What was that, David?' asked Gold.

'What's in the glass case? What's he looking at?'

'I checked,' said Feldman. 'It's an illuminated manuscript from the tenth century.'

'Watch,' said Gold. 'Watch, watch this, watch Flint's hand. He points at the door and Paul turns on his heels and walks out through the door like a little robot.'

They watched the footage again and again. There were good, clear shots of Paul's and Flint's faces. And there were two clear points of connection between them.

Rosen felt in his jacket pocket for his phone. Seeing it sitting on his desk, he went over and collected it. He dialled St Mark's but the line was dead. He tried again. It was an unreachable number. A sickening fear grew within him.

'St Mark's near Faversham, Carol. We're going to bring Father Sebastian in for questioning. Goldie, keep Interview Suite One clear approximately four hours from now. We're in for a long night.'

As Rosen and Bellwood made for the door, Harrison called from his desk, 'Sir?'

Rosen stopped. 'Yes?'

'There's acres of stuff on the internet about the Church of the Living Light.'

'Well, good, keep looking.'

Harrison laughed. 'It sure ain't the kind of church my granny used to go to, I can tell you that right now.'

Harrison's voice followed Rosen as he hurried out of the incident room.

———

TWO MINUTES AFTER Rosen and Bellwood left, Karen Jones, Rosen's civilian IT contact, arrived in the incident room with a pen drive.

'Feldman, where's your boss?'

'He's gone to pull in a suspect for questioning. He'll be a few hours.'

'Can you give him this?' She handed over a pen drive. 'I need to see him asap, so can you tell him when you see him?'

Usually calm under all manner of fire, she seemed agitated and upset.

'What is this, Karen?'

'It's not nice . . . It's called *A*. It's a book of sorts. Rosen called it the Capaneusian Bible.'

'The boss just mentioned that.'

'First thing, me and him, OK?'

'Honest to God, Karen, I'll pass your message on,' said Feldman.

Feldman looked across the room and asked, 'Something amusing you, Robert?'

'Yeah,' said Harrison. 'The Church of the Living Light.'

40

As soon as he pulled up outside the main door of St Mark's, Rosen knew for sure that something was wrong.

A sleek black BMW was parked at an angle to the wide-open main door.

'A visitor, a somewhat important and unexpected visitor,' said Rosen, indicating the car to Bellwood as they entered the building.

As they made their way towards room 11, Father Sebastian's ascetic den, the sound of raised voices hurtled down the corridor towards them.

Just outside the closed doorway of Flint's room stood three men: Brother Aidan in front of a tall man with a grey beard and, beside him, a young priest in black.

'Look, he's here!' Aidan pointed at Rosen. 'He's here already!' Aidan looked and sounded as if he was in the initial stages of mental collapse.

'Come on, Aidan, come on now, Brother.' The tall man behind him oozed authority and kindness. He placed his hands on Aidan's shoulders but Aidan shrugged him off.

'He's gone!' said Aidan. 'If you've come to talk to Father Sebastian, you can't, Rosen. He's gone.'

'When was the last time you saw him?' asked Rosen.

'When he left for London yesterday morning.'

'He did come back here last night. One of my officers drove him here from the station and watched him come in through the front door.'

'Well, I didn't see him, no one did, ask them if you like—'

'Aidan, stop being so aggressive to the police officer. He's only doing his job. Flint must have been here. Who else would have damaged the phone line to cut off all outside communication?'

Aidan span around and looked up at the grey-bearded man.

'I don't want to go back to gaol, ever, ever, you understand?'

'You haven't done anything wrong, have you?' responded the taller man.

'Who are you?' Rosen addressed the speaker.

'I'm Cardinal Francis McPhee,' the prelate replied to Rosen but holding Aidan's gaze, his hands on both Aidan's shoulders, not looking away.

'If you're going to search his room,' Aidan erupted, 'you'll need a search warrant.'

'No, they won't,' said Cardinal McPhee. 'These are good people. We're going to help them and they're going to help us. Aidan, the buck stops with me. If there's a problem here, I promise you, it's me not you who has to think on it.'

'Aidan,' said Rosen, 'could you help right now by making us some coffee?'

'Grand idea. What do you think, Aidan? Time out.'

Cardinal McPhee caught Rosen's eye as he ushered Aidan away. *Me and you, talk later.* 'In the meantime, Detective Rosen, if there's anything we can do to help your investigation . . .'

Rosen turned the handle of Father Sebastian's door.

Almost at once, a blast of cold air flew out of the room.

The window was wide open.

'He told me the window couldn't be opened, it was overpainted and jammed,' said Rosen.

Looking around, he could see no other visible change except for a picture on the wall, just above the bed, the picture Flint had held in his hands during Rosen's visit but hadn't allowed him to see.

'That picture has his fingerprints all over it.'

It was hard to make out the detail from the corridor but the central figure was Jesus Christ seated against a green rectangle, in an image shaped in an arch.

Bellwood moved into the room and squinted at the inscription beneath.

'It's 'The Mocking of Christ' by Fra Angelico.'

It's part blasphemy, part mockery. Flint's words about the Capaneusian Bible rang in Rosen's head.

'Fra Angelico was a Dominican monk and one of the finest painters of religious scenes of his era,' continued Bellwood.

'How do you know that?' asked Rosen.

'It says so in very small print along the bottom of the poster. Not for resale. Free gift with *The Sunday Times*.'

'I'm declaring this a crime scene,' said Rosen.

'What crime took place here?' asked Bellwood.

'Conspiracy to murder,' Rosen replied.

She looked at him.

'I want every single item in this room removed as forensic evidence. Call in Parker and Willis from Scientific Support.'

Bellwood pulled out her mobile.

'The books, the toothbrush, the glass, the toothpaste, the hand towel, the bedside cabinet, whatever's in it, the closet, the clothes in it, the bed, the bedding. The one thing we're looking for will be the one thing we won't find. A connection to the internet. He's using the internet. He's got a laptop.'

On the pillow, open and face down, lay a book. William Blake's *Songs of Innocence and Experience*.

Rosen picked up the book. It was open at pages 22 and 25.

'A missing page.' All that remained of pages 23 and 24 was a jagged edge. He laid down the book.

On her mobile phone, Bellwood spoke to Eleanor Willis and told her where they were. 'You'll need a van to get all this stuff back to London and . . .' – she looked around the room and did a quick estimate – 'twenty-five-metre roll of bubble wrap, no, be on the safe side, make it thirty-five. St Mark's, it's near Faversham. We've more or less just got here ourselves.'

She ended the call and saw Rosen pointing to the Fra Angelico print.

Jesus Christ, his closed eyes just visible beneath a gauze mask that covered the upper half of his face, seated on a box and surrounded by four disembodied hands, one holding a rod close to his face and head, ready to slap, poke and beat him. To the left, a disembodied head, a male in his mid-thirties, hat cocked in mock respect, almost within kissing distance, but with a thick stream of white phlegm streaming out of his mouth in the direction of Jesus Christ's face.

'This is what Sebastian Flint must've stared at every night as he went to sleep. This must be the image he took into his dreams.'

The wind blew in through the open window and the clothes closet creaked ajar. A ragged jogging top and single pair of jogging bottoms were suspended from wire hangers like discarded skin. The once-white T-shirt hung from a third hanger: a sorry array of clothes in the darkness that housed them.

On the floor of the closet were Father Sebastian's odd trainers, two different makes, worn-out souvenirs of a life spent running, running, running.

Rosen considered the contents. Two separate brands of running shoe but they form a pair. One man, two makes; a contradiction in terms like Father Sebastian himself. *The poor godly priest*, thought Rosen, *and whatever's lurking beneath his skin.*

———

When Craig Parker and Eleanor Willis arrived with bubble wrap and a two-wheeled removal trolley, Rosen was quietly astonished to find that two almost silent hours had passed in Father Sebastian's room.

The only significant interruption in that time was a call from the DNA database. Not only had Flint's water bottle sample drawn a blank, but his DNA matched none of the samples that had been found at any of the five scenes of abduction and drop-off. Rosen was disappointed, but not entirely surprised by the news.

Rosen positioned himself in the doorway of the small room to allow Willis and Parker as much space as possible to get on with their work.

To begin with, all that could be photographed was photographed. All that could be logged was logged. Anything that could be secured in small bags was taken away first.

The furniture was of the kind seen on the pavements outside down-at-heel charity shops on sunny mornings, rubbish that no one bothered to bring inside when the rain hammered down in the afternoon; exactly the sort of furniture he had grown up with. His mother had done her best, always her best, under impossible circumstances, and Rosen's heart saluted her memory as Parker and Willis moved on to the large items in the room.

The wardrobe was bubble wrapped and removed, then the bedside cabinet.

The bedding – each of the two sheets and one blanket and pillow separately wrapped – had been stripped from the bed.

Everything and anything, except the two things Rosen hoped they'd find: a laptop and an old, diabolical book.

Parker positioned himself at the foot of the single bed and Willis at the head. Together they pulled it out from the wall on the count of three, stopping when the bed had been moved a metre.

'Is it heavy?' asked Bellwood. Rosen started at hearing her voice, having almost forgotten that he had not come alone.

'Nothing we can't manage,' said Parker.

Now that the bed was clear of the wall, something was visible on the plaster, something that had hitherto been concealed.

Willis peered into the gap and pulled a face. 'That's sick, that. It's only a drawing on the wall, but that's macabre. Come on, come on, Craig. Let's get the bed away. One, two, three . . .'

They lifted the bed clean away from the wall.

Rosen peered at the drawing that had been revealed. After a wretched silence, he tilted his head towards Bellwood and said, 'Carol, go and ask Cardinal McPhee to come here, please. He may be able to shed some light on this. Explain about the position of the Fra Angelico. Make sure Aidan remains in the kitchen.'

Parker pulled the bed further into the middle of the room.

Rosen stared at the drawing on the wall and murmured, 'Jesus.'

Willis's camera whirred, its flash exploding and dying as she photographed the scene depicted there.

Within minutes, Rosen heard Cardinal McPhee's footsteps approaching, his big frame weighed down further by a heavy heart.

As the prelate stopped in the doorway and stared at the drawing, Rosen took stock of him. His clothes, though clean, were less than brand new. Rosen was struck with the intuition that he was seeing the private, humble individual who, at public masses and official church events, hid behind the elaborate purple robes of ecclesiastical office.

Rosen spoke. 'What does this mean, Cardinal?'

'It's an imitation, a line drawing, based on Hans Holbein's portrait of the Dead Christ.'

A thin man, bearded, tortured, eyes open and staring up, slack jaw, mouth open, lying on a slab.

'He's shaded this in with infinite care and – is there a print of this in the room?'

'No.'

'If he's done this from memory, it's – it's incredible. It's a remarkable forgery.' McPhee scrutinized the wall drawing, squinting.

'What do you think it means?' Rosen asked.

'This is Christ in the tomb, crucified, not risen. I can only speculate about Sebastian's individual pathology.'

'He has slept next to this each night and lay on the bed, no doubt for hours, during the day, thinking, dreaming.' Rosen paused for a moment, choosing his next words carefully. 'I've heard a story about Kenya. Of Sebastian in Kenya.'

'Yes, he was beaten to a pulp. We know this because after he was rescued, we spent a year fixing his wounds as best we could.'

'We?' probed Rosen.

'We, the Catholic Church. The brutal assault, our recovery of him afterwards, are the only facts of the case. The rest, the exorcisms, is simply unproven.'

'Are you Scottish, Cardinal McPhee?'

'Yes.'

'Were you a lawyer by trade?'

'I studied at St Andrew's University.'

'What did you say the stories were?'

'Unproven.'

McPhee's shoulders sank. The lifelong marksman had managed to shoot himself in the foot.

'An interesting verdict.'

'In Scottish law—'

'I know about Scottish law, Cardinal McPhee. Guilty, not guilty . . . and unproven. Not enough evidence to convict, not enough lack of doubt to acquit. Thank you. There were murder allegations against Father Sebastian, no?'

'Yes, but he was never charged by the Kenyan police.'

Rosen gave Cardinal McPhee a long, hard look.

'We're ready to shift the bed back,' said Parker.

———

IN THE KITCHEN of St Mark's, Rosen recalled Father Sebastian's masterful performance as the IT virgin, his other-worldly awe and wonder at the marvels of the internet, and was glad that the people presently assembled had not been there to see him so completely gulled.

'Where else did Sebastian go, apart from here and his room?'

'Two places. The chapel.'

Rosen caught Parker's eye. A small, clearly defined space, easy to examine. That was good.

'And the grounds. He used to spend ages running round the grounds.'

The two police officers calculated the cost in time and labour to forensically comb such a huge space. They exchanged a blank stare that, articulated, would have been spelled out in obscenities.

'Let's start with the chapel. Lead the way, Brother Aidan.'

———

As WILLIS DUSTED the surface of the altar, Parker bagged the chalice and communion plate, saying, 'We'll treat these vessels with the greatest respect.'

'When can we have them back?' asked Aidan.

'They'll have to keep them for some time, I would imagine,' said Cardinal McPhee, his temper evidently fraying. 'You have replacements, Aidan.'

'Flint said mass here every day?' asked Rosen.

'Yes.'

'Did he ever preach?'

'No. He just went through the motions of the service itself.'

'Oh, Craig . . .' Willis, dusting away at the window of the chapel, stopped and spoke over her shoulder to Parker to get his attention, then picked up her camera. *Click click click.*

'Yes, Eleanor?' Parker squinted from the altar, then moved to take a closer look. Rosen followed him over to the window, where something had been exposed by the fingerprint powder.

Click click click clickclickclick.

Rosen gazed at the pattern on the glass. It was a word, a single word, drawn by a single finger.

He read two syllables, 'Sa' and 'an', with a one-digit gap between and, on the final 'n', the merest trace of an ascender turning 'n' into a possible 'h'.

Rosen felt suddenly as though his knees might give way.

He turned to Brother Aidan.

'Do you know who wrote this?' he asked, as he headed out of the chapel.

'No. Where are you going in such a hurry, Rosen?' asked Aidan.

'I'm going to make a call.'

Rosen walked down the stone corridor, looking at the time on his mobile phone display. It was two-thirty-four. She'd be teaching.

'The mobile phone you've called is currently unavailable. Please try again later.' It was strange she hadn't called that day, left a message or a voicemail.

He called the school office, listened for an eternity of keypad options and finally got one of the administrative officers.

'It's David Rosen, Sarah Rosen's husband.'

'Oh, yes, I know who you are.' The intention was clearly friendly but it made him feel exposed and vulnerable.

'Could you ask Sarah to ring me, right now?'

'I can't do that, she's in class, teaching.'

'Well, as soon as she comes out of class. This is an urgent matter.'

'I'll pass your message on. Will that be all?'

'Please make sure she gets this message.'

The line went dead.

41

Harrison had two sets of keys, his most expensive set and his second most expensive set. Under the brightness of a full moon, he took out the second most expensive set – for the Ford Mondeo he'd been forced to compromise on because of the most expensive set, which was for the flat he rented in Brixton – and wondered for the umpteenth time about the wisdom of transferring to the Met. *If I was still in Southampton*, he thought, turning the key in the door, *I'd be driving a car that truly reflected who I am, what I am . . .*

'Are you thinking what I'm thinking?'

The voice, coming out of nowhere, shocked Harrison. He hadn't seen a soul in the car park on his way to the car. The speaker was right behind him and he turned to face him. Harrison took a second to match the voice to the man before him, the same one who'd been at the scene-of-crime tape at Albert Bridge Road that morning.

'I said, are you thinking what I'm thinking?'

'Depends what you're thinking,' said Harrison.

'Is this a fucking murder investigation going on here or what? My name's Daniel Taylor. I'm from the Professional Standards Unit, Greater Manchester Constabulary.'

Harrison felt a reflexive urge to vanish into thin air at the bald announcement that in front of him stood an officer whose function was to police other policemen. He adjusted the glasses on the bridge of his nose and tried to match Taylor's tone.

'So what the fuck do you want with me, Taylor?'

Taylor half smiled and half shrugged as he held out his hand. Harrison shook it with as much cold indifference as he could muster, given the buzz of intrigue that ran up and down his spine.

'All right, Robert, I know it's little consolation, the way you keep getting the shitty jobs to do; jobs that are not commensurate with your talent. A big indicator of the mismanagement of this case . . .'

'Rosen,' said Harrison.

And Taylor echoed, 'Rosen . . .'

A light went on inside Harrison, setting off others. There were rumours about the PSU's covert tactics. There were always rumours in the police, but as the case dragged on, rumours solidified, taking on substance.

'Why are you in London?' asked Harrison, a thrill running through him.

'I've been drafted in from Manchester to conduct a covert investigation into the management of this case. Your Commissioner directly contacted our chief. How tight can you keep it, Robert?'

'Go on.'

'Well . . .' Taylor was still, a silence seeming to emanate from him that made Harrison feel as if he was shrinking with each passing moment. 'What is going on here?'

'Superintendent Baxter,' Harrison blurted out.

'Rosen's superior officer?'

'I've been giving Baxter information on a daily basis . . .'

'Yeah, I know that, Robert. But what the fuck's been done with your information?'

'Baxter's called a peer review.'

'So what? Baxter has let you down as well, Robert. Listen, even he doesn't know about me because, frankly, Baxter's messed up as well. He should've called a peer review two dead bodies ago, but he didn't. Because of his personal beef against Rosen, he held out to give Rosen time and space to really hang himself. You're the only one on the team who's got a balanced view of Rosen's failures. I'll be blunt. I need your help. We're looking at the safety of women and children, right?'

'Why should I trust you?'

Taylor smiled. 'I've been digging around on every single member of Rosen's team. That's why I came looking for you, Robert, because *I* trust *you*. You will trust me because I'll earn that trust. This is too big, too fucking serious, life and death, and no time. Mistrust your doubts, not me. Help me, Robert.'

Harrison stared into the blueness of Taylor's eyes, which seemed to draw the moonlight.

'Can I ask you a question, Robert, about the consequences of your not cooperating with me? said Taylor.

'Go on.'

'Suppose this farce of an investigation throws up another mother and baby abduction and you haven't helped me. How are you going to feel for the rest of your life?'

Although Harrison hadn't invested any personal feelings in the case so far, he said nothing.

'Or, put it another way, how shit are you going to look? I'm not asking you because I care one way or the other; I'm asking because you're the right man. But I'm not begging you, right? Don't sabotage your career, Robert. You're either in this with me or you're not.'

'I'm in with you,' said Harrison.

'You've just made a good decision.'

'What do you want me to do?'

'What have you got on Rosen? Anything? You know the drill, no detail too small.'

'I've got something.'

'Yeah?'

'His wife's expecting a kid. From the bits and pieces I've heard, she had a kid but that kid died.'

'A kid?'

'A baby . . .'

'Called?'

'Hannah. It was a cot death, I heard. Turned her into a whack job. She's well enough nowadays to be working as a schoolteacher. She's pregnant again, at *her* age. I get the feeling it's all top secret, this pregnancy.'

'Who knows about it?'

'As far as I know, no one. I haven't even told Baxter. Yet.'

'Well done. Don't tell him. How do you know about this?'

'I intercepted a voicemail message on Rosen's phone. He went out and left it on his desk. He went out on business related to the case and left his fucking mobile behind – sums it up.'

Taylor laughed and Harrison joined in.

'This ties in with a whole load of other shit.'

'I thought it might,' Harrison bluffed.

'What did she say on the phone, Mrs Rosen?'

'She said she'd got an antenatal clinic appointment.'

'Where and when?'

'St Thomas's, ten in the morning tomorrow. Explains why Rosen keeps pissing off every five minutes.'

'Well, I guess their secret is our secret. Ten o'clock, St Thomas's. You got Mrs Rosen's number?'

'Yeah.'

'Give me your mobile number and hers.'

Harrison reeled off the numbers and Taylor filed them on his phone.

'No, Robert,' he anticipated before Harrison spoke. 'You don't need mine yet. You're on the way up. Well done. But you're back on Planet Rosen, right now. You're my eyes and ears. I'll be in touch with instructions but, for now, just keep watching and listening.'

They could hear two sets of footsteps approaching in the darkness beyond the car park.

'I'll be in touch, Robert. As of now, you're working for me, right?'

'Right.'

Taylor turned and walked away. As Harrison watched, it took an effort of will not to trail after him and ask question after question.

Harrison dialled 118 118 as his gaze followed Taylor turning the corner.

'I'd like the general switchboard, Greater Manchester Police. Get the number and put me straight through.'

The moon slipped behind a bank of cloud as the blueness of Taylor's eyes sank into Harrison's memory, while his future flowed before him like a river.

He got the switchboard and asked to be connected to Taylor's line in the PSU. The phone rang and the answering machine kicked in.

'You've reached the voicemail of Chief Superintendent Daniel Taylor.' Harrison recognized his voice. 'I'm out of the office on holiday until the eighth of April. If it's urgent, contact Superintendent—'

Harrison ended the call and made a mental note of the date. It was 24 March. He noted the date because he was filled with an inner certainty that this was the day his life turned around.

42

It was after ten o'clock at night when Rosen finally got home.

On entering the house, he could tell from the whole feel of the place that his wife was already in bed. The downstairs felt empty and he wondered, as he headed quietly upstairs, whether Sarah was already asleep.

The bedroom was in almost complete darkness but he could discern her shape in the bed from stray light on the landing

'Sarah?' He spoke softly, so that if she was awake she would hear him but if she was asleep he wouldn't disturb her. She didn't respond.

Rosen went to the bathroom and took off his jacket, catching his reflection in the mirror and wondering at what point in his life he'd started looking quite so ancient.

He turned on the bath taps and closed the door so the sound would not wake her. When he lifted his head again, he found Sarah standing in the doorway.

'I'm sorry I'm back so late,' he said, reminding himself that, of all the detectives' wives or husbands he knew – the ones who were married to civilians – Sarah was a paragon of patience over the chronic hours kept by her spouse. And yet, tonight, there could be no doubt, from her body language and the look on her face, that she was angry.

'What's wrong?' he asked, and turned off the tap.

'You could have called me back.'

'I could have called you back, Sarah, had you called me in the first place.'

She looked past him and returned to the bedroom.

He followed her there and turned on the light. She sat on the edge of the bed.

'When did you call?' he said.

'This afternoon.'

He took his mobile phone from his pocket and scrolled through calls received and new voicemails.

'Nothing there, Sarah.'

'I left a voicemail message, for God's sake.'

'I've had five voicemails today, but none from you.'

He sat next to her.

'Do you want to see my phone?'

'Oh, don't be ridiculous. If you say you didn't get a call on your phone, I'm not going to turn this into an investigation. I honestly know I called you and left a voicemail message. But I know you wouldn't lie about such a thing.'

There was enough of a chink in her annoyance for him to place a hand over hers.

'I left a message for you at school,' he said.

'I didn't get it.'

'That's hardly surprising. Probably turn up as a slip in your pigeon hole sometime towards the end of next week. And I'm sorry I didn't call here but things have just . . . escalated today. I've worked like a dog, end of story. What did you call me to say?'

'I've got an appointment with the consultant in the morning.'

'I'll be there. What time?'

'Ten o'clock, St Thomas's.'

He smiled, while thinking about how much he had to do tomorrow. He was going to have to be up two hours earlier than he'd hoped.

'Can you make it? Realistically? If you can't, I'll go alone.'

Guilt dug its claws into him and shook him around for fun.

'I'll go into the incident room early, set a few things up, delegate and meet you there at the hospital. Quarter to ten, OK?'

She softened and smiled. 'OK.'

'Which clinic?'

'Antenatal, would you believe. I thought you'd dismissed me, thrown me down the pecking order of important things to do.'

'I don't always get it right, Sarah, in fact, I feel as if I rarely do, but you're my number one priority, always. It's just sometimes . . . It's like I have to hack my way through the jungle just to be with you. A policeman's wife's lot isn't always a happy one.'

'Better than being married to a bloody teacher.' She smiled again.

'You're right there!'

'Don't push your luck.'

'I need a bath.'

'I know you do,' she said, sniffing the air between them.

As he turned off the bath taps, David heard his wife softly snoring from the bedroom and made a strict mental note to himself not to fall asleep in the alluring warmth of the bath. Sinking into its embrace, he closed his eyes and started developing ideas on what to do with the CCTV footage from the British Library: how and when it would be best to release it.

Rosen pictured Dwyer and Flint in the British Library and thought, *Let the mind games begin.*

43

At seven o'clock in the morning, Rosen found a pen drive on his desk and a note from Gold, explaining that Karen Jones had left the stick for him the day before and wanted to see him. The words, 'Had her knickers in a bit of a twist' were underlined twice.

When he called her, Karen Jones was already on her way into work early, to try to catch him first thing. Within an hour, she stood with him in front of the assembled murder investigation team and a troupe of twelve officers drafted in to assist with the trawl through the Capaneusian Bible.

Rosen began with an account of the meeting at Charing Cross Station with Father Sebastian and his subsequent disappearance from St Mark's.

He showed the images from the John Ritblat Gallery of Flint with another suspect, believed to be Paul Dwyer.

Baxter arrived in the room just as a question came from the team.

'The Capaneusian Bible. We've got in on a website, right?'

'I'll pass you over to Karen.'

Karen went on: 'Yes and no. The Capaneusian Bible is an inverted

Bible. We have the whole of the Old Testament but I can't get into the New Testament. The password for the website is protected and I can't as yet crack it. I've called in help from Steve Lewis from Scotland Yard's Police Central e-Crime Unit.'

Across the room, Rosen saw Baxter shake his head. Karen handed over to Rosen again.

'We're going to have to root through the books of the Old Testament while Karen gets on with cracking open the New Testament. The last line of the last book of the Old Testament, the Book of Malachi, states that the New Testament will be made known only to true believers, and that in the New Testament instructions will be given to disciples down the ages and across the world. Is Dwyer getting his orders from the New Testament of Capaneus? Is Flint giving him access to it? What can we pick up from the Old Testament?'

Rosen handed out a set of papers, a memo with instructions. 'Take one and pass these on; you're each responsible for three books of the Old Testament of Alessio Capaneus. Read through, make notes, dig out anything you can, stick any names that crop up on the NCP, run it through HOLMES. If you're stuck, Mike Marsh is here to help Carol Bellwood process entries into HOLMES.'

Apart from the rustling of paper, there was the silent diligence of an examination hall.

'David?' said Feldman. 'We heard back yet on the DNA from the water bottle?'

'Blank, sorry to say. OK,' said Rosen, 'let's crack on.'

44

Sarah's phone was turned off. At twenty past ten, as Rosen hurried from his car to St Thomas's – heart jittering and head pounding with the stress of being late – he tried to call her for the fourth time since he'd left the incident room. He was running woefully behind. When he walked into St Thomas's reception, he was faced with a dilemma: go to the clinic and try to find Sarah, or stay at the reception and intercept her as she made her way out of the huge building.

He opted to stay at the main doors, hoping she wouldn't use one of the other, less obvious routes out of the hospital building.

For a whole half-hour, human life, in all its stages of glory and decay, passed him by. He reached into his pocket again for his phone, knowing that in a hospital setting hers would still be turned off, and that phoning her was as futile as it was desperate. Still, he called her and left a voicemail message.

'I'm in reception at St Thomas's. It's moving on to eleven. I've been here since ten-twentyish, I'm really, really sorry . . .'

The word *sorry* echoed sourly within his skull and, as it faded into silence, he saw her face in the oncoming tide of strangers. She was smiling and looked calm.

He raised a hand, waved, but she didn't see him. He walked towards her and her eyes met his. For a moment, it was as if she didn't recognize him. Her eyes flicked right and back again in the space of a second. But then she smiled. She wasn't angry with him, which made Rosen even angrier with himself.

'Sarah, I'm so, so sorry . . .'

She held up a hand.

'Do you know what? Everything's OK. It's a perfectly healthy pregnancy, that's what the consultant Mr Gilling-Smith said; everything's good and the baby's fine. I saw the main man himself and his senior registrar, Dr Tom Dempsey.'

Relief swept through Rosen and he felt his whole body relax as the news sank in. He had many questions but, for a few moments, he was tongue-tied by happiness.

Finally, he managed, 'Did they do any tests on you?'

'They took samples in Phlebotomy to see if my bloods are OK, but the consultant said all seems well. He agrees with the scan: I'm twelve weeks. I've got to go back to school. Go back to work and I'll see you tonight. And don't beat yourself up about missing the appointment.'

Rosen grabbed Sarah by the hand and held onto it tightly as they walked out of the hospital into the late London morning.

———

FIFTEEN METRES AWAY, a man stood still and silent, watching the middle-aged couple emerge from the hospital entrance. The watcher's blue eyes shone at the moving picture of a handful of moments of marital happiness.

As the Rosens, still hand in hand, merged into the ebbing crowd, the watcher took out his mobile phone and made a call.

The phone rang briefly.

The ringing stopped.

A voice said, 'Yes?'

'That you, DC Harrison?'

'Yes.'

'Daniel Taylor, Greater Manchester Constabulary. You're a reliable source of information, mate. I like that, I like that a lot. Listen, I've got a job for you to do. OK?'

45

When Rosen returned to Isaac Street Police Station, there was the atmosphere of a library in the normally noisy incident room. Detectives sat either alone or in pairs, hunched over printouts from the Capaneusian Bible. Karen Jones waited by Rosen's desk where a thin, pale man was seated, working at a laptop.

'David,' said Jones, 'this is Steve Lewis from Scotland Yard's e-Crime Unit.'

Lewis looked up from the laptop and, without speaking, shook Rosen's hand, then typed in 'www.a.acalpha.org'.

A black screen. A red book emerged from the darkness, looking old and battered. Lewis clicked 'enter' and the screen turned black. Points of light appeared, stars trapped in the night sky, pinpoints swelling into whole words: BOOKS OF THE OLD TESTAMENT.

'Tell me,' said Lewis to Jones. Rosen felt a presence behind him. Bellwood, Corrigan, Feldman and Gold had now gathered around his desk, taking it all in.

'The devil's side of the story. Herod's bedtime reading. Genesis. Exodus. Leviticus. They're all here.'

In one corner of the screen, the word 'Continue'. He clicked it and the image turned to red sand, which blew away to reveal the name of every book of the Old Testament.

'Take Genesis, for instance,' suggested Jones.

'What's the gist?' asked Lewis.

'The Capaneusian Bible takes a Biblical style and infuses it with the heart and soul of a guttersnipe tabloid journalist. The Garden of Eden was a twenty-four-hour drunken orgy, an abomination. Adam and Eve were created in God's image for his carnal gratification. According to Capaneus, wild animals were the physical incarnations of angels, put on earth to dominate and oppress humankind. Satan, the serpent, felt great compassion for Adam and Eve. When Eve confessed to Adam that she loved him and not God, God flew into a black rage and passed a death sentence on Adam to be fulfilled by the lions. God, you see, loved sport. Adam went into hiding. When Satan found Eve crying in the Garden of Eden, he gathered together the friendly animals – the other serpents, the jackals, the hyenas – and, under Satan's guidance, they helped Adam and Eve escape from the wrath of God. The wrath of God was turned on Satan and the other animals who'd been kind to the human beings.'

'How does that make Herod go out and kill women and their babies?' asked Lewis.

'Directly, it doesn't. That's where you come in.'

She pointed to the screen of Lewis's laptop, at the word 'More'.

He clicked 'More'. Black screen. From the centre, a blossoming red light from which appeared the words: 'To read the New Testament, type in your password,' alongside a box.

'And the password needs cracking?' asked Lewis, looking at Rosen.

'We believe this is where Herod's been getting his ideas. Can you help?'

Lewis reached into his pocket and took out a pen drive. 'Come back in, say, half an hour.'

———

LATER, ROSEN RETURNED to his desk, where Lewis and Jones were in tight discussion.

'How's it going?' asked Rosen.

'I suspect this site's got some serious encryption software,' said Lewis. 'It kind of reminds me of the NSA mainframe.'

'What's that?'

'It's the IT used by the US government's intelligence gathering services. It's not using biometric screening, fingerprint or retinal access, but whoever's put this together is a serious maths head. It's running its security off a mutating algorithmic program. NSA security programs change on a daily basis. This is changing every few minutes. Devilishly clever.'

'Is there anything you can do?' asked Rosen.

'Yes.' Lewis pulled up a briefcase and took out a black pen drive. 'Something I've been working on for another department. It's not quite finished but it's operational. We'll run it from my laptop. It'll watch your Capaneus website and as soon as a user logs on with a password, it'll relay that right back to my laptop. The moment that happens, it'll send me an alert and I'll be straight on to you. Then we'll be able to get into the New Testament.'

Rosen thought about the website and the individuals who would have access to the New Testament of the Capaneusian Bible. There was one in particular.

'In that case, we'll know exactly when Dwyer's online.'

46

Herod.

It was all drifting away from him. Beginning with time, the length of hours and the value of calendar days, the quality of night and the shifting colour of daylight.

A pulse of doubt beat within the heart of certainty.

Fifteen hours lying on the floor at one stretch, with the clearest conviction that he had merely stumbled and paused to catch his breath but would rise again in a matter of seconds, pushed on by the awful thought: Alessio Capaneus had all been a dream.

The thought caused an acute pain in his chest and he imagined his heart breaking, literally snapping like a dried-out husk.

He pulled himself up from the floor.

'I believe in Capaneus, the One True Prophet of the Lord Satan . . . I believe . . .'

Leaving up the hatch to the basement – his fear of confined spaces had returned – he walked backwards down wooden steps into the subterranean space where the hoist remained ready by the table in the dim artificial light, central to the trio of windowless rooms.

The mobile air-conditioning unit hummed, a reassuring sound that seemed to murmur to him, 'It's real.'

He opened the half-door on the wall facing the staircase. Beyond, it stank of earth, the wetness of a world fit only for worms and crawling creatures. The farmer had made a good job of compacting the walls of the tunnel with sand and cement to produce a hard-finished surface that made it possible to scramble to the manhole on the surface of the farmyard without pulling away handfuls of soil and dead roots. But on the three occasions he'd made the journey from basement to farmyard through the tunnel, he'd hated acting like a sightless bug.

He closed the half-door on the tunnel and wandered into the meditation suite where the sensory deprivation chamber remained sadly idle, minus Julia, a coffin for the living without its mentally unravelling carrier. It was strange how the hollowness inside him shrank when the carriers were present, strange how it swelled again when they were gone.

He needed the comfort, the total affirmation that his efforts had not been in vain, that he had laboured well in the service of Satan under the guidance of Alessio Capaneus.

So he walked into the room where the souls were trapped.

He took his first lingering look at Julia's foetus, Baby Caton. In spite of the waters breaking, he'd been the easiest to deliver. Herod felt a rush of pride in his growing surgical skills that blew out the fire of doubt that had burned him as he lay upstairs with his face to the floor. His doubts in Capaneus now seemed as ridiculous as the fear of his mother's footsteps in his nightly dreams.

On a wide shelf on the wall, six cylindrical jars were set out in a line, filled to the brim with formaldehyde. In five of the six jars, there were foetuses.

What was real was before his eyes. The five souls awaiting sacrifice, and the one empty space awaiting the sixth soul.

He pursed his lips at Baby Caton and wondered, what song was in his soul?

And, he wondered, what songs would burst forth from these souls when they were sacrificed?

He moved to the sixth and final jar, stared into the formaldehyde awaiting the sixth foetus, the sixth soul, and, in the dim light, saw his own face reflected in the curve of the glass, his features blurred, his doubts dispersed.

47

osen stared at the faceless model construction that John Mason had created based on the ear print and the single hair found in the loft of Julia Caton's house. He pored over the range of images of the man who he assumed was Paul Dwyer, captured at the British Library, pictures of him alone as well as with Father Sebastian.

Rosen needed to think very carefully about which images to release, and in what order. Getting the choice right was a matter of life and death.

He looked at the one of Dwyer, enraptured as he left the toilets, then at the image of Dwyer, dead-eyed and alone on his way into the British Library.

Rosen glanced at the clock on the incident room wall: a quarter past ten. Rosen felt gluey with tiredness; it really was time for home. But he stayed where he was, gazing at the images, racked by choice.

One by one, he separated all those of Flint and moved them to the edges of his desk so that they were out of his eyeline, leaving only those of Dwyer on his own: in front of the faceless, eyeless, mouthless, soulless model created by Mason.

And, as time moved on towards eleven o'clock, Rosen came to a decision about the release of the CCTV images.

The strategy would be simple.

He would isolate Dwyer. He would use the imagery to make Dwyer feel alone.

'Sir!'

Rosen was stirred from the depths of his thoughts by the unwelcome sound of Harrison's voice. He looked up slowly.

'You're working late, Robert.'

'You gave me something I could really get my teeth into. The Church of the Living Light.'

Rosen noticed that Harrison had a file of papers in his hand, as thick as a telephone directory.

'Sit down, Robert.'

Harrison placed his papers on Rosen's desk and wheeled over a chair.

'The Church of the Living Light, then, Robert?'

Harrison sat down, his gaze meeting Rosen's directly.

'Lots of stuff on the internet to begin with. In a nutshell, it was a cult dressed up as an evangelical Christian Church. The head guy was a Pastor James "Jim" Walsh. To begin with, all seemed right as rain: lots of good works in the East End of London, a growing congregation, soup for the hungry, solace for the lonely, nothing to alarm anyone. Pastor Jim, however, didn't have a single qualification to run a church; he was a self-made minister who'd actually ordained himself on the sex offenders' wing at Durham. I managed to track down a woman called Jane Rice, who coordinates Unlock, a charity for survivors of cults. She's elderly now, but she's still all there.' He tapped the side of his head with a patronizing calm. Rosen thought, *You'll be old yourself one day*.

Harrison reached into his file and pulled out the top ten sheets.

'This is a transcript of the whole interview I conducted with her this afternoon.'

'How'd you get it typed so quickly, Robert?'

'I did it myself, sir.' Harrison handed the pages to Rosen. 'I've highlighted all the key information.'

'Thanks. How did you get on with Jane Rice?'

'She's not in touch with Dwyer now. But she knew what was going on with him until round about the mid-eighties. His mother was being counselled through Unlock. She was on a combination of all kinds of prescription medication because of the hammering she'd given her body when she was a junkie. She died suddenly; the coroner's verdict was misadventure, as she'd taken too many pills within the space of twenty-four hours. I'll follow that one up first thing tomorrow. Anyway, Paul Dwyer was drummed off a medical degree course at around the same time as Mummy died. He'd done two years training as a doctor at UCL Medical School, but this is where the trail goes stone-cold. After his mother died, Paul goes out of Jane's sights but she did make one interesting observation. His mother was loaded; she'd inherited a small fortune. Paul in turn, no doubt, inherited all that cash. Do you want me to follow up his career as a medical student, or are you going to pass that one over to Bellwood or Corrigan?'

'You've done excellent work here, Robert. Why should I take it away from you after you've done so much?'

'You don't trust me, sir.'

'Haven't we been here before, Robert?' Rosen pointed at Baxter's door. 'He's trying to find failure in me and you're feeding him; that's why I don't trust you.'

'I didn't set out to become a snitch when I joined the Met.'

'So what changed?'

'Baxter. He made it very clear to me that if I didn't act as his "eyes and ears", he'd make sure my career didn't progress. If I acted as his spy in the camp, he wouldn't get in my way. I just want you to know, it's not personal. None of it's been personal.'

It sounded like vintage Baxter, exploiting the vulnerability of those weaker than himself to further his own political ends.

'Why didn't you come and tell me this at the time it happened?'

'With respect, what could you have done about it? Baxter's in the process of giving you a public spanking. But I'd like to be a part of this team, I'd like to feel like I belong here.'

'Leave it with me, Robert.'

Harrison stood up and extended his hand. 'No hard feelings,' he said.

Rosen shook Harrison's hand and released it as quickly as possible.

'One other thing,' said Harrison. 'I earwigged some of the guys talking about a missing page in a book of poetry in Father Sebastian's bedroom. William Blake's *Songs of Innocence and Experience*. I spoke to Eleanor Willis and got the details from her of the edition, publisher – Everyman Classics – year of publication 1973; missing pages twenty-three and twenty-four. I tracked it down on Abebooks and spoke to a book dealer. The two missing poems were "The Tyger" and "The Sick Rose". I printed off a copy of "The Sick Rose" from the internet.'

Harrison placed a copy of the poem face down on Rosen's desk.

'I'll see you in the morning, sir. No hard feelings.'

'Good work, well done.'

Harrison smiled and walked out of the incident room. When he had gone, Rosen turned the page over and read quietly to himself.

The Sick Rose

> *O Rose! thou art sick!*
> *The invisible worm,*
> *That flies in the night,*
> *In the howling storm,*
> *Has found out thy bed*
> *Of crimson joy;*
> *And his dark secret love*
> *Does thy life destroy.*

In the silence of the incident room, Rosen imagined the sound of Father Sebastian laughing quietly yet insistently into his face. He pictured Flint in the darkest corner of a windowless room, laughing into its pitch-black emptiness, dreaming up his next mind-bending trick, fuelled with the pleasure of his last escapade in causing human misery.

He pushed the poem as far away as possible and tried to contain the unease that made his spine tingle in a cold eruption of goose bumps.

He rubbed his eyes, grateful for the fact that he had an alternative document to look at. He started to read the transcript of Harrison's interview with Jane Rice. It was single spaced and highlighted neatly with orange marker pen. He flicked forwards to the account of Paul Dwyer's failed medical career. Rosen's pulse quickened: Paul Dwyer had medical know-how. It was enough, more than enough.

48

There was no good time to experience morning sickness and the first lesson with 10M on a cold, wet spring morning was proof of this. The class's collective heads were bent over multiple copies of the GCSE RE textbook *Faith and Action*. Sarah took out the DVD that went with the textbook, her stomach lurching violently. She gripped the edges of the table and fought down the urge to throw up, but it was a losing battle.

She flung open the door of the classroom.

'Mrs Rosen?' a pupil called after her.

She hurried to the pupils' toilet at the end of the corridor, clenching her teeth and holding her breath in an effort to keep control. She made it to the nearest cubicle before being violently ill.

Sarah rinsed out her mouth with water and splashed her face, which was drawn and red with exertion. In a mirror that normally reflected girls on the cusp of womanhood, she saw a woman in middle life, but smiled and said to her reflection, 'So, you're not too old to have a baby after all.' And she didn't care if 10M were walking on the ceiling. She stroked her belly and laughed out loud.

Her head throbbed. Still not knowing if she was going to be sick again, she stared into the mirror and smiled again.

The memory of Hannah drifted to the front of her mind, a memory she both cherished and had to fight off every day. Hannah, six weeks old, feeding from her breast at four o'clock in the morning, moonlight spilling into the otherwise dark bedroom, the moon caught like two points of light in her baby's eyes. It had been a difficult pregnancy and birth, but Hannah had been such a good baby and had grown into a bright and loving toddler. And then she had died. Two fragments of moonlight, gone.

Sarah imagined the density of her womb filling with life above her pubic bone. She stroked her belly with the flat of her hand, as if reading the landscape of a life waiting to be lived.

Then she heard them. It was the distant hum of a dreadful din. Even in a private moment, the mass will of 10M prevailed.

She hurried back down the corridor where a sixth-form prefect stood at the open doorway of the classroom she'd abandoned, attempting to steady the growing anarchy inside the room.

Teachers from nearby classrooms appeared at their doors.

'It's OK, it's OK,' Sarah pronounced, sweeping past and taking up her place again.

She stared in a manufactured cold rage at the ringleaders, a skill she'd picked up from a pitbull sergeant major she'd served under in her TA days, and which she had mastered over many years in school. She then picked off the sheep with glances, some of sorrow and some of anger. Silence descended. Then, in barely more than a whisper, she said, 'Could you close the door please, Jenny?'

The entire class was looking at her, something she was used to, but today it suddenly felt so strange.

And she had to think: what were they studying?

'Close your books,' she said.

'Mrs Rosen, can we watch the DVD?'

'Yes . . . Jenny, overhead projector, please.' She placed the DVD into the laptop and heard the whirr of the overhead projector as the SmartBoard came to life. 'Where is God,' Sarah asked 10M, 'in the face of evil?'

Ten long minutes later, the bell rang for the end of the lesson and the start of morning break. As the first of the students headed out, Sarah turned on her phone to call Rosen.

'You have one voicemail message; message one sent today at nine-forty-five.'

The mechanical voice gave way to a human one.

'Hi, I'm leaving a message for Mrs Sarah Rosen. This is Dr Brian Reid calling from the Haematology department at St Thomas's. Your notes have been passed on to me by Dr Tom Dempsey from Gynaecology, who I believe you saw yesterday. I was wondering if you could give me a ring, please. There's a complication on your blood sample. Erm . . . yes, if you call me back on my mobile, that might be easier than going through the switchboard.' He reeled off the number and closed with, 'Please call me as soon as you can.'

She tapped in the numbers, feeling a rising unease that bordered on panic. A voice said, 'Yes?'

'Is that Dr Reid?'

'Yes, yes, it is.'

'It's Sarah Rosen.'

'Oh, thanks for getting back to me so quickly, Mrs Rosen, that's really helpful of you.'

'Is there a problem?'

'Ah, well, that's why I'm calling.'

'Could you tell me what's the matter?'

'It's the blood test you provided at your antenatal appointment.' He fell silent.

'What's the problem?'

'It could be a number of things. There's nothing wrong with you as such, but we are a little concerned about your baby, particularly given the . . . your maturity.'

'Dr Reid, why don't you stop talking in generalizations and start spelling out the specific problem?'

'Mrs Rosen, calm down. It could be something and may be nothing, but we have to be sure. That's why you've been passed over to Haematology. The Haematology and Thrombosis Centre is situated on the first floor, North Wing of St Thomas's Hospital. Could you be there at nine-forty tomorrow morning? Could you do that?'

'Why not sooner?'

'Because this isn't a total emergency. You're not in danger of losing the baby immediately. Look, it's a precaution, it's Dr Dempsey being "fussy" if you like. We haven't got time to send out an appointment card, so if you just wait at the main door of the clinic, I'll send someone to pick you up, save you having to deal with the clinic clerks. I owe him a couple of big favours, that's why I'm pushing you through.'

'Well, thanks for that, Dr Reid.'

'That's OK. Nine-forty, tomorrow morning, Haematology main entrance, first floor, North Wing, just by the lifts.'

'Couldn't it be sooner?' Sarah asked hopefully.

'I'm already bending the system to hurry you through, Mrs Rosen.'

'I'm sorry. I've got that.' And she told herself not to worry.

She ended the call. It wasn't an emergency. But if it wasn't anything wrong with her, it must be the baby, and that wasn't what she wanted to hear.

Not in danger of losing the baby *immediately*? To conceive and then miscarry the child was worse than not conceiving. As the bell rang for the beginning of lessons again, she was haunted by savage disappointment, the old wound of loss made new once more. It simply didn't bear thinking about but, as she gathered her things into her bag, she knew that she would be able to think of nothing else as she went through the motions of teaching Year Seven about Moses in the bulrushes.

She walked down the corridor with one thought for company. *It's my fault if my baby dies, because I'm too old to have him.*

49

At Isaac Street Police Station, it was a full house for the five o'clock team meeting. Rosen's glance swept the room.

'Two pieces to report to you. First off, congratulations to Robert Harrison. He's tracked down Paul Dwyer's last known point of contact, which goes back to the mid-eighties. Dwyer was a medical student who didn't complete the course, but it gives him medical know-how and that, boys and girls, ties in very nicely with what we know about Herod's methodology.'

A ripple of approval ran around the room, with all eyes turned to Harrison, who stared directly at Rosen.

'Second, I'm calling a press conference tomorrow morning, that's Friday, nine o'clock. We've got two pictures of the two suspects. On Friday morning, I'm going to issue notice on one prime suspect.'

'Boss, was that suspect or suspects?' asked Harrison.

'Singular, Robert. We're issuing limited CCTV footage from the British Library.'

'Dwyer or the priest?'

'Dwyer. Let's look at the pictures of Dwyer from the British

Library. These are the ones we'll release.'

It was an absolutely clear image of Dwyer's face as he entered the British Library, his expression unemotional. His identity was impossible to deny if you knew him by sight.

'And this one.'

A shot of Dwyer from the John Ritblat Gallery, at a moment when he had stared directly into the eye of the CCTV camera.

'There's no point in shining the spotlight on Flint. Yet. We'll never get to Dwyer through Flint. We need Dwyer behind bars fast. It's my theory that Flint's been controlling him remotely, through this Capaneus website. If we publish Dwyer plus Flint, that puts Dwyer in a pair, a gang if you like, and that would give him a sense of belonging that would buoy him up. We don't want that. If he's wanted on his own, then he's just that. Alone. Picked on. I want Dwyer to feel more alienated than he does at present, more alienated than he's ever felt. For now, I want him to think there are no other suspects. Let's assume Dwyer trusts Flint implicitly. I want to drive a wedge between them. If we issue footage from the British Library where they were both present and there's no sign of us wanting Flint, then it'll hit all his inferiority and victim buttons in one go.

'Here's the upside. When we warn the public about Dwyer, we're showing Dwyer that we know who he is. Once his image is out there, experience tells us, forty-eight hours after the press conference the pressure will start to bite and he'll make a mistake.' He paused. 'Here's the downside of the ticking clock. According to Flint, he's got one more mother to abduct and he'll have to do it quickly. So, say farewell to your loved ones for the time being, because we're all on board 24/7. Any questions?'

'Are you going to show us what Flint looks like?'

'When are we publishing the priest's picture?'

'Monday morning, nine o'clock, second press conference. The images we have of Flint, from the Charing Cross CCTV at rush hour.

On the subject of pictures of Father Sebastian, I received these three from Cardinal McPhee within the last two hours. I intend to issue the third, most recent, image on Monday morning.'

Cardinal McPhee had sent the three pictures on a pen drive.

'OK, this is Father Sebastian.'

A professionally posed picture of the priest at his ordination appeared on the SmartBoard.

'This one looks most like him now, though he's older-looking.'

Rosen then clicked through to another photo – this one less recent, and taken at an odd angle.

It looked like a corpse at the side of a broken road, the hot sun beating down, flies congregating around the bloodied head. But the eyes were open.

'What happened to him?'

'This was taken by one of the tourists on the bus that came across him after the beating in Kenya. Look at the next picture. We're releasing a cropped image of his face.'

Sebastian, cleaned up and wide awake, on a white sheet in a hospital bed, wearing white shorts, his body marked by healing wounds.

There was complete understanding in the silence that greeted the image, but for one small sound. Next to Bellwood, Harrison made a noise in his throat as if something was stuck there, choking him.

Rosen showed the cropped image of Flint looking directly at the camera. Bellwood took a sideways glance at Harrison who stared at the screen, looked away and then back at the screen again.

'How'd he survive?' someone asked.

'I don't know,' said Rosen. 'In the meantime, I've already issued an all-ports on Flint and alerted Europol. If Flint makes it out of Britain, it's the least we can do to warn our neighbours. They're distributing the information and pictures of Flint direct from The Hague. We've spread his face across the constabularies at home, particularly Greater Manchester. That is where he comes from. And Cambridgeshire, where he studied.'

'Back to Dwyer now. Someone somewhere must know Dwyer. We're urging all pregnant women in the London area, if it's possible, not to be alone. Particularly after his picture's published. Any more questions?'

There were none.

'The usual health warning, folks, but with absolute rigour. None of this goes out of the room.'

Rosen eyeballed each and every officer there, pausing only at Harrison, who had turned pale, as if he was about to throw up on the spot.

––––––

BELLWOOD STAYED WHERE she was as people drifted away but kept her eyes pinned on Harrison.

He sat at his shared desk, staring into space, allowing the phone to ring and eventually fall silent. Slowly, she moved into the space behind him, out of his eyeline, and walked up to his seat.

'Good work, Robert, tracking Dwyer back to the eighties, making that medical link!' He didn't move from his seat, nor turn his head. Instead, he just tensed up, as if someone had given him a huge fright rather than an evenly worded compliment. 'Are you OK, Robert?' she asked.

He turned, offering her the most forced of smiles.

'Yeah,' he replied.

'You don't look well.'

'I'm fine.'

He got up from his desk and walked out of the incident room as if it were on fire but didn't want to appear too distressed about it.

On the other side of the incident room the phone on Rosen's desk rang. Rosen picked up and Steve Lewis from PeCU introduced himself.

'What's happening, Steve?'

'The software's thrown up a password, but the Capaneus site's been shredded. There's nothing behind the door of the New Testament –

the entire site's been erased. Someone must have guessed we were on to them. The good news is I've got a location for where the site's been run from.'

'Canterbury,' said Rosen. 'Just east of.'

'How did you know?' Lewis sounded amazed, as if his unique gem of wisdom had been suddenly devalued to that of a message inside a fortune cookie.

'Lucky guess. Thanks for trying, Steve. I appreciate all your efforts.'

Lewis hung up. As Bellwood approached, Rosen relayed the news to her.

'What's your take on it?' asked Bellwood.

'Dwyer's either had his instructions on the sixth victim, or Flint's using a different means of communicating. Either way, Dwyer could be abducting a woman right now.'

50

Asleep on and off all afternoon, he lay on his single bed in the monastic cell of his bedroom and dreamed of the woman he'd been forced to address as 'Mother'.

Mother wore gloves, long white gloves up to the elbows to cover the track marks that the other saved souls of the Church of the Living Light had noticed from their pews and complained about to Pastor Jim, who'd ordered her to cover her arms during worship. But Herod could see the fragile network of veins beneath, criss-crossing her inner forearms like a map of the London underground, a permanent record of her former sins that the long white gloves could mask but could never eradicate.

She wore them to worship, then she wore them all the time, but when Herod closed his eyes at night, all he could see were her needle-hacked veins and arms.

In his dream, she was singing at the top of her voice but all that came out was a ringing sound followed by silence, a sequence that simply repeated. He opened his eyes and snatched up his mobile phone. He pressed the button to connect the anonymous call — always, always it registered on the display as anonymous – and, as soon as he did so, the caller rang off at the other end.

The house lay mute. And then, from downstairs, something most unusual happened. For a few moments, he had to question what it was and whether it was really happening.

He headed for the stairs. The landline was ringing.

51

Rosen arrived home just before midnight, with the intention of catching a few hours' sleep. But it was to be a sleepless night. Softly, he called, 'Sarah?' as he came through the front door, but could hear nothing. The downstairs felt empty of her presence.

He went straight up the stairs, his back aching and an irrational fear drumming its fingers on the inside of his head. In the bedroom, she was asleep with the bedside light on. She opened her eyes and smiled at him.

'You're late home, David.' Her voice was heavy with fatigue.

He threaded his jacket onto a hanger and thought, *I will never take this woman for granted as long as I live*.

'It was a dream of mine . . .' she said.

He kissed her and she closed her eyes, as if sleep were stealing her away. He was tempted to prompt her to complete the half-thought she'd articulated but, over the years, he'd learned the importance of holding his tongue, the ability to make room when his head buzzed with questions.

He sat on the edge of the bed and kicked off his shoes, a tired husband. Slowly, she opened her eyes again and turned her weary gaze on him.

'I wanted to know the inside of the antenatal like the back of my hand. Each tile on the floor, each light in the—'

Ceiling. He unknotted his tie and waited.

'I wanted to go to the clinic and be examined, to find out how our baby was growing, and I know, David, I know you did too. But now I don't want to go to St Thomas's at all. I wasn't going to say anything. But I'm scared of what I'm going to find out.'

She spoke slowly; by this time he was almost naked.

'I know how serious things are for you at the moment, how it's all seeming to come to a head, and I promised myself I'd say nothing but I can't not tell you. I had a phone call from the hospital. I've got to go there. It's come out through the blood tests. There's a problem with the baby.'

Sudden fear and disappointment overwhelmed him in a moment. In the next, he turned to Sarah, his face a calm mask.

'When's the appointment?'

'In the morning. Nine-forty.'

'Who called you, Sarah?' He laid his hand over the back of hers, pressing down the anxiety that her words had sparked.

'It was a doctor . . . Dr Brian Reid.'

'It wasn't a call from the medical secretary or clinical appointments?'

'No, it was a doctor . . . Dr Reid, Dr Brian Reid.'

'Is he in the Gynaecology department?' asked Rosen.

'He's not Gynaecology, he's in the Haematology department, Dr Dempsey passed me over to him. They're doing me a favour.'

'Nine-forty in the morning?'

'Dr Reid's sending someone to collect me at the main door, Haematology, first floor, North Wing.'

'Then I'll come with you,' said Rosen. She closed her eyes and the neutral mask slipped from his face.

'I can go alone. I just needed you to know.'

'I'm going with you, Sarah. I can delegate for a few hours. Dr Reid didn't say anything else, did he?'

'They're hurrying me through the system. There's no risk to the baby . . . immediately.'

She turned onto her side and Rosen stroked her shoulders. A minute later, her breathing altered and she was asleep.

He threw his shirt, socks and underwear into the wash basket in the corner of the bathroom. He turned on the shower and thrust his head into the powerful jet of hot water, snarling, 'Christ!' Water battered his features and, for those few moments, he was in tune with the impotent rage that had stalked him down the years. But, for once in his life, it had a human face.

Sebastian Flint's face glimpsed in the tiny mirror of room 11 at St Mark's Monastery.

He kept the water on full power, beating around his head until his breathing and heartbeat subsided to normal. He towelled himself dry and, on catching his reflection in the mirror, paused, recognizing his look of suspicion.

In clean pyjamas, he settled beside Sarah and sought out her hand beneath the duvet. He linked his fingers around hers and she turned her head slightly on the pillow.

She was fast asleep, peaceful now. Rosen was grateful for this mercy.

52

Conference Room One was the largest single space in Isaac Street Police Station, and it was the venue for Rosen's press conference. The long rectangular room was packed with journalists and photographers, seated on rows of blue plastic seats. There was a buzz in the air, a rising expectation, a clamour of voices, the word 'Herod' circulating like electricity.

At the top end of the harshly lit, windowless room, a dais had been set up, with a miked-up table, and chairs, and a PA system. Behind them was a pinboard, Metropolitan blue, with the logo – two lions, a shield and a crown – and the words: *Working Together for a Safer London*.

Rosen stood in the shadows, breathing deeply to master his nerves, and listened to the sheer noise of the waiting journalists. For once it wasn't the prospect of public performance and potential humiliation that unnerved him; it was the trip to hospital with Sarah that followed it.

He'd called Mr Gilling-Smith's secretary three times from eight-fifteen but each time he'd connected to an answering machine. On the third call, he'd left his mobile number and an urgent request to call him back.

There were no empty places. On each seat, a journalist, and in their hand, a press release, a single piece of paper bearing two pictures of Dwyer: a CCTV shot and Corrigan's photo, both from the British Library

To the left of the dais, a forty-two-inch plasma screen was set up to play a brief sequence of CCTV footage. At the door on the way out, to avoid a scrum and a sprint to issue the pictures, each news organization had to sign for their own electronic footage. There was a legally and morally binding clause: no transmission of footage before 6 p.m.

Baxter, in full uniform, led the way in, and a buzz rippled through the noise. Rosen followed and sat at the centre of the table, with Bellwood on his right. Next to Rosen sat Rob Waters, press officer.

'Good morning,' said Waters. The room settled into silence.

In his jacket pocket, Rosen's phone vibrated silently, and he intuitively knew it was Mr Gilling-Smith's secretary returning his call. He focussed on the press in front of him. His phone buzzed and buzzed in his pocket.

'Why can we not broadcast the images until six?'

'Questions at the end,' replied Baxter.

'I'll take that one, Chief Superintendent Baxter.' Rosen scanned the room, imposing a measured silence on proceedings. 'But, like Chief Superintendent Baxter said, questions at the end.' He located the source of the opportunistic question; he knew and liked the journalist who'd tried it on. 'We need a favour, assistance with a strategy. We need you to build up the broadcast. Let people know there's going to be a significant release of still and moving images. We need people, as many as possible, to be sitting in front of their TV sets, actively waiting and engaging with these images. Six o'clock news broadcasts are our optimum slot. We want homecoming commuters to see this. We don't want it coming out in dribs and drabs. We want to create a media event and we need your cooperation.'

Rosen held a script, and now he turned his attention to it.

He read, 'Good morning, ladies and gentlemen. For those of you who don't know me, I am Detective Chief Inspector David Rosen.'

The vibration of his phone stopped.

'We have invited you here this morning to ask for your help and that of the public in identifying a suspect in the current murder investigation in which there are, to date, five adult female victims. We are seeking to interview the man pictured in the photographs we have issued to you, and the following CCTV footage from the British Library. We believe this man has, in childhood, gone by the name of Paul Dwyer, though he may well be living under a completely different name now. He is in his mid- to late forties, perhaps even early fifties.

'We are seeking to question this man in connection with the abduction and murder of Jenny Maguire, the abduction and murder of Alison Todd, the abduction and murder of Jane Wise, the abduction and murder of Sylvia Green and the abduction and murder of Julia Caton.

'We are using all resources available to us to locate him, including HOLMES – Home Office Large and Major Enquiry System – the National Police Computer and a team of over thirty law enforcement specialists including detectives, uniformed officers, scene-of-crime officers, forensic scientists and specialist IT civilians.'

Rosen drew breath and paused, trying to picture Dwyer's face as he choked on his bravado while watching the six o'clock news.

'We would like to thank the dozens of members of the Greater London community who have already been quick to come forward to assist with this investigation. We'd also like to thank Londoners for their tolerance and patience as we have made our extensive enquiries.

'We are clearly dealing with a dangerous individual so must advise the public accordingly. If any member of the public sees this man, they are not, repeat not, to approach him directly. They should instead inform the police via the number printed at the bottom of the press release' – he gave the number – 'or through the emergency services 999 route.

'If you know this man, or are harbouring him, we urge you to come forward now and assist us in our ongoing investigation. If you have any suspicions about anyone, maybe a friend or a member of your family who has been acting out of character or who has appeared increasingly anxious, please contact us in complete confidence.

'If you want to remain anonymous, you can call Crimestoppers.' He gave the number.

He looked up from his script and said, 'OK, let's watch the images.'

The silence, as the carefully doctored CCTV footage was shown of Herod entering the British Library, was profound. The images of Dwyer suddenly froze on screen with a final, still photograph.

'Any questions?' asked Rob Waters.

'Are you still dismissing an occult motive?'

'We're pursuing several lines of investigation.'

'Is he operating on his own?'

'It's part of our ongoing enquiry.'

There was a barrage of other questions hurled at the panel but Waters put up his hand to silence the crowd. He thanked the assembled journalists for attending and reminded them that they had to sign for their footage on the way out.

Coming off the dais, Baxter touched Rosen on the arm as he headed towards the door at the back of the room.

'Hurrying away again, *David*?'

'What do you want, Tom?'

'I hope this idea of yours, you know, not broadcasting the images until six o'clock, doesn't backfire on you.'

'Maximum focus of public attention. It gets results.'

'It would be a tragedy, wouldn't it, if another woman was snatched? Before six o'clock? Don't think I could do much to help you in that event. Think about it.'

'He doesn't operate in daylight!'

'Fingers crossed he doesn't switch MO at the eleventh hour.'

Rosen held Baxter's gaze, fixed on the speck of light reflected in his iris, and felt the coldness of the other man's malicious glee.

'Because, if a woman does get snatched today, well, David, it's only fair to say you would bear some personal responsibility for that.'

Baxter crossed his fingers and moved away, holding Rosen's eye as he did so.

53

'**M**r Gilling-Smith's secretary. Can I help you?'

Rosen's phone was on hands-free and he was stuck at a red light on his journey from the press conference to St Thomas's. So far, the lights had been with him, but close to his journey's end, this red felt like a body blow.

'My name's David Rosen; my wife Sarah's currently under the care of Mr Gilling-Smith.'

'Oh, yes, I typed a letter about her from the last clinic.' She sounded sharp, on the ball. *Good*, thought Rosen, *good, good*. 'How can I help you, Mr Rosen?'

'My wife's got an appointment at Haematology at nine-forty. She received a phone call from a Dr Brian Reid setting up the appointment directly.' The light changed to green and Rosen surged into the passage of traffic.

'There wasn't anything in the notes I typed about a problem with her bloods . . .'

'Really?' said Rosen.

'But the blood tests weren't back when I typed them up. The

notes were all based on clinical observations.'

'Whose clinical observations?'

'Dr Dempsey, Dr Tom Dempsey. He's Mr Gilling-Smith's senior registrar: he's good, very thorough. Is there a problem I can help you with, Mr Rosen?'

'Is it possible for Dr Dempsey to have referred my wife on to Dr Reid in Haematology?'

'Absolutely.'

'But you don't know anything about that referral?'

'It happens all the time here. Tom Dempsey's one of the most conscientious doctors I've worked with and I've been in the NHS for years. Dempsey and Reid are on good terms. What will have happened is Dr Dempsey dictated the notes while he was in clinic. The dictaphone comes up to me with the medical notes, at noon. That's standard. He's sent your wife to Phlebotomy to get her bloods tested after he's seen her in clinic. The bloods have gone to the lab mid to late afternoon. Tom being Tom, he's gone to the lab directly to get some early feedback, he's picked up a problem with your wife's bloods, called Brian Reid and asked for help. Hence I'm out of the loop. But it happens all the time.' She laughed briefly and with good humour. 'And then people come on the phone and say, *You didn't know about this?* And I say, *No, I'm not psychic.*'

'And the secretary in Haematology, would she not know?'

'Not necessarily. If this is something Tom and Brian have set up between themselves on the hoof, no. Like I say, it does happen. Cut out the admin to hurry things through. I'll phone Haematology, see if they know anything, and get back to you if you like.'

It was getting on for half past nine.

'It's OK,' said Rosen, pulling into a pay and display parking space. 'The appointment's minutes away and I'm just round the corner.'

'If there's anything else I can do to help, just give me a ring.'

'Thank you, you've been more than helpful.'

'No problem.'

Moments later, Rosen pumped coin after coin into a pay and display meter. He locked the car and moved as quickly as he could, weaving past people as he hurried, glancing at his watch with mounting anxiety.

———

AT THE ENTRANCE of the North Wing of St Thomas's Hospital, Sarah looked utterly anxious when Rosen arrived, red-faced and perspiring.

'I'm sorry,' he said. They hurried towards the passenger lifts inside the building.

'It's just gone twenty to, and Dr Reid's doing us a favour here.'

A handful of people emerged from the lift. Rosen followed Sarah inside and the doors closed. He pressed the button for the first floor, his heart still pounding from the journey from car to hospital.

'I'm sorry,' he repeated, feeling oppressed by the enclosed space. Sarah rechecked her watch and sighed as the lift ascended and slowed.

A computerized voice announced, 'First floor, Haematology.' The doors slid open and they stepped out.

Across the corridor from the passenger lift were broader metal doors, the service lifts. A pair of them eased open and a patient on a scissor bed was wheeled out, chatting to the smiling porter who pushed her round the corner and out of sight.

The door of the clinic was visible from the lift area.

'You'll be fine, Sarah.'

'Are you a doctor, David? How do you know I'll be fine?'

He could feel a dry heat, the embers of a stupid row that could be fanned by tension into a stand-off, so he said, 'Yeah, you're right, I'm not a doctor.'

'Turn your phone off,' said Sarah.

'I can't,' he replied. A heavily pregnant woman emerged from the clinic, a woman who at a glance looked like Julia Caton. 'Tell me again what Dr Reid said on the phone.'

'To wait by the main door of Haematology, and he said he'd send someone to collect me.'

'Hurrying you through the system,' said Rosen.

'Look!' snapped Sarah. 'I'm just doing what I was told to do. I feel bad enough about this problem with my blood, so I'm just doing what I'm told to do. That's what you do with doctors, you follow their instructions. They're doing me a favour, fast-tracking me.'

A junior doctor, a superannuated sixth former who looked closer to boyhood than maturity, passed.

'Excuse me,' said David, 'is Dr Reid around?'

'Yeah, yes, he's around.'

'Have you come to collect my wife?'

The junior doctor looked genuinely puzzled. 'No, no, I haven't. I'm a doctor, not a porter.'

'Ignore him,' said Sarah. 'We're fine as we are.' She waited until the junior was out of earshot and spoke quietly as people brushed past them in white-coated ones and twos, while patients in all apparent stages of health milled in and out of the Haematology department. 'You turn up on the borderline of late – and I *understand* the pressure you're under – but you've done nothing since you got here late other than wind me up. Maybe you should just go, David.'

His silence was deep, hiding his hurt.

'Please don't say that.'

'He could already have sent someone to collect me and I've been missed because you didn't get here on time. DNA: did not attend, no second chances, get in the queue with everyone else. That's the attitude they'll take.' She turned her back on him and there was a lengthy pause. 'I'm sorry. I shouldn't have said that. About you going.'

'It's all right,' he said, but it wasn't. 'I made you late and I'm—'

At that moment, Rosen's phone erupted in his pocket. He backed away a couple of paces to receive the call. 'Carol?'

'David, another woman's gone missing. It looks like the sixth,' said Bellwood, driving at speed.

'Where?'

'Wandsworth.'

'Road?'

'Picardie Road, number 19.'

'Any witnesses?'

'No. Husband went to the supermarket, comes home, she's gone.'

'Domestic abduction, same as Julia.'

'Same but different. She put up a fight. There's blood on the walls. Got to go, David.'

'Jesus.' He ended the call.

'I know,' Sarah said. 'Go on, go.'

'I—' The stairs would be quicker than waiting for the lift.

'Go.'

'Call me when you've seen the doctor.' He hurried to the staircase.

'David!' He turned. Then, quietly, she spoke: 'I shouldn't have said that I wanted you to leave.'

He wished she hadn't uttered those words, still feeling the visceral sting of them, but understood why. 'I'm sorry,' he said. 'I love you, Sarah.'

He threw open the staircase door and was gone.

———

SARAH FELT EVERYDAY life flowing around her in the corridor and watched seconds tick away on her wristwatch. More than twenty years of marriage to David rushed through her memory. She imagined a world in which they'd never met, in which their chance Saturday-night encounter in a grey nightclub had never been, and was visited by a piercing emptiness.

He'd disbelieved her, thinking she was joking when she'd declined his offer of a date because she was away that following weekend with her TA unit. She'd enjoyed his astonishment when he'd tried to picture her in camouflage fatigues.

What would her world be without him?

In the glass panel of the door to the Haematology department, Sarah saw the reflection of a white-coated doctor watching her.

'Mrs Rosen?'

'Yes?'

Sarah turned. She hadn't met Dr Reid before. He extended his hand. Beneath his white coat, he wore a smart black suit.

'I'm sorry I'm late,' he said.

She shook his hand.

Dr Reid held on to Sarah's hand a little too long and said, 'I don't think you should worry, Mrs Rosen. Dempsey's one of the most cautious doctors I've ever worked with.'

'Is my baby in danger?'

'We'll sort this out and send you on your way. Would you please come with me?'

Sarah felt relieved and was unsure whether it was down to Reid's relaxed manner, or Rosen's absence and the aura of tension he'd brought along with him.

'I thought you were sending someone for me?'

'I was, but we're short staffed and when I realized you'd been left standing there, I thought the least I could do is collect you. I'd like to retake your bloods just to get a contrasting reading. I suspect the raised level of adrenalin was as a result of the stress of attending Mr Gilling-Smith's clinic.'

Sarah felt better by the moment with Dr Reid's calm reassurance. He eyed the passenger lifts and the wide-doored service lifts with the digital display above.

'Passenger lift on six,' said Reid, 'Neonatal Intensive Care. Service lift, ground floor.' Reid pressed the button for the service lift and smiled at Sarah. 'Shouldn't really use this lift, but it's quicker. I'll take you to Phlebotomy myself.'

A digital arrow showed that the service lift was on its way up. The service lift hauled to a halt and the doors opened slowly.

Inside was a wheelchair marked *Property of St Thomas's NHS Trust* and, behind this, a scissor bed covered with a bunch of crumpled green blankets.

Reid smiled at Sarah and, with a gentlemanly gesture, indicated she should enter the lift before him. She drifted inside and he followed.

'I'm going to call down to Phlebotomy and tell them to have a place ready for you at the head of the queue.' He looked at his watch. 'This hour of the morning, the wait to give a blood sample can be half an hour to three-quarters.' He reached into his coat pocket with one hand and with the other kept the lift door open. 'I left my phone in clinic.' He spoke to himself.

Sarah moved further back inside the lift, closer to the scissor bed.

He looked directly at her. 'Could I borrow your phone?'

She fished her phone from her bag, turned it on and keyed in the pin number, then handed it over to him. He keyed in digits, smiling at her.

'I'm not getting a signal. Here. Let me try . . .' He got out of the lift and dialled again, keeping the door open with his foot. She glanced away from him and at the instructions in case of an emergency on the wall of the lift. He stepped away from the door.

Sarah looked up to see the doors closing in front of Dr Reid's face.

'Dr Reid?' she said.

His face vanished. The doors shut tightly.

Sarah pressed the button to open them again but nothing happened. A knock came on the other side of the doors, followed by Reid's voice. 'See you down there, Mrs Rosen.'

She pressed the button for the ground floor and, as the lift started descending, she heard the sound of breathing. It was coming from beneath the green blanket on the scissor bed. She suddenly noticed the shape of a body that at a casual glance she had thought was just a crumpled mass of NHS blankets.

'Are you all right?' she asked.

A hand fell from beneath the blanket, dangling down the side of the scissor bed, the face and head still covered by blankets.

'I'm just going to lift the blankets,' said Sarah. Newspapers were filled with tales of pensioners marooned on hospital trolleys, forgotten for hours on end.

'Don't be afraid,' she said, though she felt fear herself. The breathing beneath the blanket deepened, coarsened, as she turned back the material.

Jet-black hair, face down on the scissor bed, tiny little ears, a man, face down.

'Try to turn over,' she said, kindly.

'Like this?' he replied.

Teeth and eyes, that was all, a flash of darkness out of softly lit space and the sudden appearance of a hypodermic needle racing towards her hand. She froze. The needle pierced her flesh. She stared at him for a moment and then reached out with her other hand to the metal wall where every button waited to be touched. The tight confines of the lift suddenly felt like a metal coffin. The four walls appeared to push in on her as panic mounted rapidly inside her. Halfway to the buttons on the wall, her hand lost all momentum and fell away from its target.

The emergency phone, built into the wall, receded fast.

She tried to call out for her husband, David, as the display above her head span to the letter G for Ground. But it was too late. He set about manipulating Sarah's liquid form into the wheelchair.

Her head flopped back as he moulded her into the seat and the last she saw was the whites of his teeth and the whites of his eyes.

As she sank into the void, a voice trailed after her.

'I did not come from darkness. I am darkness itself.'

——

WHEN HE EMERGED from the service lift, pushing a dozing patient in a wheelchair, the green-uniformed paramedic turned his back to an oncoming nurse and adjusted his patient's blanket with, 'Nice and cosy for you?'

He pushed the wheelchair away from the lift and forced himself to smile, puckering his lips to whistle silently as he rolled the sixth and final carrier towards the front entrance.

'Yeah,' he said, to a question she hadn't asked. 'I was a medical student for two years. Happy days: learned a lot, I did.'

He kept his eyes fixed ahead as he passed the ward clerk returning from a break, the first person coming the other way. She didn't react and neither did the nurses who cut across his path, nor the anaesthetist who overtook him as he made his way to the exit and the ambulance bay beyond.

Sarah's left eye wasn't quite closed. A rim of white glistened up at him, an anaesthetised crescent.

The ambulance, his ambulance, was parked where he'd left it, next to another ambulance.

He opened the back doors and looked around. People were about, plenty of them coming and going. But no one appeared to be looking as he transferred the carrier into the back of his ambulance.

54

As Rosen ran towards Royal Street, a marked police car sailed towards him down Lambeth Palace Road. He held out his warrant card with one hand and waved the car down with his other arm.

'DCI Rosen. I need to get to Picardie Road in Wandsworth.' He climbed into the passenger seat and tersely explained, 'Herod. Golden hour.'

The siren blared and, within three seconds, the car was clocking 60mph, the constable weaving through traffic.

Through a red light at a junction, the police car hit 80mph. On Victoria Bridge Road, Rosen's phone rang. The constable steered through another red light, knocking the wing mirror off a car that wasn't quite far enough out of the way.

'Yeah?' said Rosen.

'David?'

'Where are you, Carol?'

'On the way to the scene of the crime. Switchboard have a problem—'

'Oh, for God's sake.'

Rosen weighed up the traffic immediately around them. There was some sort of blockage just after St George's Cathedral where, just ahead, an ambulance took advantage of the delay and cut out of Dodson Street.

'What's the problem with the switch?' he asked.

'Two problems. The mobile number that put in the Wandsworth emergency call. It's been traced as a stolen phone. The phone was stolen this morning.'

The traffic shifted. The constable slid back to seventy and clipped the bumper of another car.

'Has anyone arrived at Wandsworth yet?'

'The locals.'

'Our people?'

'Not yet.'

At that moment, Rosen instinctively knew he was in the wrong place and that it was too late to turn back.

'Carol, Picardie Road, Wandsworth: it's a hoax?'

'The locals can't find a problem.'

'It's a hoax.' In repeating the words, their significance dawned on Rosen. He wanted to scream.

'It looks like.'

'Carol, I'm hanging up.'

He called Sarah's number. It rang as buildings flew by and streets flashed past. 'The mobile number you've called is currently unavailable. Please try again later.' *She's out of coverage*, he thought, *or she's switched off*.

The constable turned into Kell Street and Rosen shouted, 'Pull up! Pull up!' The constable slammed the car to a standstill.

Rosen's mouth was cloth, his tongue a dead weight. He made a call, reaching a duty sergeant he didn't know called George Jones.

'George, my name's Detective Chief Inspector David Rosen. My wife Sarah should be on the first floor of St Thomas's Hospital. I want officers there immediately. It relates to the Herod investigation.'

'I'm acting on it now, sir. Hold the line.'

'Turn the car around,' said Rosen. 'Back to St Thomas's!'

The constable made a 360-degree turn on a pin and went back to driving at high speed.

Down Borough Road towards the roundabout with Blackfriars, Rosen clutched the phone to his ear and willed Sergeant Jones to come back on the line.

An urgent instruction poured out of the car radio backed up by Sergeant Jones's voice in his ear.

'Sir, we've deployed all available officers in the area to the hospital.'

An ambulance, its siren silent, headed in his direction. He glanced at it as it sailed away from St Thomas's.

'Call the hospital, George. Tell them to close all the doors, in and out: no one enters, no one leaves.'

'I'll do that now.'

On either side of the road, cars hugged the pavement to allow the speeding police car through.

Rosen was visited by a memory of Phillip Caton throwing up in the gutter of Brantwood Road on the morning his wife had been abducted. Caton, a self-employed plumber, had been drawn away by a genuine call for work, leaving his wife exposed to the terror of Herod.

Rosen, a detective of over twenty years' experience, realised he'd been suckered into abandoning his wife.

St Thomas's Hospital loomed large.

'Are you all right, sir?' asked the constable. 'Sir, you want me to open a window or something, sir? Sir?'

55

On the first floor of the North Wing of St Thomas's Hospital, Rosen ran through the area between the lifts and the main door to the Haematology department. As he did so, he wondered whether he'd ever see his wife again.

At reception, he asked for Dr Brian Reid, who arrived within a minute.

'Detective Rosen?'

Rosen turned and saw a short, ginger-haired man in a white coat with a standard St Thomas's NHS badge.

'Dr Reid, did you telephone my wife yesterday and tell her to come in today?'

The doctor frowned and shook his head. 'Absolutely not.'

'An unofficial appointment because of a problem with her bloods?' Blind hope drove him on. 'You fixed it up with Tom Dempsey from Gynaecology.'

'I haven't spoken to Tom in weeks.'

Rosen's phone rang and the receptionist frowned automatically.

He wanted more than anything else for it to be Sarah.

'David?' It was Carol Bellwood. 'It's definitely a hoax. Number 19 Picardie Road. I'm standing on the pavement at the gap between number 17 and number 21 where number 19 used to be. It was blown up in an accidental gas explosion and demolished years ago. We've knocked on every door in Picardie Road in case we got the number wrong. There aren't even any pregnant women on the street. This is not the scene of an abduction. Where are you, David?'

'I'm at the scene of an abduction right now. St Thomas's Hospital. First floor. North Wing. Haematology.'

'Do we know who the victim is?'

The overhead fluorescents seemed to be blinding him, and the strength to merely put one foot in front of the other drained away.

'David, do we know who the abducted woman is?'

'Yes. It's my wife, Sarah.'

56

Sarah Rosen was both blessed and cursed with insider knowledge. Before she had regained full consciousness, she knew she was in a dismal place. Waking up was not a gradual journey into the light of a brand-new day, but a progression into an understanding of the confines of the place that enclosed her: a man-made darkness that defied and overwhelmed her.

For a moment, when her fingers touched the sides of the sensory deprivation chamber, she assumed she was sick – not a sudden return from health to the jaws of depression, but that she was sick and had never been well. That the profound blackness around her was merely the coming together of all that she was on the inside in the worst moments of her life.

She said, 'David?' But her voice was swallowed by the darkness. She lifted her hands and touched the lid of the chamber, recalling Rosen's description of the rags that Alison Todd's fingers and nails had become. She had cried in their kitchen as she dried the dishes and listened, wishing her husband would shut up, and despising herself for wanting to bury her head in the sand.

Her eyes widened and she felt something like electric shock running down her spine, a power that galvanized each nerve in her being.

She was floating. It was dark. There was an abominable silence.

Her hands rolled up her thighs and across her hips to her stomach. But there was no gaping wound in her middle; her skin, her womb, her baby were all there and intact. She kept her hands in place across her womb, but the blessed moment of relief subsided.

It hadn't happened yet. But it was coming. Soon. The only way she would be removed from this chamber was so that her baby could be removed from her.

She pressed a hand to her mouth. Primal knowledge. She was safer in silence than in the scream that built up inside her. She became aware of the stuff on which she was floating, her heels pressing down against the heavy resistance of the fluid, and she was visited by a grim notion. She was floating on the blood of other women.

Sarah seized a handful of the stuff and, as she felt it slide through her fingers, a wave of panic crashed over her. It was bigger than her intelligence, stronger than her memory, better than her imagination at shaping the future. There was no hope. The others might have hoped for the sudden arrival of the police, the broken-down door and the eleventh-hour rescue, but that was the prerogative of civilian wives. She was privy to the depth of Rosen's knowledge, the weight of his frustrations.

Sarah brought the liquid to her face.

As she smelled the liquid on her finger, a single drop fell between her lips and onto her tongue: the unmistakable taste of salt and the undeniable presence once in this enclosed space of another person.

With the taste came the aroma of Julia.

With taste and aroma came the realization that she was in a place designed to block out the senses. The utter dark and total silence had not been provided merely in order to disorientate. She began to shake. With each passing second it felt colder and colder. Her teeth banged together, setting off the nerves deep inside the enamel. Pain traced down her jaw.

She knew that she had three days to live, at the outside. But she guessed she had considerably less time, that she and her child were the last souls and that, in closure, his actions would accelerate.

She clasped her hands together for a moment to stop them shaking, laid them over her womb and clutched her elbows into her ribs. She took the longest, slowest breath of her life through her nostrils and held it in her lungs as deeply as she could.

She hung on to the breath until the shaking subsided a little as she felt the blood rising in her face and head, imagined the darkening of her skin as the pressure within her rose.

She hung on until she couldn't hold on any longer, then allowed the air out through a paper-thin gap between her lips. She realized that this was how he incapacitated his victims before the kill. The deprivation of sensory stimulation over three days and nights was not enough on its own to render the flesh unresistant. But there was another factor in the equation.

Oxygen.

He starved them of air.

She touched the lid of the chamber and estimated the distance between the surface of the water and the lid, the length and width of the tank, finding a bleak calm but no comfort in the act of mathematical calculation that told her just how few cubic centimetres of air were available to her.

She raised both hands to the lid. It was bound to be locked, but she pressed her palms upwards and pushed hard.

The lid gave slightly, opening on her left-hand side, a tiny crack, a sliver of red light in the room outside the chamber. And a wisp of air. She pushed. But it was as far as the lid would go. She breathed, blinked and focussed on the dull light.

And then she heard a sound. Feet descending a ladder. She lowered the lid so that it would allow sound through if not light. And she waited. But nothing happened.

He was in the room. He was outside the chamber. But nothing happened.

She just waited in the dark.

Suddenly, there was a noise like thunder inside the tank as a sudden, angry weight slammed down on the lid above her face.

Sarah froze. *To scream is to die, to be silent is to survive.*

She waited, afloat on the saline water, wondering whether he was standing over her, unable to detect any other sign of his presence beyond the darkness in which she was suspended.

She waited. The air was thinning and she needed to make a decision. If he was still there, to raise the lid was to alert him; to leave it closed was to run out of air.

57

Sarah hadn't returned home. The phone in the house remained unanswered, and two local beat constables confirmed that there was no one in the Rosen residence.

She wasn't at St Philomena's School. A complete search of the building and grounds showed no sign of Sarah Rosen being on the premises; the day's CCTV footage showed no record of her entering the building.

As bald reality became inescapable fact, Rosen recalled a moment in time, some twelve years earlier, when the darkness in the barrel of a gun was inches from his face.

'If she has been abducted—' said Baxter.

'If?'

'I have to ask you, David,' continued Baxter over the interruption, 'has she been well, in herself, lately?'

'Has she gone mental and run away? Is that what you want to know?'

'I didn't say that.'

It was gone noon, over two hours since the hoax call to Picardie Road and since Sarah had gone missing.

'What have your instructions been?' asked Baxter. 'David?'

'Carol Bellwood's in charge at St Thomas's. Corrigan and Feldman are viewing CCTV footage from the hospital. I've got officers talking to anyone who had an appointment on or around the first floor, North Wing.'

Baxter patted Rosen on the sleeve. He didn't look up from the picture of Sarah on his desk.

'We've got three days, tops—' started Baxter.

'Do you believe that?'

'That's the precedent; let's go on that.'

The phone on Rosen's desk rang. He sat up and snatched at the receiver.

'Yes?'

'It's Corrigan. Boss, listen, we've got something on CCTV from St Thomas's. It's a brief sequence covered by two cameras, one interior, one exterior.'

'Get to the point, Jeff.'

Rosen got to his feet and the solemn noise level in the incident room dipped.

'Is it my wife?'

'Yes. I'm sorry. Yes, it looks like it is.'

Rosen felt his face fall as the last of his hope ebbed away.

'Talk me through the footage.'

Rosen walked up and down behind his desk as he listened impatiently.

'An ambulance pulls up at the front doors, only it's a slightly old ambulance. It's there for ten minutes. A woman is pushed out of the front entrance in a wheelchair by what looks like a man in a standard paramedic uniform.'

'Is it Paul Dwyer?'

'Yeah, it looks like Paul Dwyer.'

'And the woman's my wife?'

'Yes, it's your wife. Paramedic puts her in the back of the ambulance, closes the doors, gets in the cab, drives off. He heads off in the direction of Lambeth Palace Road.'

'OK, Jeff,' said Rosen. 'Get the pictures down here straightaway.'

'Johnny Mac's on his way right now.'

'Change of plan.' He spoke to Jeff Corrigan but looked directly at Baxter. 'We're publishing Flint's picture asap, and we'll release this CCTV footage from the hospital as well. But don't approach either man. Corrigan, you there?'

'Yes?'

'How did she look? My wife?'

'She appeared to be asleep. She looked peaceful.'

Rosen wondered whether Dwyer had used Pentothal as he had with his other victims.

'Was there no one else around?'

'There were dozens of people coming and going, but the scene didn't look odd. Aside from the slightly dated ambulance, but that's not that obvious . . . I guess no one took any notice.'

An ambulance? Rosen felt the rush of an oncoming revelation. As he'd come away from the hospital, leaving Sarah alone for the attentions of Dwyer, he'd seen an ambulance cutting out of Dodson Street. It had passed within metres of the bonnet of the car he'd been in, but going in a different direction.

If I'd released the picture of Dwyer sooner, the thought mocked him, *maybe, just maybe, someone in that hospital would have noticed him* . . .

58

On the morning of Julia's abduction, Phillip Caton had turned off his mobile phone usually left on 24/7.

The last time it had rung, at seven o'clock in the morning, Phillip had picked up the call partly from instinct but mostly through raw desperation. It had been an emergency, a request for a plumber to help with a flooded nursery school. As Phillip had faltered and stuttered through his apology for being unable to take the job, the lady on the other end of the line had persisted, in a gentle and kindly manner. She had all those babies to think about, all those toddlers and their mums and dads, and then she had paused as she put two and two together. She apologized to Phillip. How insensitive she was to mention babies, and she was genuinely sorry if she'd hurt his feelings but how *was* he feeling? She wanted to know. She cared, see. She realized who he was and why he sounded so, well, devastated. Had he heard anything about Julia? From the police? From the abductor even? Had he? She didn't know how he was coping. Did they have a name for the baby? It was a boy. Wasn't it?

Wasn't it?

Phillip had been overtaken by the only moment of clarity he'd experienced since discovering Julia had been abducted.

'Which newspaper are you from?' he had asked.

'The one you read, according to your newsagent,' she replied. 'So, come on, Phillip, I want to help, I—'

At that point he had switched off the phone and poured himself a large whisky.

When the coroner released Julia's body, her mother took over the arrangements for the funeral, much as she had done for their wedding, much as she would have done for the christening of their baby.

He tried to work, which he enjoyed, to finish off a central heating installation in St John's Wood, but he couldn't. He went to the pub, a place he didn't much like.

He could drink. He could pump money into the fruit machine and find a strange comfort in those spinning icons, a welcome ritual in the 'nudge' and 'hold' decisions that the machine seduced him into.

Best of all, though, no one talked to him. In the pub, at the fruit machine, it was as if he had an invisible wall around him. No one could see through that wall, and a man with a Calvinist work ethic, and a knowledge down to the last penny of what he had in the bank, happily dropped coin after coin into the belly of the fruit machine.

When he did move away, it was only when the alcohol started to wear off and he needed another drink from the bar.

'I'm sorry,' said the barmaid, a well-preserved blonde with kind eyes and a wedding ring on her finger. 'I can't serve you any more.'

'Why?' As he asked the question, he felt a little absurd because he heard the answer in his own voice. He was drunk, categorically hammered.

'Go home,' she said. 'I'll call you a taxi. Go home and get some sleep.'

'I can't,' he said. 'Sleep.'

On a television set above the bar, the six o'clock news began on the BBC. He tried to turn away but couldn't and, in looking up, he saw a face, a frozen image that went offscreen to give way to some CCTV footage from the front of a big building, with a commentary he could barely hear above the noise of the bar.

He walked backwards, his gaze fixed on the TV screen, and barked, 'Shut up!' to a couple whose table he wobbled into, almost knocking over their glasses.

'OK, that's enough,' said the barmaid.

The face came back on the screen, behind the head of the newsreader. Phillip pointed at the TV, straining to hear, as the newsreader said something about the police issuing two sets of CCTV footage: one from the British Library and one that had been taken that day outside a hospital.

Where from? Where did he know him from?

The newsreader gave way to library footage of a tree-lined street in suburban London.

'That's my house,' said Phillip. The man the police wanted to talk to was called Paul Dwyer. 'But his name's not Dwyer.' They wanted to talk to a priest as well, a fresh-faced young man by the look of him. But Phillip didn't have a clue who the priest was.

'His name's Paul but it isn't Dwyer. I did a job for him.'

Phillip's realizations made perfect sense to himself but he had enough presence of mind to know his speech sounded slurred beyond recognition.

He took out his mobile phone and, in trying to switch it on, realized he'd forgotten his pin number.

He turned to the couple he'd just shouted at.

'Can you help me?' he said, showing them the phone in the palm of his hand. They turned away as the manager arrived.

'Out you go, come on!'

'I'm going.'

There was a numbness in his limbs that made walking from the bar to the door an ordeal; the pretence of sobriety and dignity was a tall order under the judgemental eyes of the drinkers who chose to watch him.

But he ignored their staring eyes and tried to recall Paul's surname. 'I know where he lives.'

He had Detective Rosen's direct number stored on his phone.

Outside, the fresh air made him giddy. He recalled his pin number, 1204, 12 April, Julia's birthday, but in typing the digits in, he slipped on the step, falling heavily on the tarmac, cracking his skull and knocking himself out.

59

Sarah counted back from ten, both hands pressed flat against the underside of the lid. As she reached three, she felt sick at the prospect of pushing the lid up, fearing the sight of his pupils peering at her through the crack. Her chest tightened in the stale air that grew thinner with each breath. But she had to do it, she had to hear and see as much as she could. When she whispered, 'Zero!' she kept her promise to herself and softly pushed the lid.

Red light in a darkened room. No sound. No sign of him but such a tiny gap. The trickle of air was close to pleasurable, but the weight of lifting the lid caused her arm muscles to burn.

The lid was loose at the top, near her head, but showed no sign of shifting near her feet, where it seemed to be tightly locked. She raised a foot to test it and felt like crying when the resistance was just too strong. She wasn't going to be able to lift the lid and climb out. The best she could hope for was air . . .

Then there was a sound. Above her head and outside the walls of the building in which she was confined. She listened hard as it came closer. Two noises. Voices and scraping. But the voices weren't human and the scraping was made by the friction of two hard surfaces. It was the sound of cattle lowing, their hooves clattering on tarmac. Cows ambling back from their pastures. The gentle sound of cattle calling relieved her loneliness for a moment and then made her compulsion to weep sharp and unbearable.

How far away? How far away from home am I? she wondered, as the sound of the cattle passed by on the road outside. The sound had come from above. It occurred to Sarah she was being held in a basement.

She lifted the lid a little higher but could push no more than to a ten-degree angle. She held on, allowing fresh air into the chamber, and felt the tightening in her chest ease.

Slowly, she lowered the lid because she just didn't have the strength to keep it up.

She thought deeply and for a long time. Then she started to count. She would count to a hundred and raise the lid for ten seconds.

As she counted, she bit at the tips of the nails on her right hand, making the smooth edges jagged and raw. If she raised the lid and he was there, watching, his pupils peering at her, with a ten-degree angle she had enough room to thrust her fingers through the gap and scratch his eyes.

She recalled Rosen telling her of the autopsy reports and the effects of oxygen deprivation on the lungs and brains of the other women. She lay still and counted. As she passed the fifty mark, for the first time in a long time she felt an alien sensation inside her: a gentle fluttering.

Her baby was moving. Since the death of her daughter Hannah, she had dreamed for so long of this moment and, when it came, it came with the knowledge that the man who had her trapped was going to starve her and her baby of air.

As she reached one hundred, there was a black hatred in her heart.

She raised the lid to hear footsteps descending wooden stairs and above this the sound of a tuneless tune, a joyless yet lightly whistled improvisation.

She lowered the lid, holding in her lungs the fresh air she'd taken from the basement. She felt the ragged tips of her nails and pictured his eyes in the lift at St Thomas's Hospital, imagining them streaming with blood.

He was in the basement and she wondered whether he was ready.

Sarah closed the lid completely and composed herself in the pitiless blackness.

60

She raised the lid. It was by the slightest amount, but the light and noise were astonishing.

The room was full of what sounded like a huge machine, as if the room had been eaten alive and she was listening from within the belly of some mechanical beast. Wheels clattered across a rough stone floor.

The noise was getting closer. She raised the lid a little more, a fraction more light. Something dark was swinging in and out of the path of light. The noise stopped, to be replaced by another sound. His breathing was fast and uneven, the sound of exertion.

Through the walls of the house and the ceiling of the basement, a car engine was coming closer. She willed it to slow down and stop but after it passed the nearest point, the sound started fading away into the distance.

He was close at hand and there was a foul smell.

He stopped. And then quickening footsteps, moving away from her, told her that he had been suddenly called away.

He was heading up a flight of steps and then she heard his feet on the ceiling above her. Hurrying, hurrying, hurrying.

She was alone again, in the tank, in the basement.

She lifted the lid a little more, then raised her head, looking through the crack from as many angles as the confined space allowed.

A vertical metal pole and what looked like a saddle suspended in midair. She pushed hard and the small crack became wider. There was a metal arm connected to the cradle. It was a lifting device. Was it the thing on wheels that had made a racket on the concrete floor?

He was going to use it to lift her.

If she was incapacitated through lack of air, he wasn't going to kill her in the tank. He was going to take her somewhere else to do that.

She would lift the lid only for air now.

She knew enough.

She needed to conserve all her strength for what was coming.

61

In a soulless Port of Dover café, Sebastian Flint sipped a cup of
Earl Grey tea and recalled the time when he'd been lynched.
He remembered the moment when the mob had fallen silent,
assuming he was dead, the moment after the very last kick to his ribs
when the mob had drifted away, slowly at first, in dribs and drabs.

Flint recollected the carpet viper slumbering in the shadow of a
rock. Like the snake, Sebastian was belly down in the Kenyan dust. He
had opened his eyes enough to watch the serpent flick out its tongue
to collect the chemical information hanging in the air around him,
information seeping from his skin as he shed warm blood into the
thirsty soil.

The carpet viper retracted its tongue, passing its cargo to its Jacobson's
gland in the roof of its mouth, where the airborne chemicals would
be distilled, keener than smell and sharper than taste. From them, the
snake would know not to attack the man who was neither prey nor
predator.

Flint had smiled through continents of pain, the darkness of his
pupils connecting with the black of the serpent's eye. He called to

mind the carpet viper sliding from the shadows towards him. As he had drifted out of consciousness, he had watched the serpent slide across his fingers to the open wound at the base of his hand.

From the darkness around the rock, a deeper shadow had crept towards his brutalized body. Unable to speak, he had stared into the darkness as it had crawled onto his skin in the final moments before he passed out.

In the almost empty Port of Dover café, Flint observed the increasing tension in the lorry driver at the till. He reached inside his coat and produced nothing. He rummaged with both hands in his hip pockets. Empty. He tried his trousers with no success.

'Shit! My wallet.'

Flint walked over to the till. The girl behind the counter drew back the cup of coffee she'd been about to serve the driver.

'Here,' said Flint, handing a two-pound coin to the girl, who pushed the cup of coffee back towards the driver. Flint indicated the table in the corner where he was sitting and the driver joined him.

'Are you sure you didn't leave it in the cab of your lorry?' asked Flint.

'No, I bought a paper in the newsagents, five minutes back. Thanks for this.' He sipped the hot coffee.

'You want me to help you find that wallet?'

'There was only a fiver in it.'

'Got your phone?' asked Flint.

'Yeah.'

'Got your passport?'

'Yeah, yeah.'

'You need to call your credit card provider and cancel—'

The driver laughed sourly and stared past Flint. 'I don't have any credit cards. Not any more.'

'No credit cards?'

'I had several when I was married.' He looked wistful at the memory.

'I think we've been to the same place,' said Flint. The man looked back at him. Flint added, 'My ex maxed out all my cards before she left me.'

'Bitch. She wasn't called Lisa, was she?' The driver laughed at his own joke and Flint joined in, louder than his new companion but in total harmony.

It opened doors. The driver said, 'She cleaned me out; left me for some other fellah and I ended up being made bankrupt. The worst of it is, I've got a new woman in me life now; she's an angel, the opposite of Lisa. She's pregnant, and we're going to charity shops to get stuff for the baby.'

'That's just so unfair,' Flint commented. The driver drank the rest of his coffee in silence, then glanced up at Flint and smiled.

'What you looking at me like that for?'

'You're not the only one with problems, mate,' said Flint. 'Where you heading?'

'France.'

'What you carrying?'

'Flat-packed furniture.'

'Let's go look for that wallet,' suggested Flint.

'There was just a fiver in it, that's all.'

'A fiver's a fiver. Let's go look for it.'

————

A QUARTER OF an hour later, in the lorry's cab, Flint said, 'At least we tried.'

'I didn't think we'd find it.'

The water bottle on the dashboard looked old, as if it had been refilled from the tap on dozens of occasions over several months. The driver caught Flint eyeing it.

'What did you mean back in the café?' asked the driver.

'I said a few things.'

'You said, something like, *you're not the only one with problems, mate. What were you getting at?*'

'I need a favour.' Flint reached inside his coat and took out a fat brown envelope, which he placed in his own lap. He saw the excitement in the driver's eyes. 'I don't know your name, you don't know mine. Let's keep it simple,' he said. He opened the envelope to show a wad of money. 'Three thousand in fifties. Hide me in your lorry. As soon as we get to France, I'm history and you're three grand better off.'

Flint offered the notes to the driver, who looked utterly conflicted.

'What if I get searched?'

'When was the last time that happened?'

'You never know.'

'That's a point.'

Slowly, Flint returned the money to the envelope. The driver watched, entranced, his shoulders sagging as the notes vanished from sight.

'I'm sorry, I shouldn't have asked. I shouldn't have put you in this position.' Flint opened the cab door. 'I hope it goes well,' he said. 'The birth and all that.'

Jumping down, he shut the door behind him and walked away. Suddenly, the door flew open.

'Hey, mate,' said the driver. Flint turned. 'We get searched, you say you stowed away, right?'

Flint walked back, feeling the weight of the driver's wallet in his pocket.

'I'll give you fifteen hundred now, fifteen hundred when you let me out in France.'

62

I n the incident room at Isaac Street Police Station, Rosen's mobile phone vibrated as it buzzed on the surface of his desk. Exhausted and numbed by shock and tension, he watched the phone ring twice.

'David, the phone, quickly, it's important!' Bellwood thrust the mobile at him.

SARAHMOBILE. His wife's name registered on the display panel.

He took the phone from her, all eyes in the room on him, and let out a sound, somewhere between a solitary laugh and a cry of relief.

SARAHMOBILE. The display flashed before his eyes like lightning.

'Sarah, where are you?'

But all he heard was the muffled throb of a large engine and the action of water somewhere in the middle distance.

'Sarah?' He felt the absence of her voice as a sharp intense pain in the centre of his chest. 'Who is this?'

'Your landline's busy.'

'Flint . . .?'

'Is there something going on today, David?'

'Where's my wife, Flint?'

Silence.

'Where's my wife being held?'

'I'm confused and a little disappointed, David. Are you going to ask me why I'm confused and a little disappointed?'

'Why?'

'Why what, David?'

Rosen dug deeper into the pit. Flint wasn't going to directly answer the one question he needed an answer to, but as long as he had Flint on the line, there was the spectre of a chance that he might give something away. *Keep talking, keep engaged . . .*

'Why are you disappointed?'

'Because you went to the British Library yesterday and you saw me but you didn't say hello after all the help I've given you. You didn't have the good grace to come and say hello, that's why I'm confused and a little disappointed. I felt you ought to know that. I think that's only fair, don't you?' The shape of his mood was hidden behind his manicured, educated tone.

'That's not the main question,' said Rosen, 'as I see it.'

'Then, what is the main question?' asked Flint. 'As you see it?'

Rosen didn't speak for a moment. He listened hard to the sounds in the background, knowing that these would yield more than the caller. He listened to the capacity of the engine and the wider insistence of the motion of water.

So, thought Rosen, *how did you make it out of Dover?*

A memory assailed Rosen, a childhood fragment, with the caption of his response as a six-year-old to something he had witnessed in the tiny kitchen of the overcrowded tenement flat he had once called home. The family cat, something between a stray and a regular visitor, had lifted its paw from the back of a dazed mouse and allowed the little grey ball of life to run five paces before lazily reaching out to haul it back to square one. Rosen remembered thinking: *Just do nothing, stop joining in with his game; he's going to destroy you anyway.*

'Father Sebastian, we were in a library, a place of quiet reflection, where you looked deep in study. It seemed wrong to disturb you.'

He wrote the words: 'Inform the port authorities at Calais: Flint probably on ferry heading out of Dover.' He slid the note towards Bellwood.

The throb of the engine shifted as the waves grew more dense.

'Such respect for education,' said Flint. 'You do know, it would have been lost on you. If you'd been born into a good family and you'd been sent to the best public school, you'd have still come out as you are. All that nurturing would have slid off you. You were born to be what you are, Rosen, a sorter of filth, other people's mistakes, the unpalatable end of human nature. That's what you're here for, that's what you are, and I'm telling you that the little worm that gnaws inside you – What if? What if I'd had a better start? What if I'd been to a better school? – that worm in your soul is a phantom. You're a refuse collector.' Flint sighed. 'I'm trying to cut you some slack here, Rosen, I'm trying to help you, can you see that?'

Rosen looked around the room at the faces of his colleagues as he absorbed Flint's words, and realized he was on speakerphone, for the whole room to hear. In that moment, no one quite looked him in the eye.

'David, the thing about you is—'

Rosen stared at the surface of a cup of coffee that had grown cold on his desk, tormented by the need to ask again where his wife was but knowing this would feed Flint, satisfy him and reinforce his lust for manipulation.

'What's the thing about me, Father Sebastian?'

A door opened, metallic, echoing, then slammed shut in the place where Flint was, a sound that seemed to arrest his attention and send him into a momentary lull.

'You're a taker. Take, take, take. It's all you've ever done with me.'

'What can I give you, Father Sebastian, a man of your standing and erudition?' Rosen eyeballed his colleagues. Bellwood met his gaze and he felt her willing him on. 'What can I give to you?'

'Spoken like a true pauper.'

Nausea crept up from the root of Rosen's digestive system and, with it, rage.

'David, I'm sorry for your loss.'

'No, you're not.'

The waves around Flint rode higher and, as they slapped, Rosen had the sense that Flint was about to end the call.

'That's what I called to say: I am sorry for your loss.'

'If you were sorry for my loss, Father Sebastian, you'd tell me where my wife is!'

'I was thinking of quite a different loss. It wasn't that long ago.'

A door opened deep inside Rosen, a door to a different day in another year that could never come back but would never go away.

'*You have a child, David? No, no, no.* Three times you denied her in St Mark's. Remember? Funny how those little betrayals always weigh most heavily . . . No?'

'I haven't forgotten Hannah.'

'Your lost girl?'

'You know nothing about our loss.'

'Then, educate me. What does it feel like, that kind of loss?'

Rosen sat back in his seat, staring at the speakerphone on the desk, then looked at the room full of faces, like a frozen moment of life flashing before his eyes.

'Give me your loss, David,' said Flint, 'and I'll give you hope.'

'Hope?'

'I can go as quickly as I came. Your wife? Where did you leave her this morning?'

'Hannah was a beautiful child,' began Rosen.

'Where did she die?'

'She died in her cot.'

'Did you put her in the cot that night?'

'I was on duty.'

'But she was still alive when you came home?'

'I went to see her as soon as I came in.'

'Are you sure she was still breathing at that point?'

'Yes.'

'How sure?'

'I listened to her, the landing light was on, I saw her shift in her sleep.'

'Did you touch her? Kiss her before she . . . left you?'

'You're . . . you're asking me questions I can't answer, Flint.'

'You walked away from her cot?'

'I can't give you those moments.'

'Where did you go?'

'I went to the bathroom.'

'And when you returned?'

'I thought you wanted my loss.'

In the background, the muffled sound of screeching gulls suggested that, wherever he was, Flint was coming close to dry land.

'This is the door to loss. Stand at that door, David, and take hold of the very moment when you returned to the cot and all that the landing light could pick out was her stillness and you could no longer hear a thing. Did you pick her up? Did you shake her? Did you order her to come back from the dead?'

'I picked her up. I didn't shake her. I didn't order her back. I called for Sarah, I told her our baby was dead, I gave her over to her mother . . . I called the ambulance, I called the police—'

'What didn't you do in your loss?'

'I couldn't say goodbye because I missed the moment. I didn't say goodbye. I wasn't there to so much as hold her when she passed into the cold, the dark.' Rosen was almost whispering by now.

'And your wife, she lost her mind, didn't she? But, you, David? What did you lose?'

'Then . . . then, I lost hope.'

The phone in his hand fell away from his ear. He held his breath to staunch the sobs that rose inside him but tears, fierce and silent, rolled down his face.

Carol Bellwood stepped forward and placed one hand on his shoulder. She folded a hand around his and guided the phone back to his ear.

Rosen released his grief in a deep, single outbreath.

Bellwood stepped back.

Rosen heard the faintest echo of his own voice caught in the loop of the two telephones. There was a deceleration in the ship's action and the motion of the waves slackened. He looked at Sarah's name on the display of his phone and, leaning into the receiver, asked, 'When did you take my wife's phone from her, Flint? Well?'

'She has a few hours,' Flint's voice tumbled into the room. 'But not as many as the others, so you still have a few hours to reach her.'

'An address, Flint?'

'I don't know—'

'Yes, you do—'

'But I do know someone who does.'

'Where is Dwyer?'

'That's not the man you should be looking for if you want to get to your wife.'

'Then who is?'

'Brother Aidan.'

'Brother Aidan knows where my wife is?'

'Go get him, Mr Plod!'

Flint ended the call. Bellwood took the phone from him and redialled, but the line was dead.

Rosen called out, 'Kent Constabulary, we need officers at St Mark's right now.'

Gold was on the phone. 'I'm on it, boss. I've got the postcode.'

'It's a sure-fire bet, he'll be disembarking at Calais in the next hour.'

'We're talking to port authorities at Calais, and the local police.'

'We need a single phone line free to receive incoming photographic footage, and another dedicated line for oral feedback.'

Corrigan held up his mobile phone. 'I've got the latest iPhone for visuals, David.'

'And I'll block any incoming calls on mine that aren't from Kent Constabulary,' said Bellwood.

'Brother Aidan?' Rosen said the name out loud. 'What the hell's going on, Flint?' He looked around, seeing the normality of an incident room on red alert.

'David . . . David . . .' The voice, it seemed, came from far away, but it was Bellwood in his face, commanding his attention. She pointed at Gold. 'Kent have three cars on the way to St Mark's right now.'

Rosen nodded but had the cast-iron conviction that, whether cars were on the way there or not, it was already too late for Brother Aidan.

63

Local officers from Kent police streamed live iPhone footage from the chapel of St Mark's Monastery to the incident room at Isaac Street.

Holding Corrigan's iPhone in the palm of his hand, Rosen watched and listened.

'Two of the brothers died trying to escape from the chapel.'

DS Wilson, of Kent Constabulary, narrated the iPhone footage to Rosen. On the screen, two elderly men were slumped near the doorway; the others had been hacked down between the door and the communion rail. 'The rest, as you can see . . .'

At the communion rail, Brother Aidan, the top of his skull severed and not immediately visible, must have been the first to be attacked as he knelt at the rail awaiting communion. Returning to St Mark's, Flint had apparently celebrated a mass of some description.

Aidan, who according to Flint knew Sarah's whereabouts, lay in the ultimate silence, his face a death mask on the iPhone in Rosen's hand.

'Is this the guy you're looking for?' asked Wilson.

'Yes, it is,' said Rosen, his voice barely more than an exhalation of breath.

'What's that?' The voice of an unidentified officer overrode Wilson's.

'Jesus!' The image on the screen swung abruptly as the phone that was recording the massacre in St Mark's chapel was pointed in the direction of the second speaker. He was crouched on his haunches in the middle of the chapel, metres away from Aidan's corpse. 'Look at this, Tom! It looks like a body part.'

The top part of Aidan's skull lay on the ground, spongy, bloodied brain tissue nestling in the bone. Wedged in between bone and brain, a single piece of paper poked out. The beam of a torch revealed words carefully centred on the paper, printed and orderly.

It was a poem. 'Can you read that?' asked Wilson.

'No.' said Rosen.

'It's a poem. "The Sick Rose". You want me to read it to you?'

The text of the poem sharpened on the screen, making the writing clearer.

'No. What's that other writing down the margin of the page, the handwriting?' asked Rosen.

'It's an address,' said Wilson.

'Read it!'

'Caxton Farm, near Uckfield, East Sussex, TN22 6RP . . .'

As Rosen recited the address, he wrote it down. Bellwood typed the words into Google Maps and called out, 'I've got it!'

Rosen handed back the iPhone to Corrigan.

'Stay with them, Jeff. This is DS Corrigan on the line. Describe the scene as you relay it to him.' Rosen turned to Bellwood.

'It's way off the beaten track,' she said.

Rosen looked at the onscreen map.

'The A22 southbound to East Sussex . . .' Rosen could feel his pulse pumping at the side of his neck. Uckfield, small to the point of insignificance, was suddenly the centre of his universe. He looked around the room and asked, 'How many Authorized Firearms Officers here?' Bellwood and Gold signalled with their hands.

Rosen dialled the number for CO19, Central Operations Firearms Command, and called to everyone in the room, 'I want all available marked police cars to spread through central London to keep the roads as clear as possible to the mouth of the A22.'

Clarity descended as if a bright light had gone on inside him. Around the incident room, his instructions were being relayed with grim urgency.

At the other end of the line, at Leman Street Police Station in Whitechapel, Rosen was connected to Chief Superintendent Doug Price, CO19's most senior on-duty officer.

'DCI Rosen, what's happening?'

'I need support, Doug. Herod's abducted another woman. We have his location. I need firearms assistance now.'

'What do you need?'

'Three 9mm Glock 17 self-loading pistols for my team. We're going to Caxton Farm, outside a small place called Uckfield in East Sussex. We'll meet at the head of the A22, and go in one convoy. How many officers have you got available?'

'Six immediately, but we can call in as many again within the hour. They're all top marks. Is this a siege?'

'If all the information's correct, he's got a woman with him, a prisoner in the farmhouse.'

'David, leave it with me. See you soon. We'll be ready to roll in minutes.'

Rosen put down the phone.

'David . . .' It was Bellwood. 'This could be total bullshit, this address – another piece of theatre.'

'It could be,' replied Rosen, 'but it's all I've got.'

Baxter came over and said, 'David, I don't think this is right, you going anywhere near this address in East Sussex.'

'How are you going to stop me, Baxter? I'm leading this Murder Investigation Team.'

'I'm not going to stop you going. You need to coordinate the operation. But I'm ordering you . . .' He looked at Bellwood. 'Are you getting this, Bellwood? Are you hearing me? I'm ordering you not to go into the building with a firearm. I know you're an AFO and I'm guessing you've just put in the call to Leman Street. Did you ask for firearms for your MIT?'

'Yes.'

'Including yourself?'

'Yes.'

'If you go inside that building and use a gun on Dwyer, you'd better be damned sure you can justify it in a court of law. It's on your own head. Don't go in, stay outside, that's my order, OK?'

'I'll make all my operational decisions based on the reality of what's on the ground. You can't control an operation like this from a distance.'

Rosen looked around at the many faces watching him, waiting for his orders, and was consumed with a painful vision of his wife, alone, terrorized by the things he had told her about Herod's victims.

A feeling like fire swept through him. He would do *anything* to get to her.

64

The snap fastener on the lower lock lifted. A vibration on the case of the box in which she was trapped told Sarah that the hour had come. Now, there would be no turning back, no delay, no mercy.

Beneath the lid, she prepared to imitate the deadness of the eyes in the hapless men and women she'd observed at length in the day room of the psychiatric unit in which she'd recovered. She fixed the pattern of her breathing, sharp gasps taken by mouth to the tops of her lungs, the first stages of respiratory failure. *I cannot think, I cannot breathe, therefore I am no threat,* she said in her head as he raised the lid.

The red light in the basement played over her skin, and her arms came up in goose bumps, the soft hairs standing on end. A finger, his finger, touched her shoulder and arrived at her elbow in a single slow and gentle tracing. His hand settled on the back of hers in a gesture of tenderness. The motion of his head told her he was drinking in her nakedness with his eyes, her guess confirmed by a deep and hushed grunt of sensual approval.

As he examined her face, she rolled her half-shut eyes, keeping up the dense manufactured rhythm of struggling respiration.

He pressed his lips close to her left ear. 'Are you ready?'

He checked her face again and slapped her hard on the cheek. She held on to her breath and didn't flinch.

'She's all gone,' he muttered.

He picked up a hypodermic needle balanced on the nearby hoist and, half turning his back, inspected the fluid in its chamber. A bolt of fear ran through her. He replaced the hypodermic needle on the hoist next to what looked like a single spoke from a bicycle wheel.

'Unflesh the womb of its foetus and preserve the unblemished soul of the child.' It was as if he was recalling the instructions from a manual.

He threaded the harness under her back, through the saline, and pulled it up under her ribs. It supported her shoulders and the lower half of her back. As he hitched the ends to the hooks on the arm of the hoist, she felt his breath on her collarbone and winced within her staccato breathing.

She resisted the urge to wrap her hands around his throat and break his neck: he was just a little too far away to give her maximum leverage.

She felt her weight tug on the cradle of the hoist, still suspended in the saline, and from the corner of her eye saw him move out of her sight. She waited. A clip snapped and something tinkled under the soft vibration. She saw the hypodermic needle and the bicycle spoke resting side by side on the hoist.

Post mortem, she knew that the others had had minute traces of drugs in their bloodstreams but they'd had a lot longer than she to turn to jelly. Each woman had died from cardiac tamponade from a thin sharp implement. She knew she had glimpsed the murder weapon, and the thought made her want to throw up.

The lurching in her stomach grew worse when, by the flick of a switch, he raised her body from the water of the chamber. He pulled the wheeled hoist, his hands tight around the central bar from which she was suspended, the clattering of the wheels less noisy under her weight.

He's taking me somewhere else to kill me, thought Sarah.

As he pulled her through the doorway to the next room, made soft by candlelight, she glanced back and saw the oxygen tank under the sensory deprivation chamber, the low ceiling. These might have been the last things the other women had seen, depending on how far gone they'd been. At least for her it had not been an endless ordeal of waking and sleeping, and waking and becoming hysterical, before being brain dead by degrees.

The lack of natural light confirmed in her mind that this was indeed a windowless basement. Her anxiety rocketed. The thought of dying in a dark cellar at the hands of a madman made her want to cry out.

Her arm brushed the door frame and made the sling sway, making his job a little harder as he pulled her towards a table. She immediately knew that it was the place where she would be deposited. At its base sat a long metal box. It was covered with red velvet, reminding her of the altar in the chapel at the school where she taught. *Religion*, she thought. *Man and his bloody rites.*

As he twisted the contraption around, she caught sight of the top of his head, wet and black and shining round his small, shrimp-like ears.

How you hate your mother, she thought, *and how I am about to pay for that.*

The ceiling turned slowly as she span beneath it. The hoist made a whirring sound as she was lowered. Her buttocks were first to touch the surface of the table.

But there was no chanting, no noise, no artificial drama in this ceremony.

There was a door to a third room. Intuition seized her. In that room were the remains of the babies. Here, now, beneath the scent of him, she could smell the dry aroma of charcoal and the chemical reek of formaldehyde

She knew he hadn't used fire before, as there were no burns to the others.

It took all her willpower not to scream, because there was a first time for everything, including fire.

She listened to the dry scrape of a match on the emery of a box.

'Can you hear me?' he asked.

The flame hovered between his face and her eyes. He stared at her with intensity.

Holding the flame closer, he said, 'This is not for you, this sacred fire. This is for your baby. Does the name Alessio Capaneus mean anything to you? No. Why should it?'

The flame swam around the matchstick before expiring in a blue death on the narrow stem of wood, sending up a wisp of grey smoke. He blew it away, his breath hot on her eyes, easing down her face.

'Can you hear this?' he asked. He shook the matchbox, the rattle of plenty. Another match ripped into life across the coarse sandpaper. 'Can you? Can you hear it?'

65

Rosen's eyes dipped to the speedometer. Bellwood at the wheel was tipping 120mph. From the passenger seat, Rosen had felt her nerves jarring at every grind of the clutch as she'd shifted gears on the agonizing route out of central London.

The blaring siren of the lead car and those behind echoed the clamour in Rosen's mind, a place where he couldn't hide from the image of his wife's naked body, cold, vulnerable, with no defence against the stab wound to her heart and the incision to her womb.

'David?' said Bellwood.

At first he didn't respond but after some time he replied, 'Can't you go any faster?'

'David, three forces are working on the hoof to keep the roads clear between London and the South Downs. They can't guarantee every side road. If something does pull out—'

'I know, we're all going faster than it's safe to.' He paused. 'Safe for us.' *But not Sarah, not for her, not for our baby.* He turned his head and made a noise in the back of his throat, a brief rattling sound, the desperate melody of a senseless hymn.

Rosen pictured a white tent at the midpoint of Vauxhall Bridge Road with scene-of-crime tape flapping around it in some vile wind. In his mind, he crossed the tape and recalled: *this is the end where the letter A is linked from side to side*. A for Alessio, A for Alpha, the opening in which he had left her alone on the first floor of the North Wing of St Thomas's Hospital. He had been running late as usual, too late to save her from being the sixth victim.

Rosen's mobile exploded into life, its sudden ringing jolting him.

'David, it's Feldman.' Despite his urgency, Feldman sounded pleased.

'What is it?'

Rosen turned his phone on to speakerphone and felt the weight of the gun in his other hand.

'Williams and Waters estate agents, in Eastbourne. They handled the sale of Caxton Farm to a Paul White, eighteen months back.'

'White?'

'That's what he gave his name as. They keep an archive of all the properties they sell, and they've given a detailed description of Caxton Farm's interior.'

'Go on.'

'The farmhouse is large and it's got an expansive basement. Ground floor has a kitchen, living room, dining room and large hallway; upstairs has four bedrooms and a bathroom. Bill Williams, the agent who sold the property, remembered Paul well. "Weird" was the word. Seemed more interested in the basement than the rest of the house, so it was the selling point for our man. The basement consists of three interconnecting rooms. The entrance to the basement is through a hatch in the floor in the pantry, which is next to the kitchen at the back of the house. You go down a set of wooden stairs. The stairs lead down into the middle room.'

'Any other entrances or exits to the basement?' asked Rosen.

'One more.'

'Where?'

'There's a door in the wall of the smallest of the rooms. It leads to a diagonal shaft that comes out into the yard outside, via a trapdoor. It's an old grain shaft. When it was a farm, it was used to slide sacks of grain down into the basement, where they were stored.'

'Anything else?'

'No, just two entrances to the basement, one through the kitchen and down some steps, one outside the house and down a chute.'

'Good thinking, well done.'

'It was your idea, boss; you told me to phone round the estate agents!'

He recalled issuing the instruction but it felt as if he'd done so in a dream he'd once had in some past existence. The muscles in his face twitched. The sirens screamed. His throat was desert dry.

His phone went off again as soon as he ended the call from Feldman.

'DCI Rosen?' It was a voice he didn't know.

'Yeah?

'DCI Rick Murphy, Sussex Constabulary. We've closed all the roads near Berwick, but the path to Caxton Farm's going to need local knowledge. I'll take you the quick way,' said Murphy.

'Meet us on the edge of the exclusion zone,' said Rosen.

'The best place is a little north of a village called Alciston. There's a really narrow road from Cuckmere Reservoir, about half a mile from Caxton Farm. We're waiting for you. Where are you?'

'We're on the A22 heading south. We're minutes away.'

Rosen ended the call and stared at the road ahead.

66

He lit a wax taper, pausing to observe the flame, and then dipped out of her sight to the base of the altar. Whatever he was igniting was on the floor, out of her line of vision.

She reached out to the mechanical hoist, to the bicycle spoke and the hypodermic needle, but they were a thumbnail beyond her grasp. Out of the corner of her eye, she saw his outline start to rise up beside her and dropped her arm again onto the velvet surface beneath her. For the first time, she was aware of what he was wearing. White. A white shirt and white trousers. Clothes, ordinary clothes.

He walked around the altar, a wisp of smoke drifting up from the floor where he'd just been crouching. As he pulled the hoist away from the altar, the sharp spoke and hypodermic needle moved further and further away from her grasp. She ground her back teeth in frustration.

You should've leaned further forward and grabbed them while you had a chance, stupid!

There was a patch of perspiration on his back, making his shirt stick to him, highlighting the colour of his skin, the badge of his humanity.

Her arms ached from having lifted the lid to breathe.

It was quiet, although not altogether silent because of a humming that Sarah recognized as the noise of the house; each house having its own peculiar relationship with the air within it and around it. It was the sound that kept adults awake at night and fuelled the nightmares of children.

It seemed to grow louder by the smallest degree.

He hurried to the back of the altar and fell to the ground. She lifted her head to look. He was prostrate, his hands and feet scrabbling to touch particular points on the floor, his head in the dust. She saw the daubings beneath him, the only identifiable sign of occult symbol making.

It looked like some sort of triangle, or a buckled letter: an A or an N, maybe.

Her head dropped back again as she took in the hoist and the sharps, and although she was nearer to the weapons than he was, she remained unmoving. She tried to feel her legs. She had been still for a long time. When she woke up on an ordinary morning, she couldn't move quickly for the stiffness of middle age in her limbs. One sudden move on her part and he would get there before her.

He rose to his full height.

'Are you awake?' he said, his gaze heavy upon her. His eyes were close to hers, as close as David's when he kissed her goodnight. 'Are you ready?'

A column of smoke spiralled behind him.

A single fingertip on her left hipbone, a light touch that felt like a crashing fist. He slid his finger across her skin to the other side, a line from hip to hip, marking out the first incision of the Caesarean.

She breathed the smoke of sunny Sundays, the white fragrance of the barbecue, and felt the full weight of the knowledge that this was to be her fate and that of her baby: she for the spike, her baby for the flame.

His finger remained at her hip and she went cold at the realization that he was enjoying the touch of her skin. His breathing shifted up a gear, the earliest stirrings of intimacy and arousal. She heard him swallow his saliva as he brought his face close to hers.

He lifted his finger and pressed it down between her ribs. His face and finger receded. Then, the unmistakable clatter of the spoke and the needle as he picked them up from the hoist.

He coughed, swallowing a mouthful of rising smoke, and came towards her. He coughed again, this time a little more rawly, as the smoke bit deeper in his throat. He coughed as he stood over her and placed the spoke and the needle on the altar, the spoke within her reach, the needle way beyond.

He blinked and wiped his eyes. She plucked the spoke from the velvet lap of the altar while his attention was diverted.

Ready to proceed once more, his eyes scoured the altar, his expression full of confusion as he bent to search on the ground through the thin veil of white smoke.

'Is this what you're looking for?' asked Sarah.

He lifted his head, giving her his full face as a target. She aimed the spoke directly at his right eyeball but he turned suddenly and the sharp tip sank directly into his cheek.

She had sat up to maximize the power of her arms to push, holding the spoke and feeling the tip pierce the fleshy wall of his mouth, travelling further into the space behind his teeth.

He howled, a noise neither human nor animal, filling the basement. She ground the spoke in and felt the side of his tongue writhing. It was thick and hard. With her other hand she grabbed his hair to steady the target and thrust the weapon deeper into his tongue.

His hand shot up to her face, catching her in the eye. She let go of his hair and seized his right wrist, pulling his fingers towards her lips and biting down as hard as she could, feeling but not hearing the crack of bone.

She banged his skull hard with her elbow, grabbed his hair again and pushed his head down against the direction of the spoke as it wriggled through his tongue, deeper and deeper.

She felt the slide of the spoke change as it escaped from his tongue through the top surface. She pushed the spoke harder still and it connected with the inner wall of his other cheek. She forced his head down onto the altar. His left eye met hers, and she spat his fingers from her lips.

'I'm not your mother.' Her words tasted of his blood.

She pushed again and the spoke drove through his cheek, the tip piercing his skin and digging into the velvet and wooden surface beneath.

She looked for the hypodermic needle and was crushed to see it roll off the edge of the altar and onto the floor, now invisible in the smoke.

He raised his bleeding fingers to her throat but when she took hold of his wrist again he snatched it away.

The tip of the spoke sank into the wood. She turned and turned it.

A wave of weakness hissed through her, the surge of energy with which she'd fought back ebbing away, leaving her feeling light-headed. She resisted the sensation with all her being.

She held his head down on the table as the smoke curled into her nostrils and hit the back of her throat.

The spoke was firmly embedded in the shallow surface of the altar, his face pinned sideways to the velvet covering.

'These are my fingers and these are my fingernails,' said Sarah, holding her jagged nails close to his fast-blinking eye. 'These are the nails of the five women you murdered. On behalf of us all, I have a message for you.'

He shut his eye tightly. She clawed at the lid with two fingers, digging into the eyeball beneath, feeling the curve between eyeball and skull. She tried to gouge out his eye but he rolled his neck against the altar and her fingers slipped off. She formed a fist and punched the tip of his nose. She punched again and again but with each blow she could feel her energy sapping away, the force reduced with each strike of her fist.

Blood poured from the corner of his mouth onto the velvet, and he became still.

She stooped to break his nose with her front teeth but couldn't bend forwards sufficiently.

She banged her fist down on the side of his head. He made no sound.

His body sagged into limpness, his weight supported by the tip of the spoke embedded in the surface of the table, his face wreathed in smoke.

She tried to climb down from the altar but tumbled off into the gathering smoke, her legs seizing up beneath her.

They were dead from hip to toe with chronic pins and needles, but she could still feel her arms. Getting onto her hands and knees, she crawled away, her eyes stinging in the smoke, her vision blurred.

The nearest doorway. A way out. It was a basement. Stairs up. Maybe in the nearest room beyond the doorway. Light poured in, through the smoke that chased her, and she dragged herself towards it.

She glanced back at his inanimate figure impaled on the altar.

He fell down and sprawled in a heap on the ground.

In the doorway to the next room, she looked for the stairs but all she saw was a shelf. And on that shelf five dead babies in five jars, and a sixth empty jar on the end of the row, the space awaiting her child.

'David!' she called. But she knew he couldn't hear, knew he wasn't coming. If she didn't get out fast she was going to die in there, and her baby – with the other five – would be fuel for the flames of Herod's terrible needs. There was no time to mourn the dead. She turned around rapidly. Only time to save the living.

She had to get past him in to the furthest room and, in that moment, she cursed her luck for taking a wrong turn away from the altar. There must be stairs in the room in which she'd been held.

The smoke was rising to waist height, spreading out in the unventilated basement.

Sensation had returned to her thighs but not to her knees, calves or feet as she dragged herself across the ground.

She reached the doorway and pulled herself to her knees, moving on all fours through the smoke, trying hard to hold her breath, squinting through the stinging smoke.

Smoke twisted around the concrete floor. Through the doorway she could see the stairs. The way out. The spiralling smoke.

Her knees and palms were skinned on the rough surface of the floor. She picked up speed, her target the bottom step, every movement of the knee and hand a fraction closer to escape.

The bottom step. She touched it, the blessed wood of the stairway to safety; she touched the wood, staining it with blood from her hands.

The stairs led up to a door, a hatch to the ground floor above. She took in a deep breath, preparing herself to face the ascent, determined to climb on her knees and haul herself up, via the banisters, with her hands.

She caught her knee on the edge of the bottom step but managed to lever herself onto the first flat surface. She held the sides of the stair with her hands while her eyes followed the rising smoke to the hatch from where a hook hung down. The hatch was unlocked. She began to entertain the prospect of survival as she struggled to the second step.

Sarah rested her left foot on the ground but it was still dead to sensation. She could not climb the steps on foot.

On the third step, she counted another eight to go; eight steps and an open doorway, the path to life.

Then, she felt a sharp pain in her right ankle and turned.

Eyes and teeth. A hypodermic needle spearing her ankle. His face completely lanced by the spoke, entering through one cheek – impaling his tongue, which thrust out accusingly between his teeth – and sticking out through the other, its tip broken at the end.

Blood ran from the corners of his mouth and the tips of the spoke.

One eye was raw, red and swollen.

A sea of dizzy surrender washed through her.

He said something foul and incomprehensible, but the malice of his tone was crystal clear.

She was falling, beneath the gaze of the eyes, within range of the teeth.

Eyes and teeth and metal spoke. She crashed backwards, head first, her last sense to close down, hearing, catching his scream of rage as she tumbled into darkness.

67

'Can't you go any faster?' asked Rosen again. 'What's wrong with you, Carol?'

'We've got to slow down, David—'

'Do you think I don't bloody well know why you've had to slow down?'

'We may be doing just under fifty, but we've been hitting over a hundred since London.'

The sign on the road south told Rosen they were close to Alciston, where they were to meet the waiting officers from Sussex Constabulary.

He glanced at the speedometer and Bellwood was right. They were tipping 50mph in a maze of winding lanes.

'I feel like I'm betraying her,' he said, turning off the siren and watching the needle descend, to forty, thirty, twenty and below, finally reaching a standstill.

Rosen was out of the car before Bellwood put on the handbrake. A man was advancing towards him.

'DCI Rosen?'

'Yes. DCI Murphy?' A terse nod of the head was his reply.

Night was falling fast on the East Sussex road; birds were calling, nesting, under the moon forming behind a thin bank of cloud.

'Caxton Farm?' urged Rosen.

'OK, you've got two ways into the farmhouse. Front and back. The approach road at the front is a glorified farm track. At the back of the house, you've got fields, rolling South Downs. From the back of the house, he's got a crystal-clear view of anyone coming at him from the fields. Therefore, if he's got a firearm, and you've got officers approaching the rear of the house, they'll be going home to London in body bags. If you go in from the front, there are visual obstacles. If you go in from the back door as well, approach it from the front, move down the side of the building and keep tightly against the wall as you turn the corner. But be quick.'

A woman, with her back turned to him, drifted into Rosen's line of vision. Her hair, her stature, her clothes made her look just like Sarah. Hope flooded him. He opened his mouth to call her but before he could speak her name, the woman turned. Her face was completely unlike Sarah's.

Clasping a phone, she looked at Rosen and said, 'Mary Sands, primary hostage negotiator. He's got a landline but he's left the phone off the hook.'

Anguish drowned him and, for a moment, he didn't know where he was or what he was doing. A hand gripped his shoulder and he turned to the source.

It was Bellwood, with Gold standing just behind her.

'CO19 are here and already in place,' said Bellwood.

Rosen looked at Bellwood and Gold, two human beings whose lives he was about to risk.

'Gold and Bellwood, you're to enter through the front door. I'll take the other ram and go in through the back. You come in only when I'm inside and when I order you in.'

A Sussex ambulance pulled up at the back of the group, trying to negotiate the narrow gap. It moved slowly and the group shifted as one to allow it past.

The driver leaned out of the window.

'Wait at the junction,' Rosen instructed him, wondering if this was the ambulance that would be carrying Sarah back the other way, dead or alive.

The ambulance heaved back to the junction. Chief Superintendent Doug Price of CO19 stood on the other side of the narrow road.

'Front and back entrances are covered. No sign of anything moving at the windows. He's got six Heckler & Koch carbines pointing at him. He can't get away alive.'

Night had fallen and the country darkness was deep.

If he hasn't escaped already, thought Rosen. *If she isn't already dead.*

68

Running was hard. The ram in his hands heavy, the ground at his feet cracked. Potholes threw up stagnant water into his shoes, soaking his socks. He paused, weighing up the farmhouse, his breath short, his chest tight. He ran, his left ankle bending, almost but not quite twisting, in yet another of the terrain's deceptions.

As he arrived at the farmhouse, night clouds fell away from the moon and an unsteady light filtered down onto the building.

'Carol?' His voice was little more than a gasp because of his shortage of breath.

'David?' She was at the front door, in place with Gold.

'OK. I'm going for the rear entrance.'

The back of the farmhouse was now washed in moonlight, reflected in the glass of the rear door and casting an ethereal sheen on the yard. It was there that Rosen saw the ambulance parked at the back of the house, not entirely covered by the large tarpaulin draped over it.

At the back door, Rosen thought he could smell smoke. The wooden frame collapsed with one swift hit of the ram and Rosen was inside the darkened kitchen.

He shouted, 'Bellwood! Gold! Now!'

The front door slammed from its hinges and Gold and Bellwood were in the house. A point of torchlight skittered at the front.

There was definitely smoke, but no perceptible source of fire.

Rosen saw a pinpoint of light reflected in Bellwood's eye as she entered the kitchen. Her torch picked out and settled on a break in the regular wooden pattern of the floor. It was the hatch into the basement.

Smoke leaked from its four sides.

Rosen dropped the ram and raised the hatch, allowing a torrent of smoke to pour out from below.

There were steep stairs leading down, wreathed in smoke.

'Light!' he called to Bellwood.

She threw the torch and he caught it, his senses sharpened, the pain in his legs and chest evaporating, the blood banging in his head like the primal beat of a war drum.

'Listen for the call!' he commanded, descending into the basement.

He had tilted his head and caught the best lungful of oxygen available to him, and held on to it, but almost lost it when his torchbeam of yellow light revealed a bloody hand mark on the bottom of the stair.

She had tried to escape, bleeding and afraid, she had tried her best to live.

He shifted the torch to his left hand and pulled out his gun with his right.

'Sarah? Sarah?'

She didn't reply.

It was like being blind. Finding a wall, he kept his back to it, negotiating the room by the touch of his shoulder. He moved swiftly but played the light carefully over the smoke.

He picked out a shape, a coffin, he thought at first glance, but it wasn't a coffin. It was too wide.

'Sarah?'

She's dead, he thought.

Rosen turned ninety degrees, his shoulder still against the wall, and kept moving round the first corner.

'Sarah?'

She is gone. I have nothing; therefore I have nothing to lose.

There was a half-door in the wall. He opened it and shone his light into the darkness. It was a tunnel leading upwards at an angle of forty-five degrees. The grain chute.

The smoke stung his eyes and filled his lungs but he moved with increasing speed, racing around the perimeter of the room, and came to a door frame.

He shone his light into the middle room.

A machine of sorts.

His torchlight stroked the letters on the hoist. *Faboorgliften*. He had no idea what it was, other than that here it had been used as an instrument of torture.

A table and the fierce source of the heat. It looked like a huge barbecue. The flames around it licked and spat.

The cloth on the table was burning.

Rosen held his torch between his teeth, grabbed the smouldering velvet and pulled it down onto the ground, covering the fire and burning his left hand as he did so. The cry of pain stuck in his throat while the flames on the ground did battle with the suffocating velvet.

He backed away from the fire, glancing over his shoulder into the smoke, and dragged his light along the wall to the doorway of the third room. There was nowhere else she could be. When he whispered, 'Sarah?', he could feel the proximity of another human being. He sensed her presence, in a recognition that had been years in the making.

He trained the light down. Sarah was on the ground. Her face was unblemished, her body soaked in blood.

'David!' Bellwood's voice, mute and muffled, filtered through the ceiling above him. 'David! He's in there! He's just torched the stairs!'

Sarah's body seemed to be lying on a red blanket. Rosen kneeled down next to her to find it wasn't a blanket. It was her blood soaking her clothes. He shone the light in her face. Putting the torch down, he picked up her wrist to feel for a pulse.

But there was none. Then, he detected the faintest sign of one but wondered if he was imagining it.

In the dim light, he saw the desecration of her body.

He had never seen so many separate wounds on one person.

In that tortured moment, he sensed that they were not alone. A foot banged on the floor above and Gold shouted, 'David! David! Call my name!' His feeling was confirmed by a single exhalation behind him. Rosen looked over his shoulder but the smoke was too thick for him to see.

Sarah didn't appear to be breathing. He angled her head, held her nose and, breathing into her mouth, laid the heel of his hand in the centre of her chest. He started to pump at her heart, hearing an unpremeditated howl rise from the centre of his being.

Her flesh was torn, and her blood seeped through his fingers as he gave cardiac massage.

In the distance, he became aware of Bellwood's voice, and of Gold calling to him, but they were far, far away, shouting about fire and calling the name *David*, but he didn't connect it with himself. It was a call to some other person in some other place.

He slid his hand under her head to reposition it. Her face appeared clearer through the murk and, with his fingers in the dampness of her hair, he wondered how it was that after such an ordeal she could look so young. He'd left her alone that morning, and as night gathered around him, he was just too late.

'I'm sorry,' he said. 'I'm so sorry.'

Desolation overwhelmed him and for a moment his mind went blank, his concentration crumbling. Time and place vanished. There was just smoke and desolation. And then a little sound right behind him.

The sound, a footstep, brought him back. Under cover of the smoke, something was creeping up on him.

Rosen turned and stood up in the same instant.

The face seemed suspended in white smoke, a disembodied head hovering, observing Rosen as if he was a specimen in a jar.

It was the little boy in the locket, worn by time, the unspeaking face beneath the black slick of hair.

He stood impassively, holding a metal spoke. It pointed upwards, as if in accusation. He remained still and silent in the swirling smoke, blood leaking from two facial wounds.

And then he spoke, but the word was slurred and inarticulate.

'Canathus!'

'Capaneus? There's no such person as Capaneus, Dwyer.'

Paul Dwyer's face was ordinary, not that of a monster at all. But in a moment, as Rosen watched, the features of every mean, loveless, violent, grasping, lustful, self-pitying, despicable criminal he'd ever clapped eyes on manifested themselves in Dwyer's. Every thug, every child-warping paedophile, every family-destroying arsonist, every self-obsessed killer, appeared as if as one in the smoke-filled basement of a farmhouse in East Sussex.

As Rosen aimed his gun at Dwyer, he felt the sudden blast of a burning chemical in his face, flammable spirit that ate into his eyes as soon as it touched them. He slipped backwards in Sarah's blood but stayed on his feet. His gun fell from his hands as his fingers flew to his eyes. In the adjoining room, charcoal still crackled and sighed under the cover he'd thrown over the fire. Apart from this there was silence, a huge and ugly silence, broken only by a cry of agony that came from deep inside Rosen.

He swayed on his feet but remained upright, listening for the sound of Paul Dwyer moving.

Rosen rubbed his eyes, trying to soak up the chemical with his sleeves. The pungent smell became overwhelming as Dwyer threw more and more lighter fuel into Rosen's face.

It dripped down onto his clothes. Rosen had a vision of himself burning, a huge human torch alongside his wife's bleeding corpse.

He heard a rasp, then another as Dwyer struggled with a box of matches.

Rosen summoned up all the strength he possessed. He had one last weapon left.

'Flint's a liar, he's lied to you all along, he's made a fool out of you. You've been duped by a showman, Paul. Do you hear me? You're an idiot, a mummy's boy, and this time tomorrow the whole world's going to know.' He summoned up the will to laugh and barked that laughter into Dwyer's face. 'You're not some Satanic superman, you're a fucking mummy's boy! And you've been had by a third-rate priest.'

His eyes burned afresh from the fumes and he held his breath to resist a howl of pain. Dwyer clamped a hand over Rosen's mouth and he tasted blood on the killer's fingers. Raw courage held him together, courage from knowing that somehow Sarah had wounded her murderer.

Dwyer's hand pressed down on Rosen's mouth. He yanked his head away.

'You won't silence me like that, Dwyer!'

Rosen threw out an arm and caught hold of a handful of cotton. He pulled hard and could feel that he was dragging Dwyer towards him by the shirt-front, held in the grip of his fist. Hanging on tightly, he said, 'Do you want to know the truth, Paul, the whole truth about your Satanic revolution?'

'Canathus—'

'Capaneus? A for Alessio, the buckled A for Alpha, where you left the bodies; all that secret knowledge, that hidden dangerous knowledge? It's a crock of shit, Paul. Sorry to break the bad news to you, but the Capaneus scam's got about as much truth in it as the shit Pastor Jim used to peddle to your mother back in the Church of the Living Light. He's been taking the piss out of you, just like Pastor Jim used to do to your mother. There's no such person as Alessio

Capaneus – it's a fiction, and you fell for it! Like mother, like son. What a pair of saps.'

Dwyer tore himself away from Rosen's grip and Rosen heard the sound of a box of matches emptying out onto the concrete floor. He lashed out with his foot, listening for any sound from Dwyer, aiming for his head but kicking thin air.

He heard a single match being struck on the rough ground. And Dwyer's breath was in his face. A small flame sizzled in the corrupted air.

'You're flammable too, Dwyer,' said Rosen. 'I made sure of that when I held you close. Go on, torch me. I burn, you burn!'

A gunshot. The enclosed space resounded with the solitary clap of a gun. Rosen felt the air rattle close to his skull and then became aware that Paul Dwyer's body had slumped and fallen away from him, collapsing to the floor. The match expired as Dwyer fell. And, for a moment, it was as if all the sounds in the world belonged in separate compartments, not in the living fabric of the air. The ring of the gunshot was deadened in the flat acoustics of the basement. The thud of Dwyer's fallen body.

'David?' Bellwood's voice. She was moving closer, steadily, but as fast as she could. 'I'm taking you by the hand now, David.'

He felt Bellwood's hand as assertive fingers tugged his hands away from his face.

'Don't rub your eyes, David.'

'She's dead,' said Rosen.

'I'm inspecting the body of Paul Dwyer. I'm shining my torch onto his face and head. Gunshot at close range, wound to the frontal lobes of his head.'

'You shot him, Carol.'

'No. You did,' she replied. 'I was just outside the range of vision, behind the smoke, when I heard the gunshot. You shot him, David.'

'I didn't shoot him,' said Rosen. 'I dropped my gun when the little shit threw lighter fuel in my eyes.'

'Quick!' said Bellwood. 'Gold, get some water down here! Don't touch your eyes, David! Sarah? Sarah Rosen?'

And he wondered why Bellwood was talking to his dead wife.

Bellwood let go of Rosen's hand and crouched down. Rosen followed her voice.

'Sarah?' Bellwood's voice sounded like a plea for mercy. 'An ambulance, Gold, we need the ambulance.'

'How did you get in?' asked Rosen

'I came in through the grain chute. I crawled down. He set the basement stairs on fire, blocked off the entrance you came down.'

Three taps on the floor, soft sounds.

Bellwood whispered, 'Kneel down where you are, David.'

'David,' said Sarah. He turned his head at the sound of his wife's voice.

'Sarah?' His voice reached out to her.

He kneeled down and fumbled around in the dark, placing his hand gently on his wife's arm. The gun slid from her grasp. As he touched her hand, she let out an exhausted cry of pain as the fuel on his fingers entered an open wound on her flesh.

'I'm sorry,' he said.

'David. The baby?' The fading echo of a lost whisper.

He couldn't speak to answer.

'I killed . . .' said Sarah. 'David, I heard you. I saw the gun . . . on the ground. I shot him . . . in . . . the head.'

69

Two hours later, Rosen sat at his wife's hospital bedside, dabbing his stinging eyes with a cold damp tissue, his blurred vision slowly returning. Under sedation, she slept peacefully. He folded his hand over hers as it lay, scratched and torn, on top of the blanket.

He considered what she'd suffered in the basement and wished he had a god to pray to for Sarah and their baby.

In the dim glow of an anglepoise lamp, she looked peaceful, except for a crease that formed slowly on her brow. He held her hand tightly, hoping that whatever she was dreaming at that moment would dissolve into something sweet and gentle.

The crease vanished as slowly as it had appeared.

Her breathing slowed a little.

Tenderly, he rested his cheek against her womb and whispered, 'Without you, I am nothing, I am no one.'

He bent over her and kissed her brow.

As he sat in the chair at her bedside, with the whole of his being he willed her and their baby to pull through.

As DAWN APPROACHED, there was a gentle tap on the door of Sarah's room. Through the glass, Rosen saw Bellwood waiting, but not looking directly into the room.

Reluctantly, he left his wife and joined Bellwood outside.

She glanced around. There was no one about.

'Sorry to disturb you, David—'

'What's happening, Carol?'

'Parker and Willis have been all over Dwyer's place. It's a gold mine of evidence. The babies in the basement. Dwyer's printed off everything from the Capaneusian Bible, both Old Testament and New. He even kept a handwritten diary, detailing the how, when and why in each of the killings.'

Rosen nodded. 'The babies?'

'They'll be returned to their families within the next twenty-four hours. Victim Liaison have been to see all the families. They know Dwyer's dead.'

'How were they, the families?'

'Dignified.'

Rosen looked through the glass at Sarah. When his gaze returned to Bellwood, he recognized that she was troubled by whatever she was about to tell him.

'Carol, what is it?'

'Harrison, he's been in to see Baxter. He's admitted everything.'

Rosen's scalp tightened and his skin crawled.

'Go on, Carol.'

'Flint suckered him into believing he was a PSU officer. Harrison intercepted a message from Sarah on your phone. Flint set up you and Sarah with that bogus appointment at St Thomas's.'

Rosen considered the chain of events.

'But he saw a picture of Flint at the team meeting before that appointment.'

'I remember; he looked pig sick when the meeting finished,' said Bellwood.

'He didn't say anything. Why?'

'He can't explain why, apparently.'

'Where is Harrison?'

'He's in custody, being questioned.'

Silence. Bellwood looked tired but agitated and Rosen knew exactly where she was coming from.

'Carol, you'd better get back to Dwyer's place.'

'We are up the wall, there's that much evidence to gather.'

'Thank you, Carol. This can't have been easy for you. Keep me posted.'

Bellwood looked past him. Her expression changed, its solemnity lifting.

'I think you'd better go back inside, David.'

Rosen followed Bellwood's eyes.

Sarah was stirring. Her head turned on the pillow.

Rosen went in and closed the door after himself.

'It's all right, love,' he said. 'I'm back now.'

70

After seeming to take an age to wake, Sarah opened her eyes. In the dawn, her side room was lit by a downturned anglepoise lamp.

'I'm thirsty,' she said. He helped her to sit up and raised a cup of water to her lips, his eyes still stinging.

She looked lost, and he wondered how much she remembered and what she knew.

'What happened?' she asked.

'You saved my life,' he said.

She was quiet for a moment as a shadow crossed her face. 'Did he—?'

'He attacked you with a spoke.'

'But I stuck it through his face . . .' She was drifting back into sleep.

'It seems he took it out and bit down on it, bending it with his teeth. But because the shaft was bent, when he turned the spoke on you, he kept missing his aim. The tip was buckled too, so the incisions he made were superficial. You know what you gave him, love?'

'What did I give him?'

'You gave him a bloody good hiding.'

She smiled. 'Yes, I did . . . But—'

'The baby? He didn't pierce your womb, Sarah. He went for it but he didn't make it. The scan came back as all clear.'

He held her hand, feeling her fingers squeeze his.

'Tell me everything,' she said.

'Try to sleep, we'll speak in the morning. You're here, the baby's safe. That is everything.'

For several minutes, she appeared to be falling asleep again but, just as he thought she was dropping off, she opened her eyes and focussed on him.

'What did he stick in my foot?' she asked.

'Sarah, sleep . . .'

'David, talk . . .'

'Pentothal. Fast-acting, short-term.'

'Lucky for you,' she said. 'I woke up with a gun just here.' She pointed at her temple. 'On the floor. I saw your face and his through the smoke. Because he had a lighted match in his hand. I smelled the fuel. I knew what he was going to do. He was going to set you on fire. I picked up the gun, aimed it at his head and pulled the trigger.'

'What if you'd missed?'

'What if I'd done nothing?'

'I'd rather that you shot me than let that bastard burn me alive'

'I know. That's why I did it.'

Her eyes closed and within moments her breathing had slowed and deepened until she was asleep. He watched her face in the second-hand light of the anglepoise lamp that was turned to the wall, and saw in it the imprint of Hannah's, whom he'd watched sleep hundreds of times. It was the face he'd seen when he went to check on her in the dead of night, the face he'd seen when he'd found her in that final endless sleep.

Unlike his wife, in all the years that had passed since the death of their daughter, Rosen had never dreamed of the event, never seen nor heard her in his sleeping hours. Through good times and bad, and the acres in between, he could never recall encountering his lost child even though, if only in his dreams, he yearned to do the one thing that had been snatched from him in the real, cold, conscious world.

For years, he had longed to say a loving goodbye and hold Hannah before letting her go for that final time.

The light in the room was warm and the shadows were seductive.

Rosen sat at his wife's bedside, wide awake and wishing he could sleep, and to be with his daughter just one more time.

71

After seven days and nights, Rosen took Sarah home on an afternoon that promised a dramatic change from the overcast skies and rain that had dominated southern England for weeks.

In the kitchen, he marvelled as she filled the kettle, drinking in the beauty of the everyday, the joy of the ordinary.

Sarah winced as she reached up into a cupboard for teabags, and he said, 'Here, let me.'

'Sit down!' she said. 'No fussing in my kitchen.' She got on with the business of making two cups of tea.

The main window behind her gave a broad view of the sky. A weather system was moving in from the west and snow was predicted. When he'd heard the news that morning, Rosen had translated it into the fun he could have with his child five years hence, three even, two . . .

The kettle switched itself off with a gentle snap, a small noise amplified by the calm and quiet around them.

'Did you see that?' asked Sarah. 'This late in the year, this unexpected . . . Come to the window, David. '

A bank of white clouds made the sky seem, in contrast, a dense blue. The cold wind flung a cluster of dead leaves at the kitchen window, scraping it with dry fingers. An image, a recent memory of the window of Sebastian Flint's room at St Mark's, invaded Rosen's mind. He recalled the priest's words, the sound of his voice. *'It's an upside-down and back-to-front world.'*

For a moment, he pictured Flint standing on the other side of the kitchen window, looking in, staring at him, impassive, deadly. He dismissed the image. He knew Flint was out there somewhere, casting his shadow on anyone who came close. For the time being at least, Rosen sensed that Flint was done with him. But, at the bottom of his being, he feared that, one day, the priest would be irresistibly drawn back by the darkness that drove him.

He vowed never to speak of this to another living person.

At the window, he made a futile wish: never to have to leave Sarah's side, or even the house. If only the world outside would just roll on without him, forgetting he'd ever been in it. One day, he knew, at least some of his wishes would finally be granted.

She pointed at the kitchen window. The first snow was spiralling down from the clouds but not yet reaching the ground, a chaotic symphony of thick ragged snowflakes.

As he moved behind her, she took both his hands and placed them on her middle. He waited and felt the pressure of their baby kicking in her womb.

'Can you feel him?' she asked.

'I can,' Rosen said. 'I can feel him.'

The baby kicked and kicked again.

Rosen kept his hands in place and waited for their son to kick once more. Within a matter of moments, he felt the life within her stir again.

He closed his eyes to see Hannah looking up at him, their eyes locked, father and daughter. He kissed her face and whispered in her ear, a quiet blessing to the past and the love that was. Then she was gone.

'What was that?' asked Sarah.

'I just said, *Goodbye, Hannah.*'

The baby kicked and the tremor of life ran deep within his wife once more. Sarah's hand folded across his and, as hope danced on his fingertips, he blessed the child within her and the love that was yet to be.

ACKNOWLEDGEMENTS

I'd like to thank Steve Melia, former police Inspector, Rao Vallabhaneni, consultant vascular surgeon, Veronica Stallwood, Peter, Rosie & Jessica Buckman, Sara O'Keeffe and Linda & Eleanor Roberts.

Turn the page for an excerpt from

WHAT SHE SAW

Mark Roberts' latest novel.
Available from Corvus in trade paperback and e-book in 2014.

PROLOGUE

9.22 p.m.

M acy Conner knew it wasn't good for young girls to walk alone on dark nights.

As she reached the corner of her tenement block, Claude House, she saw light flickering on the surfaces of car windows in the street and felt compelled to turn.

There was a car on fire in Bannerman Square. Next to it two figures, silhouettes, moved swiftly from the flames in her direction.

If I can see them. . . She turned the corner and ran. They've seen me.

She ran as quickly as she could, panic mounting inside her with each stride. She could hear the echo of their footsteps as they followed her around the corner.

Macy lengthened her stride, gripping the £10 note she was clutching in her damp fist. But they were like lightning, striking closer with each step. She could smell them.

Macy tried to scream but her voice was trapped.

She stumbled, lost her rhythm but kept on her feet.

She could hear their mingled panting on the edge of the breeze.

No one around. Just her. A ten-year-old girl on her own. And them.

And now they were right behind her.

She could feel their anger as they caught up with her. She could smell the petrol as they surrounded her in a cage of flesh.

One behind her. One in front, massive and oozing menace.

In the distance, back on Bannerman Square, she heard the sound of a child screaming.

She looked up into a face wreathed in darkness. His hood was up. And when she turned back the other was the same.

She stared down at her feet and the shaking started.

On Bannerman Square, there was an explosion.

A pair of hands dug into her shoulders, each finger pressing into her, enjoying her pain.

A whisper in her ear, sour breath drifting over her.

'Did you really think you could out-run us, little bitch?'